Berkley Prime Crime titles by Linda O. Johnston

SIT, STAY, SLAY
NOTHING TO FEAR BUT FERRETS
FINE-FEATHERED DEATH
MEOW IS FOR MURDER
THE FRIGHT OF THE IGUANA
DOUBLE DOG DARE
NEVER SAY STY

Never Say Sty

Linda O. Johnston

BERKLEY PRIME CRIME, NEW YORK

THE BERKLEY PUBLISHING GROUP
Published by the Penguin Group
Penguin Group (USA) Inc.
375 Hudson Street, New York, New York 10014, USA

Penguin Group (Canada), 90 Eglinton Avenue East, Suite 700, Toronto, Ontario M4P 2Y3, Canada
(a division of Pearson Penguin Canada Inc.)
Penguin Books Ltd., 80 Strand, London WC2R 0RL, England
Penguin Group Ireland, 25 St. Stephen's Green, Dublin 2, Ireland (a division of Penguin Books Ltd.)
Penguin Group (Australia), 250 Camberwell Road, Camberwell, Victoria 3124, Australia
(a division of Pearson Australia Group Pty. Ltd.)
Penguin Books India Pvt. Ltd., 11 Community Centre, Panchsheel Park, New Delhi—110 017, India
Penguin Group (NZ), 67 Apollo Drive, Rosedale, North Shore 0632, New Zealand
(a division of Pearson New Zealand Ltd.)
Penguin Books (South Africa) (Pty.) Ltd., 24 Sturdee Avenue, Rosebank, Johannesburg 2196,
South Africa

Penguin Books Ltd., Registered Offices: 80 Strand, London WC2R 0RL, England

This is a work of fiction. Names, characters, places, and incidents either are the product of the author's imagination or are used fictitiously, and any resemblance to actual persons, living or dead, business establishments, events, or locales is entirely coincidental. The publisher does not have any control over and does not assume any responsibility for author or third-party websites or their content.

NEVER SAY STY

A Berkley Prime Crime Book / published by arrangement with the author

PRINTING HISTORY
Berkley Prime Crime mass-market edition / April 2009

Copyright © 2009 by Linda O. Johnston.
Cover illustration by Monika Roe.
Cover design by Rita Frangie.
Interior text design by Stacy Irwin.

ISBN: 978-0-425-22704-6

BERKLEY® PRIME CRIME
Berkley Prime Crime Books are published by The Berkley Publishing Group,
a division of Penguin Group (USA) Inc.,
375 Hudson Street, New York, New York 10014.
BERKLEY® PRIME CRIME and PRIME CRIME logo are trademarks of Penguin Group (USA) Inc.

PRINTED IN THE UNITED STATES OF AMERICA

10 9 8 7 6 5 4 3 2 1

There's usually a time gap between when a book's manuscript is completed and when it's published, or so Kendra has been told by Linda. Even though belatedly, they want to give the following acknowledgments:

Thanks to Peggy Wimberly, secretary, newsletter editor, and web manager of SCAMPP (the Southern California Association of Miniature Potbellied Pigs) for her prompt response to Linda's e-mailed inquiry about potbellied pigs, and for putting her in touch with Marlies Reno.

Special thanks to Marlies Reno for her invitation to visit her home and potbellied pig rescue facility, her unstinting answering of questions about potbellies, and her forwarding of the most delightful photos of adorable piggy noses.

All the best to *Arfriend, a Resource Guide for Human & Animal Friends*, and its founder and president, Janet Cole. Mooch, one of the pups who appears in this book, was the winner of the contest at the Arfriend booth at the 2007 West Hollywood Book Fair.

Ever so many thanks to Michelle Vega, who'd just become Linda's new editor around the time she was writing this book. Michelle's enthusiasm and excellent advice have helped Kendra's adventures keep coming.

A belated but heartfelt public welcome to the world to Blake Alexander Bartlett, son of Linda's outstanding agent, Paige Wheeler, and her delightful husband, Drew Bartlett.

And speaking of delightful husbands, Linda, as always, wants to acknowledge how special hers is, so here we go again—and Kendra agrees. Fred, you're the greatest! But don't let it go to your head.

Another belated but very special welcome to our family to Tara, Linda's older son Eric's wife.

—*Kendra Ballantyne/Linda O. Johnston*

P.S. A very special acknowledgment to our inspirations, our Lexies, and a welcome to a Cavalier puppy named Mystie, a recent addition to Linda's family.

Chapter One

"It's sooo perfect, Kendra," piped my pet-sitting assistant, Rachel Preesinger, into my ear. Or, rather, into her cell phone, as I listened to mine, propped between my shoulder and my bent head.

I was sitting in my office at the law firm of Yurick & Associates, staring at my computer. I'd been drafting a bruiser of a brief for a motion in a senior citizen case I was handling for my boss, buddy, and firm's senior partner, Borden Yurick. And, okay, I admit it: my mind wasn't exactly focused on my other incarnation and adored career—pet-sitter.

But Rachel's words absolutely yanked my attention back to animals. "What's perfect?" I asked.

"Haven't you been listening?" I could almost see the pout on the pretty twenty-year-old's face. She'd just had a birthday, so my chief helper—and daughter of the primary tenant of the large house on the property the bank and I owned—was no longer a teenager. That didn't make her mature, of course.

"Er . . . not entirely."

"Well, great. You put me into this fabulous situation, told me to work closely with Charlotte LaVerne so we can get *Animal Auditions* off the ground, and—"

"That's the name now?" I inquired, my concentration finally focused. "Cute, but not as catchy as I'd hoped."

"Well, you come up with something better, then." I felt her fuming over the phone.

I swiveled in my desk chair and stared out my office window into the crowded parking lot. Not much to see there but cars—including that stupid little sedan I was still renting—but at least it was better than trying to concentrate on my computer screen.

"I'll think about it. Okay, now you've got my full attention. Start over."

A second of irritated silence, and then, "I'll keep it short, so you'll get it. Everyone loved the concept of a reality show starring animals. Remember?"

"Absolutely," I agreed. After all, it had been my idea.

I'm Kendra Ballantyne, attorney-at-law as well as professional pet-sitter. Because of my dual adored interests, I often take on law cases involving pets. That's what had happened here. Disgruntled customers had sued my client, Show Biz Beasts, claiming they hadn't made good on their promises to get their pets film industry auditions. As always, I came up with my own form of ADR—usually considered by lawyers to stand for alternate dispute resolution. In my case, it's animal dispute resolution.

This time, it consisted of creating an idea for a possible TV reality show—and had gotten those persnickety plaintiffs off our client's case.

Plus, to my delight and sorta surprise, the concept was catching on where it counted. My friend and former tenant

Charlotte LaVerne had been a reality show star, and was now a maven of that sector of the TV industry. Rachel, my pet-care assistant at Critter TLC, LLC, was also a wanna-be actress. The owners of Show Biz Beasts were absolutely intrigued with being associated with an actual reality show.

And so forth.

All we needed was up-front funds to get the show into preliminary production, and a little interest from a network. Well, actually, a lot of interest. Enough to give it a try for at least one short season. And—

"So Corbin and Shareen got a call from out of the blue," Rachel was saying. They were my clients the Hayhursts, owners of Show Biz Beasts. "He'd heard about the show idea, we don't know how, and he wanted to discuss it. See a session. You know."

"He who?" I asked.

"That's what I've been trying to tell you, Kendra. That's what's so perfect."

"Okay, then, tell me."

"He's hugely rich. And he's really connected in all kinds of animal industries. He even owns HotPets."

I finally knew who Rachel was ranting about. "Dante DeFrancisco?"

"Exactly. He's interested in being executive producer and chief moneybags behind *Animal Auditions*. He loves the idea. And if anyone can put money into the show to make it successful, he can. Like I said, it's perfect."

Dante DeFrancisco was the Donald Trump of the pet industry. His chain of super-mega pet stores outshone all the competition. He had a reputation for backing animal rescue organizations, including groups that saved all sorts of wildlife.

And he was interested in our little reality show idea?

Wow!

Except . . . in some ways, Rachel could be right. It sounded perfect. But in my experience, something sounding perfect always led to trouble.

"Anyway, he's on his way to the studio in Valencia. We're going to give him a demonstration."

"When?" My eyes darted from the words in the center of my computer screen to the digital time readout at its bottom corner.

"In an hour."

Could I complete this initial draft of the brief that quickly, using any semblance of legal professionalism? It would take about forty-five minutes to drive there, and I had to ensure I'd get back in time to pet-sit . . .

"See you later," I said to Rachel, hanging up and diving frantically back into my drafting.

OKAY, IT WASN'T the best brief I'd ever written. But I'd handed a hard copy to Borden for his preliminary review, with caveats—that's legalese for covering one's butt with warnings—and a promise I'd take his comments and combine them with my own careful cleanup first thing tomorrow morning. After all, it didn't have to be filed and served until later that day.

So now I was in my ugly little rental car, chugging up the 5 Freeway toward Valencia, where Show Biz Beasts had its training facility. As always, there was plenty of traffic, so I had time to think. Which I did. Mostly about Show Biz Beasts.

I'd already rallied some of my entertainment industry contacts to participate: Charlotte and Rachel, and another law client, Charley Sherman—a retired animal trainer for

Hennessy Studios. Along with the Hayhursts' and my input, we'd put together a dynamite concept for a delightful reality show.

People would enter their pets, and those chosen would work on training them in a specific scenario. Initially, we'd attempted to complete each concept in one show and choose a champion, but that soon seemed too rushed. Instead, as in many reality shows, the test would now continue for several weeks. Some contestants would be booted off after each episode for lack of skill or popularity. The last animal standing would take home a grand prize yet to be determined, perhaps a role in some upcoming show on the network that aired our auditions.

I finally got off the freeway, inching along behind a bunch of slow vehicles in the direction of the warehouse area housing my client. Soon, I turned into the driveway behind the long, low stucco structures. Building B was home to Show Biz Beasts. I parked and slipped inside.

The entry area was, unsurprisingly, empty. The day's activities had begun. The place was a typical waiting room, à la a vet's office, with a beige tile floor, neutral-hued walls, and pseudo leather seats. But I wasn't about to sit there. Normally, people had to be buzzed in, but I happened to know where that button was. I slid the glass window into the receptionist's area ungently aside, then leaned over and groped till I found it. I pushed it and was rewarded by a loud click. The door to the inner sanctum slid open.

I scurried down the hall till I reached the large room where the training and auditioning had occurred before. No knocking necessary. I just walked in.

The place looked like a typical sound stage, or what I, with my lack of show biz background, had come to assume one looked like: a large room with high ceilings that could be decorated to be nearly anything. Rows of portable lighting. A sort of musty smell.

And in the middle was exactly what I'd anticipated: lots of people milling around a set. Many sat on chairs at the edges, holding their dogs' leashes. Among the dogs were a Chihuahua, a German shepherd, and two other dogs of sizes in between, neither of whose heritage I could exactly identify; one was furry with a pointed muzzle, and the other was short-haired with a blunter nose. Some participants from our first sample show were also in attendance, including the litigious bichon frise's owner, sans attorney.

I didn't see the Show Biz Beasts mascot, Dorky, or his usual handler, Larry, but entering that brilliantly trained dog in today's test festivities would definitely distort the results.

Corbin Hayhurst stood in the center of the stage. He had a pudgy face that seemed as wrinkled as his yellow shirt. His jeans hugged his thick thighs. "Okay, listen up," he was saying. "Our test scenario for today involves a pretend emergency. We'll act as if this is an actual show we're filming. Our staff"—he pointed to the people at the fringes of the set, including Charlotte, Rachel, and Corbin's wife, Shareen—"will vote on who does best. Of course, this is just a demonstration, but you'll get to see how it goes."

Corbin faced a participant, the one with the German shepherd. I looked more closely—and saw that this was one handsome dude. Those around him were ordinary mortals with unkempt hair and clumps of wrinkles. But he sat tall. His hair was dark, wavy, thick, and all there. His chin was strong beneath well-defined cheekbones. And that mouth. Rather, that wry grin—he appeared to be having the time of his life, perhaps enjoying a joke that no one else got.

And then I got it. My suspicion was confirmed an instant later when Corbin said, "Like I told you, Mr. DeFrancisco, some of these people have brought their dogs in for lessons before, so you may want to try Wagner out on the scenario once or twice."

"Not necessary, Corbin," said Dante DeFrancisco oh, so smoothly. "But thanks for the offer. Wagner will take his licks if he can't cut it, just like any other dog here."

"Okay, then. Here we go." Corbin turned to a guy I didn't recognize who stood next to a cameraman and jabbed his finger in a gesture that seemed to mean "Do it."

"Fire!" that fellow yelled.

Immediately, chaos ensued. The Chihuahua stood and barked and attempted to drag her hefty owner offstage.

The furry middle-sized dog and the bichon both just looked around, as if bewildered at all the sudden activity.

The medium short-haired pup leaped toward a wastebasket in the corner of the set that appeared to be smoldering. Had he been trained to pick it up and drag it far from vulnerable people? Looked that way, since that was what he did.

But the German shepherd was the dog that got all my attention. He rose fast and glanced at his owner. Dante nodded and said, "Fix it, Wagner."

So he did. Wagner ran to the wall of the set and leaped into the air, knocking to the floor what looked like a big, red fire extinguisher. Wagner grabbed it by a woven black strap, carrying it to Dante and offering it up to him.

Dante did as his dog directed, grabbed the extinguisher, and went through the motions that would have directed foam from the contraption into the seemingly smoldering wastebasket that the other dog had moved. Wagner gave a final, excited jump, then sat down and watched his master expectantly.

"Good dog." Dante DeFrancisco bent down to pat his dog's head. And then the guy looked directly at me, as if awaiting my approbation.

Well, hell, how could I do otherwise? I hurried toward them and dropped to my knees at Wagner's side. "You're a hero," I told him, giving him a big hug. Maybe not the best idea with a dog I'd never met before. After all, some German shepherds are taught to attack strangers. But Wagner simply lolled out his large tongue, then rewarded me with a big slurpy kiss on the cheek.

I stood. "You've got quite a dog there, Mr. DeFrancisco. He's wonderful." I held out my hand. "I'm Kendra Ballantyne."

He looked at me with that same amused expression in his dark, dark eyes as he clasped my proffered hand and held on, instead of shaking it. "I know," he said.

Okay, he could have been acknowledging what I'd said about his dog. But I somehow sensed otherwise.

He knew me. But how?

And why did that send shivers of anxiety and anticipation through every synapse in my suddenly quivering body?

Chapter Two

SHOW BIZ BEASTS had a perfectly nice inside office we could have borrowed for our conclave. But did we?

Nope, because big shot Dante DeFrancisco wanted a fresh cup of coffee. Not one brewed right there at the beastly facility, either. Instead, he loaded Charlotte, Wagner, and me into his sleek silver Mercedes and drove us to a nearby chain coffee shop. Now, we sat outside, Wagner at our feet, where the entire world of other patio drinkers could eavesdrop on our negotiation.

Gee, do I sound peeved?

Well, there was no sense blowing a perfectly plausible business opportunity for my friends, clients, and business associates just because a guy with mega power decided to rub it in our obviously eager faces. Instead, I assumed my most professional lawyerly cool.

"I'm sure you're aware I'm an attorney," I said to him as I sipped my luscious and rich café mocha. Charlotte had ordered a decaf caramel coffee concoction. Wagner had a bowl of water lying beside him on the sidewalk. And Dante sipped a grande-size espresso, no milk or other frothy flavorings, with those full lips that now irked me with their frequently cynical smile.

"Yes, I know of your reputation, Kendra," Dante said, which made me all the madder. Was he telling me he was well aware of that embarrassing situation a while back, when I was unjustly accused of an ethics violation and temporarily lost my law license? "You're becoming well known in the pet community for helping people resolve their differences amicably—like with your clients, the Hayhursts."

Oh. Of course he could have known of my ADR that resulted in the pet reality show idea. And as a pet mogul himself, owning all those wonderful HotPets stores, he undoubtedly kept up on anything else interesting in the animal community.

Not that my small animal dispute resolution triumphs were trumpeted everywhere. Still . . .

"I doubt I'm becoming well known," I said. "And I bring up that I'm an attorney only because it makes sense for you to have your lawyer present, too, in any negotiation about your proposed financial backing."

"I know your ethics require you to disclose that," he said. "And if necessary, I'll sign something that says you did in fact warn me. But I'm perfectly capable of negotiating my participation myself, and my team of lawyers knows that. They'll help us paper the deal once we've settled on terms. First, let's talk about my requirements." Uh-oh. I preferred his untrustworthy smiles to the unyielding stare of his deep brown eyes.

And his assertion of requirements strongly suggested they weren't subject to negotiation. But, hell, I'm a lawyer.

Lawyers always negotiate to improve their clients' positions. Or at least attempt it.

"Fine," I said with a chilly grin of my own. "Tell us what you'd like, and then we'll discuss what you'll get."

"Er . . . Isn't she a wonderful attorney, Dante?" Charlotte had been staring at Dante, then me, moving her head fast enough that her long braid of dark hair swung from side to side. "Always ready to argue. But of course we want to hear everything you have to say." Her tone turned gushy. Which made me feel like throttling Charlotte, though I realized that what she was doing—attempting to throw the guy off guard by flagrant flirtation—might actually be advantageous to me.

"Thank you." Dante looked only at her, although the words that poured next from his again-smiling lips were clearly aimed at me. "I'll need to see a proposed budget for the initial season of *Animal Auditions*. I'll pay for those costs, if the budget makes sense and contains projections that show how I can make a substantial profit if all goes as we anticipate."

Charlotte was nodding as she stared straight into those sexy eyes that Dante kept directly on her.

Well, fine. She could have him. And maybe if she did, I'd get him to budge off the unreasonable conditions I was certain he was about to present.

"And your desired terms?" I inquired. I shouldn't have used the word "desire." Not with a guy who looked like that sitting beside me. It only reminded me I hadn't had sex for weeks, not since my former boyfriend, Jeff, had first disappeared. Sure, he'd returned to town, but he'd really wounded me with his attitude when he resurfaced.

Maybe lack of sex was exactly why I thought about it

now, in the presence of a guy as great-looking as Dante DeFrancisco. But now that I understood my attitude, I'd deal with it.

"Here's what I want." He took a sip of espresso, then returned his cup to the glass table. His movement apparently disturbed Wagner, who sat up beside him. Dante distractedly stroked his dog's head as he said, "First, this studio is too far away for easy filming access. I have a nicer and more convenient place we can rent in—where else?—Studio City."

"That's fine, isn't it, Kendra?" Charlotte said, her usually friendly face wearing an expression that suggested she'd go for my jugular if I disagreed. Apparently, she really wanted to please this guy . . . in more ways than one?

That idea made me want to dig in my heels, but I'd wait and choose my arguments. This demand actually had some appeal.

"Let's hear the rest," I said sweetly, "so we can determine what needs negotiation." Like Dante's autocratic attitude.

"Fine." Charlotte would have hissed and aimed her claws at me if Dante hadn't started speaking again. And this from a lady who'd always annoyed me with her hugginess.

"Second," Dante said, "I enjoy finding new and different things to do to amuse Wagner, so even though he won't be a viable contestant, I'd like for him to be included in at least some of the training sessions for dogs. Offcamera is fine, of course."

Wagner grasped that we were gabbing about him. He moved away from his owner's stroking hand and around the table toward me. His leash was long enough that he had no problem reaching my side. Like Dante, I started petting the friendly pup as I pondered this part of the proposal.

"As long as it doesn't slow down the production," I said. "And if you're willing to pay for any additional staff time, facilities, and other expenses, that may be all right. Depending on the rest of your . . . suggestions." I still wasn't willing to openly acknowledge that they were demands.

"Only a couple more. The next one's a deal killer, though, if you don't agree, but I'm sure it's the most obvious."

I drew in my breath, defensive even before I heard what it was. I always got that way around so-called deal killers. They too often tended to be unreasonable. And unreasonable demands never made it into contracts that I got involved with negotiating . . . unless they were mine. Good thing I was first and foremost a litigator.

"What's that?" The mistrust and irritation in my tone evoked another glare from Charlotte, a stiffening of Wagner at my side . . . and another sardonic smile from Dante.

"My backing of *Animal Auditions* appears a no-brainer, considering I'm in the pet supplies business. HotPets will be the major sponsor, or there'll be no show. And there will of course be no competing pet-related retailers' ads. Period."

Again his gaze hardened. His broad jaw grew tauter and more belligerent, as if he anticipated an argument.

But why would I object? The condition seemed reasonable—not that I'd concede that to him.

"Any final suggestions?" was all I said.

He didn't exactly relax. But one corner of his mouth quirked up almost imperceptibly. "Yes. Dogs are delightful subjects for this show, but to bring in a wider audience, I want you to agree to have other pets participate as well. That'll help differentiate *Animal Auditions* from other pet reality shows, especially with the kinds of ongoing training scenarios you've already introduced. We want it to stay unique. And I'll assist in coming up with scenarios for training and showcasing other kinds of animals."

A good idea—one we'd already considered—but I still considered digging my heels in, so as not to appear to be a pushover. "What other kinds of animals?" I demanded.

"I'll think about it. But you're an animal expert, too, Kendra. With your law practice, and especially with your pet-sitting, you work with many kinds of creatures. What's your suggestion?"

My mind flitted among ferrets and kitties, iguanas, ball pythons, and macaws. Macaws? Maybe. I'd considered them all. But then my thoughts stopped on something I'd seen only a few weeks ago. My friend and former law-firm co-worker Avvie Milton had shown me a heck of a performance by her pet, Pansy.

"Potbellied pigs," I proposed.

That garnered a grin from Dante. And a relieved look from Charlotte as she observed his pleased demeanor.

"Done," he said. "And the other 'suggestions' so far?" He stressed the word "suggestions" as if he was simply humoring me.

Which he most likely was.

"We may need to discuss how to accomplish them," I said slowly, considering the move from the Valencia sound stage, the staging of Wagner's participation, and the inclusion of noncanine contestants, "but I haven't heard anything unworkable."

Which made Charlotte relax and take a deep swig of her coffee drink.

"Oh, and one more thing." The challenging expression in Dante's expressive eyes suddenly made me freeze. And grow hot. At the same time. How did that happen?

"What?" I asked as casually as I could . . . expecting the worst.

Which I got. Kinda.

"I'll back the show only if you'll have dinner with me tonight, Kendra."

"SO WHAT ELSE could I do?" I asked Abra a while later. The female Siamese kitty glared at me in the kitchen, since I had been so rude as to interrupt her dinner. Her cohort and co-cat of the household, Cadabra, a pretty tabby, at least looked at me with a shred of sympathy before returning to carefully pick over the morsels of kitty food I'd put in her dish. Their human, Harold Redding- ham, was a long-term pet-sitting customer of mine. The felines had decided to put up with me when Harold was out of town—which he often was—though they sometimes played games like hiding to scare the silly pet-sitter who appeared daily to do their bidding.

They obviously had no answers for me, so I next headed to Stromboli's home. The shepherd mix seemed happy to see me, but offered no suggestions as I walked him along his street. His neighbor Maribelle Openheim, who'd be- come my friend, came outside with her wiry terrier, Meph, after I called to let her know I was in the area. I considered telling the hairstylist, whose own coif now had a lovely layered look, my dilemma, but decided to lay it on her later, if at all. I'd already made my bed, so to speak—I'd ac- cepted Dante's dinner invitation.

"What're you thinking about?" Maribelle demanded, staring straight into my face. She wore her middle age well these days. When I'd first met her, she'd been going through an awful emotional time, but now she was essentially happy with her life—and ready to organize mine. "You look like you've swallowed something awful."

"I'm fine," I told her. "I'll tell you all about it soon."

"Oh, one of those dirty attorney confidentiality dilemmas," she surmised with a sigh. "Glad I don't have to deal with such things."

I didn't disabuse her. Instead, I took Stromboli home, made certain he was comfy, and, sitting in the car, jotted my latest pet-sitting notes into my Critter TLC, LLC, journal. Then I hustled to pick up my darling Lexie from doggy day care, and headed home to feed her. And hug her. And feel sorry for myself for as long as I could.

"You feel sorry for me, too, don't you, Lexie?" I asked her as she sat on the bedroom floor, watching me prepare for an evening without her company. But good sport that she is, she wagged her long tail and stood on her hind legs to hug me.

I didn't have a whole lot of leeway here. I'd enlisted a lot of people to participate in this cute reality show concept, but it would shrivel away to naught if we didn't secure sufficient funding.

Martyrdom? Maybe.

In any event, a while later, I sat across from Dante in an intimate booth in a delightful, upscale French restaurant only a couple of miles from my home. The place was moderately crowded, but the wait staff was utterly attentive, the aroma of the cuisine made it worth waiting for, and the acoustics were fine for a private conversation.

Dante had picked me up at my place in a limo driven by a liveried chauffeur. A bit much? You bet. But impressive nonetheless. And if he'd been surprised that I'd told him to meet me at the bottom of the stairs beside the garage after buzzing him through the wrought iron security gate, instead of at the entry of the main house, he didn't mention it. I had to assume, since he knew who I was, that he had also learned that Lexie and I live in the apartment over the garage and I rent out the beautiful big residence on my property so I can hang on to it all despite the hefty mortgage.

Of course dogs weren't invited on this outing. I'd attempted to explain that to Lexie, but she'd still aimed a hurt look at me as I'd left.

Now, I sipped a deliciously tart yet fruity Bordeaux that cost a bundle more than the house wine. Dante had ordered, with my prior okay, chateaubriand for two—one of the priciest items on the menu. Was he itching to impress me? Well, hell, he was succeeding—and not simply by all the expensive accoutrements.

No, what was really impressive was *him*.

"So you brazened out that whole ugly situation after losing your law license," he said in a tone that sounded surprisingly impressed, considering all this guy had accomplished so far in his successful life. He wore a black suit, crisp white shirt, and navy patterned tie, an outfit that suggested a whole lot of sexiness beneath. Not that sex was what this business meeting was about. But geez, his eyes sure suggested otherwise as he seemed to study me all over.

"What choice did I have?" I asked rhetorically as I shivered beneath his stare. "Lexie and I had to eat. And a really good friend came to my rescue by referring me to some of his doggy day care clients who needed nighttime petsitting, so, voilà." Not that I actually spoke French, but it seemed appropriate to toss in one of the few words I know here, in this mini château.

"Brave woman." He aimed a smile at me that would

have made me melt as much as his gaze if I'd decided to take his flirtation personally. But this guy had to have every woman in the universe swooning at his Ferragamo-shod feet. He was undoubtedly used to encouraging them, either to lure them between his sheets or for practice till he found someone worth luring.

Which wasn't me.

Well, okay. I'd dressed for the occasion, too, in a snazzy, slim cocktail dress that dipped way down in front and back. It was black and sequined and showed off my relatively slender figure. My ordinary, shoulder-length brown hair had been blown into a flattering coif that framed my face.

Odd, though, how his continued appreciative stare, no matter how practiced, somehow made me feel attractive. Well, hell, I'd enjoy the charade for this evening.

And even engage in a little flirtation myself. What would it hurt?

Except that I'd learned my lesson too well. The most attractive men could hurt the worst.

"I'm not brave," I said. "Just practical. But tell me about *you*. How did you wind up getting into the pet product business?"

"Practicality, too," he said, taking a sip from his wine goblet. "And the fact that I care about animals. My career could have taken many different directions, but I wanted to focus on something important to me, preferably products I could sell to everyone, of all economic levels. And what is it that people, no matter who they are, indulge in most these days?"

"Their pets, of course."

"Of course. You've found your niche—or should I say niches? You pet-sit, and apparently excel at that. But in addition, you've modified your law career to incorporate that additional interest. I'm most definitely impressed."

So how had we gotten back to talking about *me*? Hell if I knew. I didn't press the subject of Dante DeFrancisco until after our salads were served.

"Okay," I said after swallowing a mouthful of greens bathed in delicious whipped vinaigrette. "So you looked around and decided to sell stuff to pet owners. How did you get started?"

"Small at first," he said. "A store here, and when it did well, a store there. I especially enjoyed selling the upscale end of things—jewel-studded dog collars and leashes, for example. But I always made sure there was also an adequate supply of ordinary nylon ones. And rhinestone-decorated accessories for in-between."

"Smart," I said. "But . . . well, forgive me for being nosy." Or don't. I didn't care . . . did I? "How did you start in the first place? Did you have investors?" Or were you already wealthy?—though I didn't ask that. Nor did I ask whether, if he'd already had money, he had earned it by honest means.

Somehow, I had a sense that this man could accomplish anything he imagined—but didn't necessarily have the scruples to wait patiently while dribs and drabs of ordinary income flowed his way.

"I chose to start conservatively," he repeated, "and do it all on my own. And I was lucky."

And smart. And . . . a scintilla crooked? But I didn't ask. I'd no reason to assume so—except for an indefinable yet unignorable intuition.

"That's impressive," I said.

Soon, we were discussing the merits of dog breeds. And rescued animals—of utmost importance to Dante. I'd already discovered, after Googling him, how many shelters he supported. Most took in pets for adoption—and had an inviolable no-kill policy. Other shelters took in injured or otherwise endangered wildlife that could not be released back into the wild.

The chateaubriand was scrumptious. So was the company.

Later, we lingered over coffee and crème brûlée. Then, all too soon, it was time to leave.

The chauffeur brought the limo to the door as we exited. He drove slowly back into the Hollywood Hills—not to my home, but up to Mulholland Drive, where he pulled into a turnout, and Dante and I observed the mega-acres of lights illuminating the eastern San Fernando Valley.

Was I surprised when this man drew me into his arms and gave me the hottest, sexiest kiss I could recall having in forever? Not. But would I have torn off his clothes and mine had we been inside and alone?

Not. I knew exactly how awful my judgment about men was. I'd only recently ended a relationship I'd thought would never need to end.

It was way too soon to tango.

Plus, as amazing as Dante seemed to be, there was too much about him I didn't know.

Mostly, how gently would he handle my badly bruised heart and ego, if I ever left either vulnerable to him?

Which I wouldn't.

"Oh, Kendra, you are such a surprise," he breathed as we ended that kiss.

"You don't know the half of it, Dante," I replied, my lips still settled against his. Okay, I could flirt even if I'd no intention of it going anywhere.

"But I will," he said with no dribble of doubt.

Don't count on it, I thought. And I was all but certain I stomped on his enormous male self-esteem when, at my place, I kissed him goodbye at the front gate without inviting him inside.

But I'd done my duty. I'd had dinner with him, satisfied that condition of his backing our baby reality show.

Sure, I'd see him again. At negotiations for the actual agreements that would be needed before filming could begin. On the set. Wherever.

But as sexy and appealing as I found the man—and as sleepless as I remained that night, hugging only my dear Cavalier Lexie in my arms and thinking about dinner and its unfulfilled sensual suggestions—I knew better than to dream about having Dante DeFrancisco insinuate himself further into my highly satisfactory life.

Chapter Three

"So ALL THAT buildup, and you haven't heard back from the guy?" asked my best bud in the whole world, Darryl Nestler.

A week had passed since my dinner with Dante. Now, I sat in the messy but comfy office of Doggy Indulgence Day Resort, where I'd come after my morning pet-sitting rounds to drop off my beloved Lexie. She needed some extra indulgence, which here involved playing with other pups when she felt like it. If not, she'd relax in her favorite of the large room's multiple pet-pampering areas: the one with the plethora of people furniture.

And I needed some TLC, too, via talking to the tall, lanky guy who'd been my moral support through all sorts of upsetting situations over many months—not the least of which was that I'd become a murder magnet. But fortunately, after helping to solve the last one, a few weeks back, I was free of felonies to figure out.

Darryl had also introduced me to the Hayhursts and

made some suggestions for our initial *Animal Auditions* ideas.

"Nope, haven't heard a word." I didn't intend that to erupt as a grumble, but it did. Which irked me even more. I should feel relieved. Of course, I had a meeting scheduled tomorrow with Dante's attorney to go over final details of the agreement we'd been negotiating. All the conditions he'd asked for were agreed on—other than the coerced dinner with me, but that was now a done deal. But the new location, broadening the types of animals cast, and mega-promotion for HotPets were all there.

I'd also put together a nice new limited liability company for those of us involved in the *Animal Auditions* production. We were all members now—Charlotte LaVerne, with her unequaled reality show background; Rachel; the Hayhursts of Show Biz Beasts; and, of course, moi.

Oops. There was that dratted French that kept coming to mind after my evening at the château with Monsieur Dante DeFrancisco. Not that I allowed him to remain too prominently in my tête—er, head.

"I'd thought," Darryl said dryly, peering over his wire-rims, "that the guy had the hots for you, which was why he insisted on a date before committing to spend lots of money on your reality show production."

"No, he wants to promote HotPets. He doesn't give a damn about someone like me, whose role with *Animal Auditions* will be minor once we get going."

"We'll see, but I have a sneaking suspicion you haven't seen the last of him."

"Nothing earthshaking about that," I responded. "I intend to be there for at least some of the *Animal Auditions* tapings, and Mr. DeFrancisco may attend, too."

"Mr. DeFrancisco? I thought you were on a first-name

basis. Not that you told me a lot, but I had the sense, when you described your dinner, that it ended with a major clutch in the car, chauffeur chaperoning or not."

"Yeah, well, that was then and this is later, in the light of day and all that. Dante DeFrancisco is about to get the deal he wanted, so he doesn't have to schmooze the production company's lawyer—me—anymore."

"Maybe," Darryl said. "So . . ." He looked at me with a sudden, big smile lighting his long face.

"So what?" I'd known him long enough and well enough to assume that expression suggested a secret. "Spill it, Nestler."

"Spill what?" His tone resounded with assumed innocence.

"Whatever it is that you want me to pry out of you."

He raised his eyebrows above his spectacles' frames. "Who says there's anything like that?"

A knock sounded on his office door. His expression changed to an odd combo of irritation and relief as he called, "Come in."

Kiki, one of Darryl's longtime assistants, opened the door, and a couple of pups popped in at her feet. Lexie was one, and she leaped onto my lap.

"Hi, girl," I crooned, though I had to speak up since now the sounds of barks barged in from the animal area.

"Sorry to bother you, Darryl," lied the ill-tempered blonde bombshell who, like many around the area, aspired to become a star. Good thing she obviously loved dogs, for they clearly loved her back. And she hadn't been cast in anything I knew about. "An owner is here and asking about long-term pet-sitting. I explained we don't do it . . . but that you sometimes give referrals." She shot a dagger of a glare at me, followed by a too-sweet smile.

"Come on, Kendra," Darryl said. "I'll introduce you, and if it's an assignment my favorite pet-sitter doesn't want to take, you can refer the owner to a fellow member of the Pet-Sitters Club of Southern California."

"Fair enough." I deposited my darling pup on the floor as I followed Kiki and Darryl out the office door and into the enormous chamber where dogs of many sizes mingled, with careful human supervision. Before we got to the front desk I touched Darryl's arm. "Don't think our conversation is over," I said. "I want to know what you weren't telling me."

"It's no big deal," he said, but the way his face lit up shouted otherwise. "It's just that I've got a new girlfriend."

With that, he turned and started talking to the guy who stood at the sign-in desk, a golden retriever at his side.

I was too floored to join them as I swallowed my surprise. I knew Darryl dated now and then, even spoke of fixing him up with a friend once. But for the entire length of our friendship, I'd always dumped my tales of woe in the relationship arena on him, not vice versa.

Now he was not only dating, but whoever it was had been elevated to the position of girlfriend without his even hinting of it? Well, I'd hide my hurt and swallow any advice . . . for now.

I needed to know who it was—and whether she was good enough for my best buddy Darryl.

I WAS STILL a whole lot irritated with Darryl the next day, when I entered the Yurick & Associates offices. The attorney representing Dante DeFrancisco was coming in shortly to finalize our contract negotiations.

"Hi, Kendra," chirped Mignon, the Yurick firm receptionist, as I entered the former restaurant building. Perky as always, her auburn curls bobbing, she sat at the front desk in the area where greeters must once have shown hungry patrons to their tables. "I've got the conference room reserved for you all morning, okay?"

"Great," I told her. "The other lawyer should arrive in about an hour."

I was wrong. The other lawyer arrived in half an hour. His name was Glen Elizarian. He was a partner in a major downtown law firm, mid-forties, and mighty sure of himself, judging by his condescending smile. No business casual for him; he was dressed to impress in an obviously expensive navy suit and silk tie.

And he wasn't alone. Dante was with him. Well, why not? It was his dollars we'd be dealing in here. I shook their hands, showed them into the former bar that now served as the Yurick firm's conference room . . . and we came out fighting.

Guess I shouldn't have been surprised, but it took two hours to hash out final details. At times, the discussion grew so contentious that I wondered whether Dante would walk.

To his credit, he hung in and even instructed his attorney to give in on some positions. We discussed how much he'd expend and how, and the way HotPets promotion would be incorporated into our production.

And when we were done, Dante gave me a genuine smile. "No wonder your 'animal dispute resolution' seems to go so well. But I've been watching you. I really don't know how you've managed, in addition to your excellent lawyering skills, and your growing pet-sitting business, to become an amateur sleuth, too. If you explain that to me, we'll have a deal."

"What?" I stood, unsure I'd heard him correctly. Well, hell, of course I had. "My . . . unfortunate affinity for people in difficult situations"—like victims, or suspects, in miserable murder situations—"is irrelevant to what we're talking about here."

Besides, he probably knew too much already. The guy was smart. Savvy. Undoubtedly Googled many people he met. And my past connections with solving murders weren't exactly secret. In fact, I'd sometimes made use of my acquaintanceship with a paparazzo of sorts, Corina Carey, outspoken and brazen reporter for TV's *National NewsShakers* show, when publicity made sense for helping to solve a crime.

But still . . .

"Are you worried that working with me on the show might endanger your life, Dante?" I demanded oh, so sweetly.

"I can take care of myself," he replied. "But I'm interested. We'll let it slide for now, though. Glen, put what we agreed to in legalese, and then we'll be through with this negotiation. Okay?" He looked at me.

"This murder magnet couldn't be happier," I responded with a smart-alecky smile. "That's how I think of myself these days—unfortunately or not—not 'amateur sleuth.' "

"Got it, murder magnet. So, now that we're done, join me for dinner tonight."

No way. The guy took me out a week ago, then ignored me till it came time to do business. He could eat alone. Or with his high-powered, high-priced legal counsel who didn't appear at all pleased that we had reached an agreement that would contain clauses he hadn't championed.

So why did I feel so bad when I said no? "Maybe once we get this deal all signed up," I replied.

"Fine. Tomorrow, then." When I opened my mouth to protest, he said, "Glen will have the revisions by then. And you'll be at the first potbellied pig program tomorrow, won't you?"

"Wouldn't miss it," I said with all certainty. In fact, I was looking forward to it.

In a while, Dante was gone. So was Glen. And my peace of mind fled with them.

So what did I do? I went to my office. Made a phone call I had no business making.

I thumbed through the stuff in one of my too-tall piles, giving my nervous fingers something to do as I spoke. "Hi, Althea," I said too brightly. "This is—"

"You think I'd forget your voice this fast, Kendra?" she demanded dryly. Her tone softened. "Good to hear from you. How are you?"

"Fine. And you?" We went through all appropriate amenities . . . except for ignoring the six-hundred-pound gorilla in her office that neither of us mentioned.

Actually, her boss, Jeff Hubbard, head of Hubbard Security, wasn't so huge or ugly. He was a great-looking guy, muscular and not an ounce overweight.

He was also my former boyfriend, whom I'd dumped because of his really awful attitude toward me during a recent situation. One in which, yes, I'd been a murder magnet.

"I'm calling to ask a big favor," I finally said. "It's made bigger by the fact that I don't want you to—"

"Tell Jeff," she interjected. "Right?"

"Right."

"Well . . ." She didn't sound excited. "Tell me what it is."

"I'm negotiating a transaction that involves Dante De-

Francisco. I've done all the initial Googling I can, but your sources are a whole lot better than mine."

Mainly because they were supersecure. Althea, a really attractive grandma who'd become my good buddy over the last many months, was an A-one computer hacker.

"That rich guy with all the pet stores?"

"That's the one. Will you do it?"

"I admit I'm intrigued. He's interesting. But . . . okay, I'll do it . . . on one condition."

"What?" I anticipated what she would say—and it wasn't something I'd like.

"You'll talk to Jeff. Maybe have lunch with him or something. See if there's any way to mend fences."

"There isn't, Althea," I said. "But if that's the only way I can get your help, I'll speak with him. We'll have to figure out a reason, though, besides my enlisting you to do something he'd never approve if he knew."

"We'll think of something," she said.

I knew we would. But I wasn't exactly excited about talking again, even one more time, with Jeff Hubbard. Maybe I could put it off while Althea worked . . .

Like forever.

Chapter Four

"THIS IS UTTERLY amazing," I stated to Lexie at one o'clock the next afternoon. We sat in my office at the Yurick firm. Although we'd had our usual great time pet-sitting first thing that morning, I hadn't accomplished a whole heck of a lot of lawyering, since my mind was whirling around what would happen later in the day.

A piggy audition.

But before I could pack up my pet paraphernalia and head to the new filming location in Studio City—yes, Dante had come through that fast in booking the perfect spot—I'd gotten an e-mail with an attachment from Glen Elizarian. Dante's attorney had put together a revised version of our agreement.

I'd opened it, and had simply stared as I perused it. It looked exactly like what we'd agreed to yesterday. No attorney gamesmanship as I compared it with the prior version and my meeting notes. Fantastic!

I phoned Glen immediately. I didn't project my enthusiasm about his excellence in judgment, though. No sense giving the guy more of a swelled head than he already had.

"It looks acceptable," I opined. "I'll go over it with the other members of the LLC later, at the filming. If all goes as I anticipate, I'll get their signatures then."

"Good," Glen said. "Dante's ready to execute, too. He'll be there, so we can put this puppy to bed. So to speak." He talked a slangy sort of legalese, but must have figured someone with my canine connections would assume he meant genuine puppies.

"Great." As I hung up, I remembered the other thing this meant: I might be committed to having dinner tonight with Dante. I'd told him I'd do it again once we had a signed contract.

How did I feel about that? It had been on my mind a lot, but I couldn't state my opinion with certainty. No matter. For now, I had potbelly pig auditions to attend.

One more call before we left—to my friend and piggy expert, Avvie Milton. She'd been an associate at my former law firm of Marden, Sergement & Yurick. She still was, although it was now just Marden & Sergement. Bill Sergement, the senior partner who'd seduced first me, then her, had recently dropped her in favor of his wife. Right now, I figured Avvie wasn't long for that firm.

"Hi," I said when she answered her cell phone. "You on your way?"

"I sure am. I wouldn't miss this experience."

"But you still don't want to enter Pansy in the audition?"

"Nope," she said. "It would be unfair competition. I'm friends with the management—that means you. Plus I know some of your other friends. And . . . you want to know the main reason?"

"What's that?" I inquired.

"My potbellied pig is the smartest of all, and she'd win no matter who else is there. That's what would really make it unfair."

I laughed as I hung up, but couldn't disagree. I'd met Pansy. Had pet-sat for her a few times. Had seen how smart she'd gotten as she grew bigger, the amazing tricks she picked up awfully fast. It might indeed skew the competition to toss her into the mix.

I peeked into elder partner Elaine Aames's office to exchange goodbyes with her—and with Gigi, the Blue and Gold Macaw. I waved at the Yurick firm staff as I hurried out the door.

Then, I drove my ugly little rental car east from Encino, toward Studio City.

Do you get the impression I wasn't happy with my ride? I was narrowing down the search for a replacement for my beloved but totaled BMW. I couldn't afford a new Beamer without a lot of economic pain, and the lovely sedan I'd had before didn't suit my lifestyle of today. I now had my sights set on a small-to-midsize SUV, one that didn't guzzle too much gas. Maybe a hybrid. But till I made up my mind, I was paying for the rental, since my insurance had run out.

On the way to the studio, which wasn't far from CBS, I dropped Lexie off at Darryl's, partly because I didn't think she needed to participate in a pig audition. And also so I could sneak in and see my buddy Darryl again, maybe catch him off guard, get him to spill his guts and give up the name of his new girlfriend. But he was busy interviewing potential new employees, so though he waved through his office window, he didn't step out to say hello.

So I went to the studio somewhat miffed. But mostly a

whole lot excited. Amazingly, Charlotte had already received a commitment from a notable cable network to air episodes starting with today's. Almost live—taped this afternoon, and shown in a scheduled spot tonight. Tonight! They'd taken a chance on us getting a sponsor so fast, and now we had one—as soon as we executed the contract with Dante.

Which had me wondering. Which came first? Had Dante engineered this exciting twist even as we were negotiating?

There were several buildings on the SFV—San Fernando Valley—Studios lot. Our show was to be shot in the first. It was sexier than most I'd seen: three stories, with offices inside at the front and the rear converted into several smallish sound stages. One side of the frontmost sound stage contained stars' dressing rooms. Fortunately, they were versatile, since at this moment the stars housed were of the porcine persuasion.

Ten potbellied pigs were about to start their audition adventure. They'd been recruited fast, thanks to assistance from a local pig owners' club. From what Avvie had told me about piggies, although they were pack animals of sorts, it sometimes took them a while to warm up to strangers of their own kind.

Charlotte LaVerne, now the reality show maven of L.A., had dressed for her producer activities in a sleek and silky peach pantsuit. She held a clipboard in her hands, and the instant she saw me, she dashed over and gave me her usual effusive hug. "Oh, Kendra, I know we put this together quickly, but it's going to be great! As long as . . . ?"

I knew what she was inquiring about. "Yes, we've got a deal with Dante."

"Wonderful," she squealed, and hugged me again. "They

were asking." She tilted her head toward some guys gabbing nearby who wore blue knit shirts with Nature Network
logos. My surmise about Dante's fixing this with the cable
station was most likely correct.

Of course, since Dante hadn't yet arrived, we'd have to
execute the agreement later. But apparently that hadn't
stopped him from setting everything up.

My pet-sitting assistant, Rachel, was in attendance as
well. She was less demonstrative but equally enthusiastic
as she greeted me. "All the contestants are here," she said.
"So are the Hayhursts." The Show Biz Beasts principals
were to teach pet owners to train their charges to participate in scenarios created for this ambitious but potentially
excellent reality show.

I stuck my nose into a couple of dressing rooms and
laughed at the large, adorable noses that seemed to study
me as well. The pigs, primarily black, white, or a combo,
appeared to be mostly belly and nose, although each also
had interested eyes. And thin, wagging tails, though their
nether appendages weren't as expressive as doggy tails.

At the third room, I stopped. And stared. There were
two people inside, and two pigs. One of the people was
someone I'd met up with often—perhaps more to his cha-
grin than mine.

"Hi, Ned," I said to Homicide Detective Ned Noralles
of the LAPD. "What are you doing here?"

"Kendra! I hoped I'd see you." He headed toward me
and shook my hand heartily.

Ned was the detective I came up against most in my
unwanted sideline of being a murder magnet. The first time
was when this nice-looking African American cop had
tried his damnedest to prove I had slain two people. I was
able to uncover the actual criminal. Since then, he had

been involved in many cases where I helped friends and acquaintances who were accused of murder . . . sometimes by him. I absolutely identified with their angst, so what could I do but assist them?

He'd been sympathetic when my former boyfriend, Jeff, had apparently disappeared, even though the two of them had been enemies of sorts. Ned and I had developed a mutual respect, or so I thought. But now . . .

"Is everyone around here okay?" I asked in a lowered voice.

"Oh, he's not here as a detective," said the woman with him. She was attractive and poised and seemed to resemble Ned. His sister? She confirmed my conjecture as she approached with her slender hand outstretched. "Hi. I'm Nita Noralles. This guy's my brother. And don't you think it's the cutest thing ever? My brother the cop isn't just a pig. He owns one. So do I." She introduced me to the two cute black-and-white potbellies on the dressing room floor. Porker was Ned's, and hers was Sty Guy.

"So you're here because . . . ?" I began, although the answer was pretty obvious. I looked at Ned.

"We love our pigs," Nita responded. "And we live near enough to Hollywood to get involved in stuff like this. We'd love to become stars—or at least for our pets to succeed."

Ned's smile was a whole lot too bright. Somehow his sister had coerced his participation, and I guessed he wasn't overly excited about it.

Maybe it was because any of his cop friends or superiors who didn't already know of the irony of a policeman having a pig for a pet would learn about it now.

"Isn't that right, Ned?" Nita goaded.

He said strongly, "Absolutely." One thing I'd learned about Ned: he could be a good sport—if he wanted to.

Even when he was shown up by someone else solving the crimes he was assigned to. Like me.

"Well, that's great," I said. "I'll look forward to seeing how you do."

Things were getting organized around the sound stage. Rows of seats were set up for an audience, which for now would probably consist mostly of contestants' friends and families. I saw several familiar faces, including cops who'd obviously come to cheer Ned on.

As on many reality shows, a line of tables was set up for judges. The center stage was the focus of the cameras. And soon, the animal stars would emerge.

Charlotte buzzed around, speaking with people, appearing official. And frazzled. I found myself a folding chair along the fringes of the room, out of the way and most especially out of camera range. Then, it was time to begin.

A man in a suit strutted into the main area. "Hi, everyone. I'm Rick Longley, host of *Animal Auditions*." He looked slick and smooth, used to facing the TV camera, but I instinctively glanced for a nonexistent weather map behind him. I'd never met him but knew him by reputation. He had been a successful local weatherman who'd heeded the call to potential fame and sallied forth to New York for a slot on network TV. Unfortunately, he had washed out. His slink back home had been about the time Charlotte starred in the reality show in which she'd had to choose between ostensibly true love and heading her own production. She'd smartly chosen the latter, and Rick had apparently enlisted to host anything Charlotte got involved in.

In a moment, a lovely young lady, clad in a snazzy cocktail dress, strolled to his side. I couldn't suppress the huge grin that slid across my face. "And I'm Rachel Preesinger," she said, smiling for the camera. "Welcome to *Ani-*

mal Auditions." I couldn't be prouder that my pet-sitting assistant and daughter of my main house's tenant was to co-anchor this show.

The two of them introduced the production's judges: Matilda Hollins, a veterinary psychologist; Eliza Post, who had a radio talk show on pets; and Sebastian Czykovski, who was well known as a dog agility trainer and judge, and made the TV talk show circuit showing his skills.

Then it was time for the pigs to make their preliminary appearances. They'd be brought out one at a time, at least for their initial instruction.

As the first pig entered, I noticed someone slip into the first row of the audience. Dante.

The heck with keeping a rational distance, playing hard to get. Protecting my bruised psyche. If I'd been able to sidle nonchalantly in that direction, I'd have done so. To get the contract signed, if nothing else. But, I admitted to myself, I genuinely wanted to see him.

But not now, with everything occurring onstage. Plus, there wasn't an empty seat near Dante. I stayed where I was. At least I could stay offcamera and get a good view of him. And maintain my dignity where he was concerned.

"Here's how things will work," said host Rick, and no thunderstorm pelted us as he spoke. "As with all sequences on *Animal Auditions*, all our potbellied pig contestants will be trained in the same scenario. The first week will be education. The second week, they'll run through their new routines, and two will be chosen to go home, partly based on votes from our viewing audience. That's how it will go until we have two finalists, who will compete during our last week to become champion and win prizes worth fifty thousand dollars from . . . who else? The world's best pet store: HotPets."

So our grand prize was identified at last. I glanced toward Dante, who smiled his pleasure. We were fulfilling our contract's promotional obligations even before it was fully executed, and he was likewise fulfilling his. Excellent!

Except for the fact that he still hadn't appeared to notice my presence. Well, who cared?

Piggy number one was told to come to center stage. The owner was a slight-looking lady, particularly compared with her chubby pig. Rachel greeted them and told them where, initially, to stand—near the trainer-in-chief, Corbin Hayhurst. The scenario: pigs are in fact highly intelligent animals, and they also have a hugely developed sense of scent. That's how they locate truffles in Europe, and they'd even been trained to unearth explosives in Israel. That was our pretend setup. Our pig contestants were to learn how to find things hidden in onstage props by their scent, and distinguish them from other objects.

The first pig, Randall, portly yet plucky, appeared confused, but he obviously loved his mistress and meandered around the stage on a bright red leash that matched his harness, sniffing things on command. When he was finished, the judges were called on for comment. The two ladies, Eliza and Matilda, appeared to me to be animal aficionados. But as always with these reality shows, at least one judge had to be a fault-finding grump. That was Sebastian.

"Pigs." He shook his head and scrunched up his nose as if something smelled bad. "They can't compare with training dogs, but even taking that into consideration, your pig's performance was terribly flawed," he criticized in a clipped voice.

The owner smiled bravely for the camera despite the sorrow in her eyes. "Randall and I will practice hard this week," she said. "We'll be better next time, I promise."

Randall appeared chastised, nose down toward the floor, and I stifled an urge to hurry over and hug his bristly hide.

The second contestant's situation was similar. Confusion but good intentions, tugging on his nylon lead without appearing the slightest bit sure of his assignment. The judges reacted much the same, too, and Sebastian's critique was even stronger.

The third was Nita Noralles with Sty Guy. I was genuinely impressed by that particular pig's attempt to please. And Ned's Porker seemed even smarter.

Even so, Sebastian snidely and nonchalantly sliced their performances to pieces.

Nita had remained silent when her own act was criticized, but when her brother was reamed she spoke up from the side of the stage where Sty Guy and she still stood. "Your judgment sucks!" she complained oncamera.

"So does your slipshod training of your less than stellar pig, and our latest contestant's, too," Sebastian retorted, which made Ned clench his fists. But he was wise enough to stay silent.

Not poor Porker, though. He shrieked an ear-splitting piggy wail till Ned finally convinced him to waddle offstage.

None of the other eight contestants seemed to me to do as well as Porker or Sty Guy, but of course I was biased. Good thing I wasn't one of the judges.

Sebastian remained uniformly nasty to everyone. Big surprise. Would he be kinder to canines, his approved animals? Maybe, maybe not. Perhaps his attitude would encourage outstanding TV ratings, and that was important to the show's success. I hoped so, but also hated it for the pigs' sake, not to mention their despondent owners.

When it was all over, I sighed with relief and prayed everyone would return next week despite their obvious dismay. Then, I finally had the opportunity to get the group of production proponents together, discuss our contract, and get it signed.

Right after, Dante greeted me warmly and signed without the slightest hesitation, trusting me not to have altered his attorney's language. Which of course I wouldn't. I'd already been punished for an alleged ethics violation I hadn't perpetrated. I wasn't about to actually commit one.

Except for differences of opinion about Sebastian, everyone seemed excited. And pleased.

With luck, we'd have a huge TV hit with *Animal Auditions*.

Okay, the show biz bug had taken a bite out of me, too. One of the hazards, I guess, of living in Hollywood.

As everyone started to walk away, I stood to one side with Dante. I waited for the dinner invitation I was sure was coming. After all, he'd issued it before, and I'd told him sure—but only after we had a signed agreement.

"This was fun," I said.

"Yes, fun." His tone was husky, and those dark eyes of his sizzled into mine.

But no invitation.

Well, I wasn't exactly shy. Maybe he was, somehow, way inside. Or his masculine ego had been bruised when I hadn't accepted his earlier invitation on the spot.

"So," I said, "care to celebrate with dinner tonight?"

"Ah, Kendra, I would love to."

I heard the "but" before he said it. And felt humiliated that I'd even—

"But I can't. Not tonight, unfortunately. Something came up, and I'll have to take a rain check."

And this in sunny Southern California. No wetness in any upcoming weather that I knew about. Maybe I should ask Rick Longley for a forecast.

"Sure." I made sure my smile seemed somewhat genuine.

"I can't tell you how sorry I am." He sounded surprisingly sincere for a guy who'd just scorned a nervy lady's somewhat nervous invitation. "I have to fly to Pennsylvania tonight to check on one of my warehouse facilities first thing in the morning. Although . . ." He smiled and snapped his fingers. "I've got it. Come with me, Kendra. I'm going by private plane, and there's room. For Lexie, too. I'm bringing Wagner. I'll be there a few days, but if that's too long, I could send you back and have the jet return for me. What do you say?"

Well, hell. That was an invitation almost too good to be true. A spontaneous vacation with one heck of a sexy guy. To Pennsylvania? I could think of worse spots. But still . . .

"I'm the one who needs the rain check now," I said, sure my real reluctance showed. "I have pet-sitting to do right now, and also first thing in the morning. Not to mention a couple of law client meetings tomorrow, and a hearing on a motion the next day to prepare for. But maybe some other time, with a little advance notice. That sounds like fun."

"Definitely some other time," he said, and right there, in front of all the people and pigs who still milled around, he bent and gave me a deliciously sexy kiss.

But it was interrupted by some shouting off to the side. Who was involved?

Guess. Nasty Sebastian, of course. Dante and I dashed toward the judges' table. Several contestants screamed at the judges. Their piggies squealed even louder than if they were emergency sirens blasting in the background.

"You're so unfair!" shouted Nita Noralles, somehow audible over the porcine din. She saw me and shook her head. "That S.O.B. Sebastian told us that Ned and I will definitely be booted off the show unless we really get our acts together this week. He said we looked like asses on camera, so we should be the ones in training, not our poor piggies."

"*He's* the ass," Ned hollered, "and he'd better watch his behind. I'll make sure we find something to haul him in about. Then he'll see what it's like to be on the short end. And if the rest of you judges stick up for him, I'll be after you, too."

How utterly odd! Ned's reaction was clearly extreme, especially for such a usually laid-back kind of cop. His concern for piggy feelings must be particularly keen. Or maybe it was his sister's emotions he endeavored to shield from any unfair judging.

"See what you did!" Formerly almost nice Matilda turned to Sebastian. "I don't need cops snooping around my business."

Interesting comment. Did she have something to hide?

Apparently Ned wondered the same thing, since his suddenly cool gaze settled on her.

"I'm terribly sorry everyone is so upset," Eliza said in her soft British accent. "You know we all love animals, but part of the fun of this kind of show is to be critical."

"Critical, yes," Nita cried. "Not personally nasty."

"Suck it up and take it, you nobodies," Sebastian said with a sniff. "I'm leaving." He stood and dusted off his suit, as if someone had spilled something nasty on it. "But I'll be back for our next scheduled filming. If everyone's still so sensitive, it's your tough luck." He shot a glare first at his fellow judges and then toward the contestants—especially Ned and Nita.

Before he got far, Dante confronted him. His face utterly impassive, he said to Sebastian, "You're being paid well, and this show will do great in the ratings. Be hard and heartless if you want, but don't lay it on too thick. If our viewing audience hates you enough not to watch, you're out of here."

"Just who do you think you are?" Sebastian demanded. But then one of the guys in the blue Nature Network shirts sidled up and whispered in his ear. Which made Sebastian smile sickly and hold out his hand. "Oh, how do you do, Mr. DeFrancisco."

"That," Dante said after a brief shake, "may be up to you."

Fortunately, the camera crew had already packed up, so none of this nonsense was recorded for posterity.

My production gang exchanged farewells in the parking lot. Dante promised to stay in touch. Yeah. Right.

In any event, my concern for the show was rampant. But it was time for me to go pick up Lexie, escape into petsitting rounds . . . and ponder the pitfalls of all this.

I WATCHED THE show on TV that night and loved it! I prayed the viewing public felt the same. Charlotte called first thing the next day, praising our preliminary ratings. Our piggies rocked!

No need to get into the angst I felt that week, even as I threw myself wholeheartedly into my enjoyment of pet-sitting multiple pooches and pussycats—unfortunately, no especially exotic pets just then. Lexie often came along for company, since she'd gotten to know some clients, including Piglet the pug, Stromboli, Abra, Cadabra, and others. I hadn't yet taken on the golden retriever I'd been referred to at Darryl's, but that seemed forthcoming soon.

I also accomplished a whole lot of lawyering. Even won the motion I'd been preparing for that had been my main reason to refuse Dante's intriguing invitation.

Dante. Althea told me a couple of times that she'd not found anything especially exciting about him—but that I should come to the office anyway, so she could show me all she'd uncovered, such as it was.

Reading between the lines, that meant she wanted me to see Jeff. And I wasn't ready to do that.

I got a number of calls from Dante that lit up my psyche and proved that he had been genuine about keeping in touch. But he was delayed in Pennsylvania. So, nothing exciting happened in that area of my life either.

Probably a good thing.

The next week rolled around. So did the filming at SFV Studios of the next edition of *Animal Auditions*. It was as much fun to watch as last week's, to see the piggies in training for undercover sniff work.

It was also as excruciating as before to hear Sebastian superimpose his opinions on those of all the other judges— right oncamera. Two piggies—not, fortunately, Ned's or Nita's—were booted off the show, as anticipated. But it did not seem accomplished with fairness or flair.

Unsurprisingly, another free-for-all ensued after filming ended, with contestants and production staff and even Dante, who'd gotten back to town, participating. Leading the very vocal charge against the judges were Nita and Ned.

This didn't bode well for the success of our endeavor, despite Charlotte's assumed cheerfulness about how audiences always appeared to love tough judges. What if our contestants all quit? Those who remained appeared ready to mutiny. Even the Nature Network attendees appeared frazzled.

All of us on the production staff, including Dante, agreed to meet the next day. But before we got together, I received an absolutely frantic phone call from our producer in charge.

"Kendra!" Charlotte sounded especially hysterical, even for someone as emotional as she. "It's terrible. And I don't know what it'll mean for *Animal Auditions*."

"What's terrible?" I asked soothingly, attempting to calm her down.

"It's Sebastian Czykovski. He and I were scheduled to meet for lunch to talk over maybe toning down the way he comes across on the show, and how he acts with the contestants afterward. I got to the studio just after noon. I went into the judges' office and . . . Oh, Kendra!"

She didn't have to finish. Murder magnet that I was, I knew what I had to ask.

"Charlotte, did you find Sebastian—"

She interrupted with a shrieked exclamation: "He was dead!"

Chapter Five

I CONSIDERED REMAINING megamiles from the crime scene. I didn't need another murder in my life.

But, heck, there *was* another murder in my life. My own involvement with *Animal Auditions* said so. Many of my friends and acquaintances had spent mucho time and money on this concept. And, in fact, it was mainly my brainstorm.

Maybe, because of some incomprehensible quirk in the universe, I was somehow to blame for what had occurred, murder magnet that I am.

Better yet, maybe that nasty Sebastian had brought this one on himself, without my involvement at all.

I was at my law office. Lexie was at Darryl's. Fortunately, I had no court appearances that day, nor any pleadings that required immediate drafting.

Even so, as frazzled as I felt, I stuck my head into my senior partner's office. "Borden, you'll never guess what happened."

I love his antique desk and the eclectic mix of client chairs facing it. I sat my butt down in one and stared sadly at the silver-haired man who'd been so sweet to take me in as a law partner some time ago. Never mind that he was quirky and always wore Hawaiian shirts. Today's was black with yellow flowers.

"Don't tell me there's been another murder," he said in his high voice, a frown of concern creasing his aging face even further.

"How'd you guess?" I asked in amazement.

"You get a certain look in your eyes." He shook his head. "Murder just seems to follow you, Kendra. It's amazing. You should write all this in a book someday. A series of books."

"Who'd ever believe it? Borden, I'm afraid it's dangerous to know me."

He knew all about *Animal Auditions*. He'd loved the idea but hadn't chosen to buy into it. I had kept him informed about the first filmings, and he'd helped me laugh, instead of cry, about Sebastian and his cruel criticisms.

When I told him who the victim was, he was anything but amazed.

"So you have to find out which of the people you know are suspects." He nodded sagaciously.

"More like I have to figure out which ones *aren't* suspects. Anyway, I've got to look into it."

"Good luck," he said, and I was on my way.

I DREW IN my breath before I opened the outer door to one of the rear SFV Studios buildings. I'd already had to show an ID to authorities to get onto the lot, and the main building where we shot our show was completely cordoned off.

I'd been directed to come straight here. The place was, unsurprisingly, crawling with cops.

I wasn't exactly surprised when, walking inside this building and directly onto a well-lighted stage area, I spotted Detective Ned Noralles in the midst of others in suits, whom I assumed were also cops.

"Hi, Ned," I said, in a weak semblance of cheerfulness. "So now we have another murder case in common. You ready to solve this one for a change?" Okay, teasing the guy wasn't especially tactful, but after all our history I couldn't resist.

His face froze, and I could have bitten off my tongue as the two cops I recognized suddenly approached and stared at me.

"Hello, Ms. Ballantyne," said Detective Howard Wherlon. He'd been Ned's sidekick when I was a murder suspect and in some cases afterward. Seeing him in context reminded me I'd last seen him here, too—definitely not in detective mode. He had been among the cops in the *Animal Auditions* audience, observing his buddy Ned, Nita, and their adorable boars get lambasted by the current murder victim. I'd barely recognized him out of the typical gray suits he wore, like now.

Some other people I thought appeared familiar in the grandstand were also cops. Ned had attracted his own fan club.

But Howard wasn't simply observing at the moment. In his mid-forties, the detective had dark, bushy eyebrows, a receding hairline, and perpetual bags beneath his eyes. I'd gotten used to his decidedly glum expression, but this time he appeared determined. And inquisitive. And accusatory, although his next words weren't especially nasty. "So you've done it again. Another murder within your sphere of influence. It's got to be pretty tough on you—unless, of course, you're guilty this time." When I opened my mouth, he smiled. "Which you aren't. I'll assume that for now, unless the evidence starts pointing otherwise."

"Thanks," I said, certain that at least some relief spilled from my soft tone. "Do you have any suspects in mind yet?"

"Sure he does," Ned said with a surly scowl. "At least a couple. Right, Howard?"

Wherlon shrugged his shoulders. "Could be."

"And they are . . . ?" I asked, and had a sinking feeling I knew exactly who Ned meant.

"Nita," Ned said. "And me."

I should have known better, after all the times I'd been involved in murder investigations, but I heard myself giggle guilelessly. "Right. A police detective and his sister considered as possible killers of a nasty TV personality. Sounds like an episode from some silly comedy series."

But I was the only one laughing even a little. And that stopped immediately, as I stared into Ned's bleak brown eyes. Howard had, after all, most likely heard Ned shouting at Sebastian, leveling threats. But they were cop kinds of warnings, not murder alerts. Still . . .

"Okay." I drew out the word to show it wasn't okay at all. "I'm assuming you're considering all our contestants as possible suspects—at least those who dared to yell at Sebastian for being such a nasty judge."

"We're still considering all possibilities," Wherlon affirmed. "Contestants, staff . . . whoever."

Meaning me? Maybe—notwithstanding his earlier comments to the contrary.

"Where's Charlotte LaVerne?" I asked. "Is she still here? I need to speak with her." And Rachel, and the Hayhursts, and everyone else involved with our show. We needed to compare notes. Protect our production—as long as no one obfuscated the truth, whatever it was.

"She's being interrogated right now," Wherlon said. "And before you speak with anyone, I want to talk to you."

In other words, he intended to interrogate me, too. I supposed that was okay, as long as I was careful. I surely hadn't any secrets . . . at least not pertaining to the demise of Sebastian Czykovski.

We went into one of the building's small offices. The desk and chairs seemed to be generic, wood-grained vinyl. Around the room's edges were video monitors and much other high-tech stuff I couldn't identify.

"So," Howard said, "I saw you around here last week when I came to watch what Ned was up to. Of course I prefer seeing trained dogs, but the pigs did okay. And you—what's your connection with the *Animal Auditions* show?"

I hadn't held an especially high opinion of Detective Wherlon when he'd been on murder cases where I'd investigated—er, snooped—to seek out the real killers. Not that he'd done anything especially stupid, but Ned had always been in charge.

For now, I'd give Howard the benefit of the doubt and assume he was an indomitable detective of Ned's ilk—which meant that he was probably quite competent, yet egotistical enough to zero in on a suspect and be certain he was correct. He would work impressively hard to prove his case without, however, keeping an open enough mind to consider the genuine murderer. And he couldn't be all bad if he loved dogs . . . could he? We'd see.

Did his suspects seriously include the Noralles siblings? Absurd, of course. And yet, I hadn't sufficient facts to absolutely eliminate them from my personal suspect inventory.

In response to Howard's question, I explained how the idea of the *Animal Auditions* show had originated, and why I'd stayed involved—partly because I'd helped to assemble the cast of characters who were now behind the production. I responded to his inquiries about the filmings I'd attended, my limited acquaintance with the ill-mannered victim, my obvious opinion that he'd most likely made more enemies than tolerant friends by his attitude— assuming he always acted, in real life, as he did in the role of animal judge.

"That Sebastian guy seemed to like giving people and their animals a hard time, but did you have any particular reason to harm him?" Howard's bushy eyebrows were raised, and I assumed, especially after what he'd said before, that this wasn't an entirely serious question. Or did he use those brows as props to put people off guard and obscure what he really thought?

"Nope," I replied in all sincerity. "I might have thought him an utter ass, but his kind of general nastiness might actually help attract sympathetic audiences to reality shows. A lot of them have judges like him, after all."

"So I've heard," Howard said, "although I prefer to watch sports and game shows."

"I like cop fiction," I said somewhat snidely, pleased to notice his pained wince. And then I figured my interrogation was coming to an end, so I might as well take advantage of this contact. "So how was Sebastian killed?" I hoped I sounded more nonchalant than intrigued.

Wherlon peered at me with a sudden scowl. "Don't get involved with this one, Ms. Ballantyne. Detective Noralles developed a tolerance for your interference, mostly because you had a run of luck in resolving difficult cases. And he's the one who wound up being patted on the back by the department for successful case solution. But I'm not Ned. I won't go after the wrong suspect. And I do not put up with any kind of meddling. Do you understand?"

I considered standing and saluting smartly. But that wouldn't earn me tolerance from this cop who was obviously swellheaded about being in charge. "Yes," was all I said. I swallowed the sarcasm that sped to my lips. "May I go now?" Oh, did I sound like the perfectly pliant and chastised interrogatee. Okay, so I couldn't completely sublimate my sarcasm. But he seemed to buy it as genuine acquiescence to authority.

"Yes, as long as you understand, and I repeat: Don't stick your nose in my case. Got it?"

What I got was that there was a whole lot of antipathy between Detective Wherlon and me. I simply nodded before I could say anything I might later regret, then slunk irritatedly out of that office.

Where I ran into a cop in casual clothes whom I'd seen at last week's filming: Detective Vickie Schwinglan. I'd met her previously in a different situation I'd happened into as a murder magnet. She'd helped Ned investigate the killing of one of the lawyers at my new law firm, a guy with nearly as winning a personality as our current victim.

"Hello, Ms. Ballantyne," she said with a sardonic half-smile turning up the corners of her narrow lips. She was at least a half-foot taller than my five-five, and it wasn't just her navy suit that made her look a lot thinner, too. I recalled her nondescript light brown hair being tied behind her head before, but now it was cut in a short, layered style that wasn't any more becoming to her ordinary appearance.

Okay, so I was being catty, but having yet another cop glare at me as anathema wasn't doing much for my mood.

"Detective," I responded with a nod, and started to walk past her, down the hall toward the open sound stage area.

"I'm sure Detective Wherlon made it clear to you," she said, "that we will not accept any interference in this case." Her glare could have punctured an entire parking lot full of tires.

Well, hell. I'm an attorney. A litigator. I'm used to swallowing all kinds of irritated responses generated by a judge staring down at me from the bench. But I'm paid to do that. And these repetitious orders to stay away were getting old.

No one was paying me to maintain my frazzled temper here. On the other hand, failing to do so could land my butt in jail as easily as a contempt of court citation. Maybe even easier, with this bunch of bullying cops.

"I get it." I attempted not to unleash my irritation. And then I eased past her and opened an obviously soundproof door, since as soon as I did, I was surrounded by noise.

The large stage area was filled with people. And pigs, all harnessed and leashed. Some screamed in dismay at being there with no exciting performances to execute.

There was to have been a general rehearsal today for all who wished to participate in an extra practice, without cameras or backstage people. I was told this area, not within the building containing the murder scene, had been cleared first by the crime scene techs. The decision had been made to allow all the contestants to come to this convenient locale to be questioned individually—and pigs were permitted to accompany them and let the rehearsal go on, at least for now.

I sidled toward where Charlotte and Rachel stood with

other folks I'd gotten involved in all this. No Dante, though. I felt both relieved and sorry not to see him. Not that I considered him a suspect, but he was now an integral part of this reality show team. Maybe some moral, as well as financial, support from him would help us all survive this awful situation.

"Oh, Kendra!" Rachel moaned as I reached them. "This is so terrible! I know you're used to it, but I've never been treated like a possible murder suspect before."

"I can't say I'm actually used to it," I responded dryly.

"That makes two of us," Charlotte said. I'd helped to find the real killer once when she and some ferrets had been accused of doing away with a guy she'd known from her first reality TV experience.

The Hayhursts, too, bemoaned their potential suspect status. Which was when Ned and Nita joined us, with Porker and Sty Guy waddling, leashed, by their sides.

"Okay," I said softly, huddled among them. "Someone tell me how Sebastian was killed."

Nita started crying softly. She limply lifted the loop of the brown leash she held, then let it sag once more.

"He was hit on the head," Ned said, shaking his head. "And then supposedly strangled with a pig harness."

Poetic justice, considering how nasty he'd been to our potbellied contestants? Perhaps.

"And before you ask," Ned continued, "all of us have our harnesses accounted for."

Maybe, but that harness had to come from somewhere. Not that I had to be the one to figure out where.

Unless that became the only way to protect *Animal Auditions*.

Chapter Six

As I PONDERED the strangulation possibilities, my cell phone rang. Saved by the bell. Well, by the ring tone. Even though I was getting tired of the song, I still was serenaded by "It's My Life" each time someone chose to call me.

Was it Dante at last? I'd left him a couple of voice mails after I'd heard about the awful event at the *Animal Auditions* set. Since he was an integral part of the show—at least his money was—I figured he should know.

But when I pulled the receiver from my pants pocket and glanced at the caller ID, it was someone else's number. Someone I didn't always want to talk to.

What the hell? She'd helped me a few times in difficult situations. For a price. Corina Carey was a reporter for the TV scandal show *National NewsShakers*. If I gave her scoops, she gave me leeway not to get mentioned in the media, at least by her, till I was ready. Which could not, unfortunately, be never.

I nodded my apology to Ned and hustled into a hallway

where real pigs weren't squealing and reputed pigs—cops—were only directing indoor pedestrian traffic, not demanding answers to unanswerable questions.

"Hi, Corina," I said softly into my phone. "What's up?"

"You tell me, Kendra," she retorted. "Why didn't you call me the instant you knew about this latest murder?"

In the world of nosy reporters, news travels faster than the speed of TV feeds. "Sorry," I said somewhat sincerely. "I don't honestly know much yet, but I'll give you a little."

"Good. I'm right outside on the street with my cameraman. The cops won't let the media through. Come out and talk to me."

"Only if I'm a 'reliable source' and not someone on-camera."

"Done."

But when I headed for the door, my way was immediately blocked . . . by Dante. He'd obviously shown sufficient credentials to convince the cops to let him in.

"Kendra," he growled, "what the hell happened?"

"Sebastian's dead," I said, not exactly spewing patience. I'd told him so in my phone messages. "He was murdered."

"Yeah, I got that." He grabbed my arm and propelled me down the hall in the direction from which I'd come. "I need to know how. Who. And we have to get the production group together to make alternate plans—and figure out the best way of turning this into positive publicity for *Animal Auditions*."

I stopped and stared—and nearly lost my arm, since Dante didn't ease up on it. His eyes were icy as he glared back . . . and then they softened.

"Poor Kendra," he said, much more softly. "I'm sorry. I forget you're not just an attorney. You have a heart, or you wouldn't also be a pet-sitter. But you've taken impossible situations and turned them into opportunities. That's what I've learned to do with everything."

All I'd wanted was to protect the show. He wanted to turn Sebastian's demise into a publicity opportunity. Maybe we weren't so far apart. But who was he, really? What experiences had turned him into this wealthy, powerful opportunist?

One with heart, too. I could tell by how his attitude had suddenly grown sympathetic. He'd loosened his grip and wrapped a strong arm around my shoulder. And then, suddenly, I found myself teary-eyed with my head leaning on his hard chest.

"Come on," he said quietly. "We'll learn what we can. Even if he was a heartless, pig-and-people-hating bastard, we'll give him a huge send-off. Okay?"

"Okay," I sniffed. And felt Dante's kiss on my forehead.

I started walking at his side . . . till I heard "It's My Life" singing in my pocket. I pulled out my phone. Corina again.

"Where are you, Kendra?" she demanded. "And can you get me an interview with Dante DeFrancisco? I saw the cops let him inside. I know he's bankrolling your pet show—a natural, of course. He's probably even more camera-shy than you, but still . . . Bring him out, okay?"

"I'll ask him." I looked at him, and his expression immediately grew leery. After hanging up so Corina couldn't eavesdrop, I explained the situation to Dante, including my longtime love–hate relationship with this pesty but practical media personality.

"A contact like her could be helpful to the show," he responded slowly, and I could almost see his brain synapses processing the information. "But this isn't the time to talk to her. See if you can set up a time later. Maybe dinner. My treat."

His smile was so beguiling I almost bit. But then I recalled how he seemed to use dinner invitations for his own, undisclosed ends. Corina was a reporter definitely appealing enough to hold her own oncamera with the prettiest of celebs. Would Dante find her attractive?

And why the heck should I care? I didn't want this guy, great-looking and hellfire hot though he was.

"Sure," I told him, and stalked into a corner, clutching my phone. I called Corina back and told her the good news. "He'll talk to you. Let's set up a time for the two of you to have dinner. His treat." Okay, I'd done my duty. Acted as messenger. Irritated intermediary. Enough.

Only . . . "You'll join us, of course, Kendra," Corina dictated. "I'll want your perspective on this latest murder. You always have such interesting commentary. And my viewers recognize you each time I cover a new killing when you're involved. That's how many now?"

"Too many. And I'm making no promises about joining you. I'll check my schedule." And my mood. Would I want to watch the two of them—powerful, debonair Dante trading flirtation and pseudo facts with this glib and great-looking reporter?

When Dante's Inferno froze over.

I said goodbye, hung up, and swore softly under my breath. Being a murder magnet really sucked, in more ways than one. Who needed a leechlike reporter as a persistent acquaintance and occasional friend?

Who needed an utterly appealing hunk like Dante De-Francisco as a business acquaintance who oozed sexuality even as he kept questions circulating through my mind?

Did he honestly sense some attraction between us, or was it all a game to him? Worse, was it because he wanted something from me—like my affiliation with *Animal Auditions* and the publicity it might garner for HotPets? Especially now. With the murder of its irritable, outspoken judge Sebastian, the show's ratings might go through the roof, even though only two episodes had aired.

I stalked back down the hall toward where I'd parted company with Dante. He wasn't there, so I entered the decibel-enhanced sound stage. At least most potbellies had settled down. Perhaps that was because Corbin Hayhurst, bless him, had apparently recommenced scent-trail lessons, most likely as a diversion.

I suspected that the cops, some of whom stood at the edges of the stage to keep an eye on things, might regret their initial decision to allow the rehearsal to go on even here, in a building beside the actual crime scene. Sure, it might have been a convenient way to corral some suspects and interrogate prospective witnesses, but with the piggies here it stayed prohibitively chaotic.

A couple of less adept contestants were sniffing stuff to locate later. Ned, Nita, Porker, and Sty Guy stood together near the doorway I entered.

I watched for a few seconds, then said, "This is a great scenario. I only hope the show can go on without Sebastian. Maybe we can dedicate the rest of the episodes to him."

Ned glared, but Nita said, "That would be a nice gesture, even if he was an awful S.O.B. I'll bet your boyfriend would approve."

"What boyfriend?" I'd recently dumped my last one, Jeff Hubbard, for being a jerk. I was fairly certain Ned knew it, too.

"That handsome Dante," Nita answered. "You two obviously have something going on between you."

"Just this show," I said. "By the way, where is my so-called boyfriend?"

"With my buddy Wherlon," Ned said irritably. "His turn to be interrogated, I guess."

"I'm sure he's enjoying that," I said with sarcasm. I went back to watching the latest pig scenario as my mind kept flashing to imagined images of Dante's interrogation.

Who would get the better of whom?

DANTE EMERGED TWENTY minutes later from the office in which Detective Howard Wherlon had ensconced them for their little discussion. He soon stood beside me at the edge of the stage where the piggies were once more absorbing lessons. Other production people milled around, including some wearing Nature Network shirts. No camera folks, though. This was simply a rehearsal—at least as far as we, and not the cops, were concerned.

I looked at Dante sidelong. He wasn't smiling.

"How'd it go?" I asked over the orders being given to the potbellies snuffling the floor in front of us.

"Well enough," he replied. "Oh, and by the way, we're each other's alibis. You need to confirm that we spent last night together. At your place. Got it?"

I turned and stared. His demeanor didn't disclose that he'd just told a huge lie to the cops. Or underhandedly gotten me involved. If I allowed it.

"Are you nuts?" I whispered angrily, hoping no network reps were eavesdropping. "For one thing, they already asked me a whole bunch of questions, and your name came up only in the context of helping to back the show."

"Helping?" he asked wryly.

"Okay, gang," called Corbin Hayhurst from the animal congregation area in front of us. "All trainers take your pigs' leashes and start walking them around the edge of the stage area. Meantime, Shareen will hide small containers of different-smelling items in the boxes in the center. Then we'll see how they do picking out particular odors."

Cute scene, watching those waddling characters in shades of black and white, all leashed and all, fortunately, acting obedient and not shrieking in piggy pandemonium.

"Well, okay," I confirmed to Dante as I watched. "I did tell them you're the money behind everything. But that's it. I certainly didn't suggest we had a sexual relationship." I turned my gaze toward him and glared.

"Who said anything about sexual?" he said softly, his dark eyes smoldering as they stared into mine. "Although if you're offering . . ."

"Forget it," I said through my teeth, even as Detective Wherlon whisked up beside us. I nodded my greeting. His glance darted between Dante and me and back again.

"Time for you both to leave," Howard said. "We're going to start clearing the whole site." Which gave credence to my assumption that the cops had decided that massing witnesses here hadn't worked out well.

"We're on our way, Detective." Dante put his hand in the small of my back as if having the right to escort me away.

"In a minute," I said sweetly. "I need to say goodbye first." I maneuvered adroitly away and headed toward the stage, where Ned and Nita Noralles were coming toward me with their pigs. Shareen Hayhurst had stopped sticking scent packets into the boxes and stood at the side of the stage with her husband. Most pig people were directing their pets toward the rear exit.

"I'm leaving now," I told Ned and Nita. "Will you be okay?"

"Sure," Ned said. "One thing, though."

"What's that?" I asked.

"We've talked it over," Nita said. "If we're both thrown in jail, would you pet-sit Porker and Sty Guy for us? We had nothing to do with that miserable Sebastian's death, but the damned—er, those nice coworkers of Ned's haven't quite bought that."

"You're not serious! There are plenty of people who yelled at Sebastian." But when I looked at Nita's face, I saw fear there. Realistic or not, the cops were apparently treating them as potential suspects. Or at least the Noralleses assumed so. And who would know better than Ned? "I'll make sure these adorable guys are well cared for if for some reason neither of you can do it, but that won't happen."

When I glanced into Ned's eyes for confirmation, his expression was definitely desolate. Yep, he apparently assumed they were genuine suspects. And I empathized.

Impulsively, I hugged them—both Noralles siblings, and each of their adorable potbellies. The pigs both moved their noses in my direction, as if scenting a friend as well as something amiss.

"Take good care of yourselves," I told them, then headed back toward where Dante and Detective Wherlon still stood chatting. As if they were friends.

And why not? If Dante had convinced the cop that he had an ironclad alibi—me—why wouldn't they get along just great?

"All set?" he asked as I reached them.

I nodded curtly.

"I was just assuring Detective Wherlon that neither you

nor I had any motive to kill Sebastian Czykovski, even if neither of us has any easy way to prove we were home alone last night."

I stared at him. Obviously he'd just been pulling my chain earlier. He'd never told Wherlon we were each other's alibi.

"Judging by the excellent ratings for our first televised shows," Dante continued, "our audience enjoyed Sebastian's nastiness. I'd venture to say it wasn't anyone concerned with getting the show produced who killed him."

"Unless they had a motive other than high ratings," Wherlon said dryly. "And let's wait and see the ratings for your next shows, now that people's interest might be increased because of the judge's murder."

I didn't respond. Detective Wherlon could be correct. Morbid curiosity was a major attraction for some people's prurient interests.

And I wasn't thrilled that I might be enhancing it by my possible commitment to dine that night with Dante and a tabloid-type reporter.

Chapter Seven

I CONVINCED MYSELF I could get my mind off the Sebastian Czykovski killing if I threw myself into my law work that afternoon. I therefore called Tomas and Treena Jeong.

They were a recent referral from Geraldine Glass, another Yurick firm partner. Like our founder and most of our other attorneys, Geraldine was a senior citizen. Her practice did not include pet law, so she had asked me to work with the Jeongs.

The Jeongs had a Brittany spaniel with acute separation anxiety. At the moment, they were out of town and had a friend's college-age daughter house-sitting. But the young lady had things to do besides sit at home with Princess at all hours, and I'd gotten a frantic message from the Jeongs. Some neighbors had called Tomas on his cell phone to complain that Princess was once again crying her heart out or at least the wife had.

The same neighbors, a childless couple, had previously called some fortunately overworked and underinterested authorities who'd declined to enforce a countywide ordinance against inordinate barking. Then, they threatened to sue for damages for diminishment of property value and emotional distress. They'd told Tomas that they'd have their lawyer file the complaint soon unless Princess shut up, pronto.

The Jeongs adored their Princess. Hated that she was so distressed when they were away from home that she shrieked, not barked—even when they were in town. Also hated the idea that they might have to pay a whole lot of money if there was a lawsuit. They'd already tried a few avenues of canine training and psychology, but so far nothing had helped. Could I do something legally to attempt to appease their neighbors, at least till they got home from their two-week trip?

Sounded partly like a pet-sitting problem . . . maybe. But hopefully, since I both lawyered and pet-sat, I could help.

In any event, I needed to see the situation for myself. I headed my rental car in the direction of where the Jeongs lived—west of L.A. along the 101 Freeway, near Thousand Oaks. I located their address and parked on the street. It was a nice, relatively new development, and the house was large and modern. Its windows were arched, its roof, of brown tiles, over a beige, multilevel structure with a jutting entrance.

When I rolled down my car window, I heard what the neighbors complained about. A shrill, sad cry like an animal in pain emanated from the Jeong home. I exited my vehicle and strode toward the sound. The yard had a nice, green lawn in front, a short driveway at the side, a two-car garage, and a tall gray fence at the rear. The cries came from the backyard.

"Princess?" I called, but the cries continued. I raised my voice. "Princess!" She must have heard me then, since she quieted momentarily. I half expected her to bolt toward the front of the fence, since surely she was loose in the yard, judging by the volume of her wails. But I didn't see her.

I called the house's phone number but got no response. I also saw no sign that the house-sitter was home. I tried her cell but got voice mail. No assistance there—at least not now. But I'd at least seen the lay of the land.

And heard the pitiful wail of the poor, lonesome pup. I wished I could get into the yard and give her a huge hug.

The crying started again, and a neighbor's door opened. A woman, maybe mid-forties, clad in jeans and a loose gray T-shirt, glared as if I was the source of the sound. "Isn't that awful? Those people have no regard for anyone. That dog is so pitiful. It should be taken away from them."

This had to be one of the complaining neighbors—presumably the wife. I couldn't talk to her, thanks to legal ethics, since I believed she was represented by counsel. But I absolutely disagreed with all she said. The Jeongs cared a lot about Princess. That's why I was there. So, I simply shrugged and gave a half-friendly smile. "You'll be fine, Princess," I called. "I promise." Which amazingly caused the crying to stop. And earned the neighbor's quizzical look along with her irritated glare.

I remained where I was a few more minutes, but Princess kept her sorrow to herself. The neighbor disappeared back into her house. All was calm, at least for now.

Maybe Princess's plight could be eased by hiring someone to stand outside and call her name. Or finding a house-sitter who'd be utterly housebound, since apparently Princess cried every time no one was home.

Impractical? Probably. But at a minimum, I could let

my mind churn on these and other ideas for animal dispute resolution in this sad case. And right now, I could head home to reclaim my own little Lexie from her day at play.

As I CHUGGED toward the freeway, I noticed an auto mall I hadn't visited before. I really had an urge to dump this darned rental car back where it belonged. But I hadn't yet settled on what car to buy for my own.

Not another Beamer. I doubted I could afford one, unless it had a lot of miles on it already, which wouldn't bode well for longevity. My preference was buying new and hanging on to a vehicle forever. Or until it got wrecked, whichever came first.

I hoped to find a car that wasn't a gas guzzler, maybe even a hybrid. Something roomy, since I often transported animals hither and thither in my pet-sitting career. Something not too expensive to start with. Probably something that didn't exist.

I stopped to look at a few cars. Some kinds I'd seen before and hoped I'd change my mind about. That didn't happen. Foreign cars were far more popular these days than domestic ones, which often meant more expense, especially for additional amenities.

Then I saw a U.S.-made one that definitely captured my attention. Not that it was gorgeous or gaudy, but it was attractive. And practical. An SUV in which I could get a whole bunch of awesome options, including a super navigation system. What made it stand out most was that it was a hybrid. Its gas mileage could be great. Its name? Escape. And although I'm the kind of person who always faces up to reality, I really liked the idea of being able to sneak into my vehicle and . . . escape.

Of course I had to look it over closely. Price it with the stuff inside and out that I wanted. Ouch.

It could be majorly worse, I informed myself, as I fought off the assertive salesperson rubbing her hands in glee at finding someone excited about one of her autos. I told her I had to think about it. Long and hard.

Which I did on my drive back east toward Studio City . . . and reality. My law practice was a lot less lucrative than when I'd bought my Beamer way back when, as a new law associate at a major L.A. firm. My pet-sitting sideline was definitely a help, but it wasn't exactly a pathway toward financial wealth.

If I bought a car like that, I'd be making substantial payments for ages. Was it worth it? Could be. But I'd need to consider it for a while before leaping in and incurring the additional debt.

SINCE IT WAS only midafternoon, I had time to head to my law office before my late-day pickup of Lexie and performing our pet-sitting. I was nearing my freeway exit when my cell phone sang. I glanced at the caller ID. Since I generally program in phone numbers for my clients—legal and of the pet-sitting persuasion—I immediately knew it was the Jeongs, checking up on my visit to their Princess.

"Hi," I said. "Tomas?"

"No, it's Treena. What did you find out?"

I explained how mournful Princess had sounded, how I'd wanted to soothe her, and how I'd also met one of their nasty neighbors. "I didn't like the neighbor's reaction, but I can sort of understand it. We need to figure out a way to keep Princess occupied when she's alone, or another solution to her separation anxiety."

"Yes!" Treena sounded jazzed. "What would you suggest?"

I'd been hoping she'd toss out some ideas of her own, but no such luck. Instead, she expected that her hired pet expert would act as a canine psychologist as well as an attorney and pet-sitter. And hadn't she already taken that route unsuccessfully?

"Maybe if you fixed it so she didn't get in the yard, she wouldn't sound so loud," I said.

"But she's trained to use the doggy door. We tried keeping her inside for a while, but that did awful things to her housebreaking skills. And she still cried loud enough that the neighbors complained." Treena paused, as if waiting for me to come up with an idea that was a whole lot better.

"Well . . . let me do a little research," I said. "You can do some, too. And Tomas. Maybe, among us all, we'll figure out a way to help poor Princess."

"Sure." Treena sounded dejected and defeated. "We'll figure it out."

"What about your neighbors? Any chance of enlisting them to visit Princess and keep her company instead of complaining about her? Or are they animal haters?"

"I don't think they hate all animals," Treena said. "They used to have a dog, but he got old and they lost him. They haven't gotten another one, so maybe they're still in mourning. But I haven't asked them to help because I'm afraid, with their attitude, they'd do something awful to keep Princess quiet."

"I'll try to come up with something," I assured her— although I wasn't sure what might work.

Almost immediately after she hung up, my phone rang again. Had she come up with a brilliant idea in an instant?

No, this time the screen identified Althea Alton, my

friend and former computer consultant when I'd been up
close and personal with her boss, P.I. and security expert
Jeff Hubbard.

"Hi," I said brightly. "How are you, Althea?"

"I've finally found some stuff on Dante DeFrancisco,"
she responded with no polite preamble. "Interested?"

"Absolutely."

"Good. Come here tomorrow around noon, and I'll spill
it all." Althea could hack computers like a pro—which she
was. A lovely, young-looking grandma, she'd also perfected
the art of manipulation. Or so I felt certain at this moment.

"I assume Jeff will be there," I replied dryly. Since we'd
last seen each other, he'd called and left me multi messages. I'd responded only to the first, to ask him to quit calling. But Althea had apologized on his behalf and clearly
aspired to play arbitrator. Get us back together.

Not going to happen.

But I had to humor her to get the info she'd unearthed.

"Of course he will," Althea said cheerfully. "Wasn't that
the deal? I find data you're after, and you humor me and say
hi to Jeff. If nothing comes of it, at least I'll have tried."

"Okay," I said with a sigh. "But tell him to be on his
best behavior. And not to expect me to act anything but
civil to him."

"That's a start," she said, and hung up.

As I ENTERED the long, low building housing the Yurick
firm, Mignon, the receptionist, looked up and smiled. "You
have a visitor waiting in your office, Kendra," she chirped.

Over the months I'd worked here, I'd come to read the
numerous nuances of Mignon's perkiness. Mostly, she was

simply an amazingly happy person who wasn't ashamed to let it show. Other times, she feigned her usual demeanor to hide what was really inside at that less-than-delighted moment.

This, I felt certain, was one of the latter times.

Her lack of genuine enthusiasm told me Dante couldn't be my caller. "Who is it?" I asked, waiting for her to suggest it was Detective Howard Wherlon or his sidekick in the Sebastian Czykovski murder investigation, Detective Vickie Schwinglan.

"It's that nice detective," Mignon twittered. My heart sank as I realized my clairvoyance was in champion mode that day. I attempted, as I walked down the hall between attorney offices on one side and support staff cubicles on the other, to prime myself to handle another interrogation with resignation and ease.

But when I got to my office, inhaled a huge, calming breath, and looked inside, a different detective sat there: Ned Noralles.

Interesting. I didn't think he was in investigator mode on this particular murder, but maybe he'd convinced his superiors of his innocence, so they permitted him to participate.

"Kendra!" He sounded a whole lot heartier than he tended to be when he planned to rake me over the coals of his questions. "Got a few minutes?"

"Sure." I sounded nearly as perky as Mignon. "What's up?"

He wasn't in his usual dark suit, but still wore his leisure attire of earlier that day when he served as potbelly coach.

"I'm just looking for . . . well, some suggestions. I've been a cop for a long time. A detective who conducts investigations. But . . . okay, let me just say it. How does a person whose background is in the legal field—whether a police professional or an attorney—deal with being a murder suspect, even if not at the top of the list? I mean, how did you live with that?"

His face had fallen with each new attempt to spit out what was on his mind. I'd always considered him good-looking. He still was, but his handsomeness was absolutely strained by the difficulties he was dealing with.

"It isn't easy, Ned," I assured him sadly. "There's this prevailing sense of paranoia, like everyone's buying into those absurd allegations. Sometimes a feeling like, even if you did nothing wrong, you're being punished for something, but you don't understand what it is. At least that's how it was for me."

"Yeah," he said. "And there's this other thing with me. I know how cops think. Sometimes we do stuff to fool suspects into confessing. We can tell lies if we'd like. But of course we have to Mirandize people when they're actually taken into custody. At least I haven't undergone that particular indignity. And neither, fortunately, has Nita."

"Your sister's an actual suspect, too?"

"Sure. My buds Howard and Vickie made that clear right away. The Noralles siblings both had their feelings hurt by that S.O.B. judge Sebastian and decided to do something about it—one acting alone or both, doesn't matter. There'd be at least collusion and co-conspiracy." He shook his head sorrowfully. "They'd even hang it on Porker and Sty Guy as conspirators, too, if they could. Maybe the potbellies worked together to wind that damned harness around the guy's miserable neck and pull it tight. Pigs are smart, so why not try to convict them, too?"

That latter question was obviously rhetorical, so I didn't attempt to answer. "I don't know what to say, Ned, except that I empathize. And if there's anything I can do to help. . . ."

His expression immediately lightened. Uh-oh. I had the awfullest sensation that I knew what he was going to say.

Hadn't he once—and not completely in jest—suggested that I act as unofficial consultant to the LAPD in my murder magnet mode?

"That's why I'm here," he said. "I know you're not a pro, a trained detective. All you go on is guts. And intuition. And . . . well, persistence when you think there's injustice being done. I'll be working on it, too, of course, unofficially. And this isn't easy for me, but. . . . Please, Kendra, I'd be eternally grateful if you'd turn your usual insight and whatever the hell else you've got going on in our direction. Help me figure out who killed Sebastian Czykovski before Nita and I are hauled in for it."

Chapter Eight

TALK ABOUT TOPSY-TURVY situations. LAPD Detective Ned Noralles was actually asking the attorney he'd snubbed and snarled at for being too nosy to do exactly what he'd gotten upset about. More than once.

Solving a murder.

But what could I say? We'd developed more than a mutual respect . . . or so I thought. "I'll try, Ned." I was surprised to see his dark eyes dampen.

"Thanks, Kendra," he said softly. "I'll owe you. And if you would especially look for. . . . Well, never mind."

I *did* mind. What else was he thinking? I needed all the extra ideas I could get. But when I pressed him slightly, he just shrugged and thanked me all over again.

Even assuming I was successful in determining who'd disposed of Sebastian—a huge assumption—I'd no idea how Ned thought he could repay me what he claimed he'd owe. A Get Out of Jail Free card? I sure as heck hoped I'd never need one of those again, like I had a while back as a suspect in multiple murders.

Meantime, I figured he was probably just being paranoid. There was no indication—at least, that I'd seen—that Nita and he were any more suspect than the rest of us. Even so, I could understand his concern about being on the other side of a murder case.

"Let's just hope your comrades in arms come to their senses and find Sebastian's real killer themselves," I said. "Soon."

And I'd also hope they'd forget how adamantly they had insisted that I butt out.

AFTER NED LEFT, I stared at my computer screen for what seemed like eons. I pulled up my e-mail, but my mind wasn't on it. Instead, it swirled around Sebastian Czykovski and his slaying.

Who hated him enough to hit him hard, then choke him with an animal's harness? I'd learned from media accounts, my own interrogation, and Ned's additional insights that whoever it was had apparently taken Sebastian off guard and slammed him against the wall, knocking him unconscious. Thus, the killer wasn't necessarily someone with strength enough to fatally tighten a strap on a nylon harness around the neck of a healthy, medium-size male who'd be fighting back in self-defense.

I Googled Sebastian once again, but now most of what came up immediately involved his death. Nothing stated emphatically who hated him enough to kill him, although online postings contained multiple speculations on that subject. The upshot was that, as I'd suspected, the less-than-kind Sebastian had earned a lot of enemies in his proudly public animal training and judging life. He had been highly involved in canine agility trials—training dogs for them, judging competitions, and talking about them on lots of TV interviews. He'd even seemed somewhat revered in that field.

Glancing toward the bottom of my computer screen, I discovered I was running late. Time to hurry from the Yurick office to pick up my pup from Darryl's. I'd hoped to go home and change clothes and freshen up for this evening's activities—dinner with Dante and Corina.

Maybe that was exactly what my subconscious mind had been saying by not fussing about the hour: I was a fruitcake for agreeing to accompany these two on an evening out. What could it be but a verbal sparring match between the smart, powerful Dante and the subversive, also intelligent, paparazzo?

And then I got an idea for a potential diversion. As I waved my farewells to the office staff and fled, I called Dante.

"Hi," I said when I reached him immediately. "We still on for tonight?"

"I'd rather it just be you and me, and not your friend the reporter." His voice was low and husky, and sent shivers through me that made me glad I wouldn't be alone with him. Which was another reason I'd called.

"I have an idea where to eat tonight, and why," I told him.

"Good idea," he said when I was done. "See you there in an hour."

THE PLACE WASN'T extremely convenient, though I didn't have to go home to leave my exuberant Lexie alone. I headed over the hill after picking her up, departing the San Fernando Valley and heading for Melrose Avenue, one of L.A.'s most trendy locales.

Fortunately, since it was July, the evening temperature was moderate, which meant the outside setting would work well. We were dining alfresco, with dogs.

I'd spoken with Corina, who'd been delighted with the venue, particularly since she'd expected my call meant I was calling off our conclave. "Just wish you'd told me before," she said. "I'd have hopped home to get my doggy, too. But it's probably better this way. Three dogs would be even more of a distraction to my interview than two."

I parked, and Lexie and I headed down the sidewalk to Regalio's on Melrose. I noticed immediately that my dinner companions already sat at a table in the crowded outside patio area. Dante rose gallantly as we joined them. Wagner traded eager sniffs with Lexie.

"Good to see you, Kendra." Dante kissed me lightly on the lips in greeting. "Sit here." He motioned to the chair beside him, facing the street. "I've ordered a chenin blanc from a winery I visited last year in France. I hope that's all right with you."

Corina Carey, who'd also stood, hadn't said much after "Hello, Kendra" and "Hi, Lexie." She wasn't exactly a shy violet. Tonight she watched Dante—not a difficult chore. The guy was absolutely easy on the eyes. He'd worn a dark suit that went utterly well with his deep brown eyes and black, wavy hair. His smile smoldered as he passed it between Corina and me.

"The wine's great, Kendra," Corina informed me as we sat down. Corina, too, had dark hair. Hers was styled in a cute shag. Her soft brown eyes tilted enough to suggest some Asian ancestry. She wore an emerald green pantsuit to show off her slinky figure that looked so good oncamera. I looked around, half expecting to see one of her prize photographers lurking in the background, but one of Dante's conditions for tonight's interview had been no pictures. Not this time—and probably not ever.

I sampled the wine. Smooth. Seductive. Seemed utterly appropriate for this small crowd.

We ordered first—salads plus exotic-sounding pasta and chicken dishes to be served family-style.

"Too bad I didn't know further in advance that we'd be eating here." Corina leaned over to pat Lexie. She turned to Dante. "I told Kendra I'd have loved to bring my dog, too."

Dante responded with the obvious. "What kind do you have?"

"A Puli." Corina's smile revealed her bright, white teeth. "It's—"

"A Hungarian sheepdog," Dante interjected, clearly stealing her thunder, since her smile started to droop.

She obviously expected us to be puzzled, but even I had heard of Pulik—the plural of Puli. "They're smart," I said. "Good herders. And that hair of theirs—I like how it resembles dreadlocks, depending on how they're brushed. Or not."

"I brush ZsaZsa's often," Corina said. "She's got black fur, and she's beautiful."

"You'll have to show her to me sometime," Dante said.

"Me, too." Okay, I'd heard of them, but I'd never seen one.

"Sure," Corina agreed.

Our salads were served. And as we started to eat, Corina initiated her interrogation.

Dante answered frankly that he was the deep pockets

behind the new reality show that I'd helped to dream up—and he'd been pleased with the initial ratings, even before they might balloon because of Sebastian's death. As they chatted amiably, I allowed my mind to wander, until—

"So you had an argument with Sebastian Czykovski the day before he died?" Corina said.

I glanced at Dante, who'd paused with a forkful of greens near his sensuous mouth. Instead of appearing affronted or defensive, he smiled, took his bite and chewed slowly. "If you're asking if I killed him, or even had a motive," he said in a few seconds, "I'd hardly admit either to you."

"But—" Corina began.

Dante changed the subject to his pet projects, pun intended: HotRescues and HotWildlife. The first saved pets and placed them in new homes, and the second saved wild animals, releasing them into the wild when appropriate, and nurturing them for life when it wasn't.

Dante handed business cards to Corina and me. "We do damned good work, and my staff should get all the public kudos possible. Come to HotRescues or HotWildlife anytime, Corina, for one of the best personal tours you could ever imagine. Just think of what a great TV show that would be."

Since her affiliation was with the tabloid show *National NewsShakers*, I suspected she'd be a whole lot more interested if Dante could guarantee a nice, juicy, oncamera big cat mauling. Even so, she seemed surprisingly enthusiastic. "Love it!" she exclaimed. "I'll absolutely be in touch. Oh, and if you happen to be there on the day of the filming, that would be a major plus in getting it onair faster."

"I'll see what I can work out."

"And you'll be willing to talk about your HotPets stores as well as the pet rescue organizations?"

"Of course." Dante twirled pasta around his fork and raised it to his mouth. "Offcamera."

Corina opened her mouth to object but closed it again. The guy obviously didn't like being oncamera, and if she pushed now, he might rescind his open invitation. Or so I assumed.

Why was he so determined not to be shown on the TV screen? That was another question mark in the mystery that was Dante.

Corina apparently got the message—no on-the-record interviews. We finished our meals chatting amiably about animals, and Corina engaged Dante in additional verbal sparring. Soon, it was time to argue over the tab. Rather, Corina and Dante did. Corina could charge it off as a business expense. Perhaps Dante could, too. In any event, he could clearly afford it. And even if I could arguably chalk the charges off as business, I was too busy saving for a new car to enter into this affable argument.

Dante won—or lost, depending on how you looked at it. The treat was on him.

As all five of us, dogs and all, started strolling down the street, Corina's cell phone rang. "Oops. Got to run." She sounded disappointed.

Dante walked Lexie and me to our car, parked a block away.

"I've been meaning to ask," I said, "since you have so many contacts with people who deal with animal issues, could you recommend any who might have suggestions on dealing with dog separation anxiety?" Maybe someone would come up with an idea that the Jeongs hadn't yet tried.

"For Lexie?" Dante knelt and let my Cavalier come close. I smiled fondly at them as I bent over to give mega attention to Wagner.

"No," I replied while snuggling the German shepherd. "It's for a legal case I'm working on."

"I'll ask around," Dante promised. "But a couple of good sources might be our remaining judges. Matilda's a pet psychologist, of course, and Eliza, with her pet-oriented radio show, might have referrals if she has no answers herself."

Of course I'd thought of that, but now I could drop Dante's name before requesting a discussion with them. And if I happened also to sound them out about Sebastian's murder . . . why not?

"Thanks for the great suggestions," I said.

Dante stood up and smiled. "You're welcome. Oh, and if you figure out that either one or both is guilty of murdering Sebastian, would you give me a heads-up before calling the authorities? I'm already working with Charlotte to find one replacement judge, and if we need more I'll want time to deal with it."

"What makes you think I'd figure that out?" I demanded. I hadn't told him I'd be investigating this killing. How had he jumped to that particular irritating conclusion?

"How many murders have you solved in the last few months, Kendra?" he inquired smoothly. "By my count, it's over half a dozen. I figured that adding Sebastian's to your lengthening list would be child's play for you."

"A pretty nasty child," I retorted. Still, I felt a strange frisson of pleasure, combined with nervousness. For whatever reason, Dante had spent some time learning about me.

Well, I'd learn even more about him tomorrow, when I reaped the fruits of Althea's computer hacking on my behalf.

And would see Jeff Hubbard, too. That thought quickly quashed my good mood. It was a confrontation I wasn't exactly anticipating with eagerness.

Dante, the dogs, and I soon reached my rental car. I opened the door, and Lexie hopped in.

"I pictured you in something bigger," Dante said, staring at my leased wheels.

"Me, too," I told him. "And I've been looking. But I've needed something to drive while I decide on a replacement for my BMW that got creamed."

He nodded, then bent toward me. My heart sped up like a racing car. He kissed me, hard. I kissed him back, harder.

And as I finally got behind the wheel and started to drive away, I realized that my mind was absolutely bemused . . . by Dante DeFrancisco.

Maybe I'd avoid him in the future, letting others involved with *Animal Auditions* keep in primary contact with him.

Or . . . maybe not.

Chapter Nine

WHEN LEXIE AND I arrived home, I didn't see Rachel's car. Not her dad Russ's, either, though that was the usual state of affairs. As a studio location scout, he was nearly always on the road seeking suitable locales for film shoots. But I'd hoped to speak with my assistant at Critter TLC, LLC, about how her pet visits had gone that day, as I always did.

I also wanted to make sure she was dealing as well as possible with the ongoing excitement about being on-air hostess of *Animal Auditions*, especially now, when it was on the news for the wrong reasons. Plus, even if she hadn't been overly fond of Sebastian—who was?—it was always a shock when someone you knew was suddenly erased from your life . . . especially by murder.

But all that would have to wait, for now. I didn't want to call her and give my concerns greater emphasis than happening to run into her and asking. And we had exchanged our daily minimum chat on who was caring for which pet first thing this morning.

"Okay, girl, this is your last chance to empty yourself tonight," I told Lexie, who immediately acknowledged the idea by squatting at the side of the driveway. Fortunately, no poop-cleaning detail was required. And then we headed up the steps beside the garage to our over-the-top apartment.

Exhausted, I vegged out on my comfy beige sectional sofa in front of the TV, Lexie in my lap. The nightly news didn't mention *Animal Auditions* or its deceased judge. And *National NewsShakers* wasn't on until tomorrow morning after I headed for my morning pet calls, so I'd simply have to trust Corina not to breach the confidentiality she'd promised Dante this evening. She did have *some* scruples, after all. More important, she was intelligent. She knew that if she wanted any shot at on-air interviews with Dante—or any scoops, should I be the one to unearth the killer—she'd need to stay discreet.

I'd showered and started for bed when my cell phone sang. I froze at my bedroom door, staring at the phone on my nightstand as if it was suddenly coated with slime.

Okay, so I'd agreed to meet with Althea tomorrow. That meant seeing Jeff, too. And this was the hour he'd always called when we were together. *Grab it anyway, Kendra*, I ordered myself. I wasn't a coward. Even more, failing to fix the situation immediately could lead to additional unwanted calls. I strode with determination toward my bed, a puzzled Lexie at my heels.

I grabbed the phone, preparing to say something nasty . . . until I glanced at the number on the caller ID.

Not Jeff's.

Dante's.

Was I about to embark on a similar series of pre-bed discussions with the new man in my life? *Was* he in my life?

No doubt about his being a man.

"Hi, Dante," I said. "Did you forget to tell me something? We were together only—"

"Fifty-seven minutes and ten seconds ago. Eleven. Twelve."

I might have felt an enormous amount of affection for a guy who paid attention to something as trivial—and as potentially important—as the time we'd been apart . . . if he'd sounded happy about it. Instead, he sounded pissed.

"That seems about right," I responded cautiously.

"I'd no intention of giving a damn, Kendra." His tone was curt and cutting. "You're not the kind of woman I want to be thinking about constantly. You're pretty, you're sexy, and you're smart—all that's just fine. But you're nosy—partly by profession. You're a lawyer." He spat that out as if he'd just used the most obscene epithet in the English language.

Maybe he had.

"And you're—" I started, unsure what I intended to say. Something sounding equally repulsed. At least that was my plan.

"Hear me out," he interrupted. "You're also friendly with the media. And the cops. You're a murder magnet, for crying out loud! Which means I should be avoiding you. But I'm thinking about you. Too much. And, heaven help me, I want you. For all your shortcomings, you're sexy."

"You're repeating yourself," I said coldly, though the more this sexy guy referred to sex and me in the same breath, the more my body simmered.

"Maybe if we just had some mind-blowing sex I'd be able to get you out of my system. Willing to give it a try? I promise I'll make it memorable. And—"

"Cool it, Dante." I suddenly started to laugh. "I've had obscene phone calls before, but this one wins the prize. Am I in lust with you? Most likely. Do I intend to act on it? No way. I'm afraid you'd be like dark chocolate."

That stopped him for a second. "Bittersweet?"

"Addictive. I wouldn't be able to stop at just one session to get you out of my system. So here's the thing. We have a business relationship, thanks to *Animal Auditions*. And I'm honored"—yeah, right—"that you find me attractive or whatever. But let's leave it at that. Thanks for calling. Good night." The last I said lightly, as if he'd truly been a business acquaintance I'd spoken with during daylight hours about something utterly trivial. And then I hung up.

And thought long into the night about hot, animal sex with Dante DeFrancisco.

I CALLED RACHEL on the way to my morning pet-sitting visits, and we confirmed who was doing what. "You okay?" I inquired. "I mean, with all that's gone on at *Animal Auditions*—"

"Charlotte and I are talking later. She wants to continue filming next week, with both potbelly and dog scenarios. We'll need a new judge, but she's working on that. It's horrible, of course—what happened to Sebastian. But if anyone had to get . . . well, you know what I mean."

Indeed I did. "I'm not sure that 'The show must go on' is always in the best of taste, but, hey, it's my first real venture into showbiz, so I'll leave that up to those of you who know what you're doing."

Okay, so she was nearly as new at this as I was. But she cared about showbiz and had been in a few commercials and minor productions. And I really liked the young lady, so giving her a few strokes was fine.

Lexie seemed as happy as I to visit Stromboli, Piglet the pug, and some of our other canine clients. And, yes, I had started to sit for the golden retriever—her name was Beauty.

Then, I headed for Doggy Indulgence to indulge my beloved Cavalier for another day.

Darryl was at the front desk checking canines in, and I couldn't resist the dig that had become a daily routine. "So who is she?" I whispered as I stood on tiptoe to give him a greeting kiss on his smooth-shaved, skinny cheek. As always, he was clad in one of his green Henley-style shirts with a Doggy Indulgence logo on the pocket.

"Don't worry about it," he replied with his now familiar secretive smile. Which made me want to strangle the answer out of him.

That reminded me of Sebastian, who'd had the actual *life* strangled out of him. . . .

"Of course I worry about you," I responded softly, my irritation in check. "Tell me."

"Maybe someday. See you later, Kendra." He started toward his office. I sighed, said goodbye to Lexie, and left. Darn the man! Why wasn't he telling all to me, his best buddy?

After last night's call from Dante, my concerns over Rachel and *Animal Auditions*, and my non-discussion with Darryl, I wasn't exactly in the most wonderful of moods when I reached my law office. I nevertheless accepted the chirpy greeting from Mignon with a smile, then called the Jeongs to assure them I was still researching a solution for Princess's separation anxiety. Next, I inquired about appointments with the two remaining *Animal Auditions* judges, explaining my legal issue with Princess in generalities. I was unlikely to be breaching client confidentiality by going into detail about this particular pup's separation anxiety, but didn't want to chance it.

Then I buried my nose in legal briefs for an upcoming court appearance . . . and attempted not to note the too quick passage of time.

But noon inevitably rolled around. That was when I had to hurry to Westwood to meet with Althea at the Hubbard Security offices . . . and to see said Hubbard himself.

Althea was first out of her office as I entered the central waiting area. "Jeff wants to take you to lunch, and then you and I can talk."

I'd sort of figured lunch was in the intended schedule, since my appearance was to be at noon. Did I want to spend that much time with him?

Did I have a choice, if I wanted Althea's information?

Just then Jeff strode out of his office. He was still one hunky dude, despite all the stuff he'd been through when he'd had to remain deep undercover to determine who'd attempted to kill him.

He had even hidden his presence from me. But that hadn't been the worst of it. He hadn't trusted me. And that had smashed my romantic interest in him to smithereens.

"Kendra!" He crossed the room and took me tightly into his arms before I could back away.

Jeff was tall, muscular, and all male. I'd been extremely attracted to him. He kissed me hard, but I didn't respond. He got it and let me go, looking into my eyes with his intense and sexy blue ones. He seemed to try to search my soul for a few seconds, then said, "Let's go grab lunch."

"Okay," I agreed without revealing my reluctance.

I glanced at Althea on our way out. She sent a sympathetic stare our way. For Jeff, or for me? Maybe both.

I wasn't surprised when Jeff led me to a Thai restaurant. Thai had always been our mutual favorite. Our sexual stimulus. Pad thai and mee krob, followed by a bout in bed.

No beds were on our agenda this afternoon, or ever again.

"So how've you been, Jeff?" I asked after we'd ordered. I stayed away from our habitual fare, instead ordering something with unspicy shrimp.

"I've missed you, Kendra," he stated. "You know I'd do anything to take back what happened. And you also know it wasn't entirely my fault."

He'd been drugged for part of the passage of time that had led us to this point. But not for all of it. And his mistrust of me had only underscored my knowledge that I was a bust in the boyfriend department. My relationship with Jeff had been the most meaningful since I'd had an affair with the senior partner of my former law firm.

Which was also why I couldn't allow myself to get too interested in the mystery man who was Dante. Although, with luck, he'd be a bit less mysterious after I had my conversation with Althea.

"I know there were extenuating circumstances," I said to Jeff. "And I don't blame you." Not entirely, at least. "But as much as I enjoyed what we had, I just don't feel the same anymore." Okay, I was being as blunt, yet as kind, as I could. Would he buy it?

Not entirely. Although we talked in generalities about his cases and mine, my pet-sitting, and the whole *Animal Auditions* situation for the rest of our meal, he put an arm around me as we walked back to his office. I pulled my muscles in tightly and remained as far from leaning on his hard body as I could, yet I chose not to make a scene and shrug him off altogether.

But I dashed through the door of his office building and then stayed far from him, especially in the elevator when we were all alone.

"Thanks for having lunch with me, Kendra," he said as we reached his company's offices. "I'd really like to do it again. Give me a chance to make it all up to you, will you?"

Obviously, he hadn't chosen to accept what I'd told him. "We can certainly be friends, Jeff." I turned to him without opening the door. Mentioning friendship was surely the kiss of death to any hopes he might harbor, wasn't it?

"I want more than just friendship with you," he said sadly, acknowledging what I'd anticipated. "But I'll take what I can get . . . for now. Go talk to Althea. I know you asked her to check out Dante DeFrancisco, since he's backing that new reality show you started. I also know you intended to keep it secret from me, but what the hell? You and I are friends if nothing else, and if you need anything from Althea or me, just ask."

"Thanks," I said weakly. What else could I do?

But he wasn't through. "I've looked over what she found. That guy seems too good to be true . . . which most likely means there's something still out there. I'll have her keep looking. Meantime, watch your back. There's already been one murder connected with your show, and I'll bet you that DeFrancisco either did it himself or knows who did."

Chapter Ten

Sure, it was sour grapes that flavored Jeff's ugly innuendos. Innuendos? Heck, those were utter accusations.

I didn't defend Dante or demand a retraction. For all I knew, Jeff was absolutely on track for figuring out Mr. DeFrancisco. I had my own suspicions, after all. But I'd reserve judgment at least until I'd gotten the information Jeff had from his expert computer person, Althea.

Deep down inside, I knew I didn't want to learn any bad stuff. Wise or not, I was smitten—at least somewhat—by the sexy pet-supplies mogul.

I thanked Jeff for lunch, agreed to keep in touch—sentiments any old friends might exchange. But I didn't allow him close enough to seal that sorta promise with a kiss.

I was pleased when one of Jeff's employees, Buzz Dulear, exited his office to say hello. Buzz was a whiz at installing security systems and had recently gotten his license as a P.I. A tall fellow with a buzz cut that emphasized his receding hairline, he'd become a fairly good friend when we'd hunted together for Hubbard Security's big boss after Jeff disappeared.

"Good to see you, Kendra," he said in a tone suggesting he was serious. Good old Buzz was definitely discreet in the way he tried to disguise how he shifted his gaze from Jeff to me, as if attempting to determine how the wind blew between us: Did it bluster to shove us far apart, or gust enough to propel us into one another's arms? He obviously got the gist of things, since he suddenly seemed rueful, yet resigned. "Sorry, got to run. I'm in the middle of designing a security system for a new downtown office building. Hope I'll see you again one of these days." But his quick handshake suggested that he strongly doubted it.

Althea appeared in the reception area. "How was lunch, you two?" She didn't await an answer—or maybe she knew it wasn't necessarily what she wanted to hear. But I'd met with Jeff, even joined him for a meal. She owed me. "Come into my office, Kendra," she said, as if in acknowledgment. "I'll show you what I found on that assignment you gave me."

"See ya later, Jeff," I said casually and strode behind Althea into her office. I held my breath while waiting to see whether Jeff would impose himself in here. This was his company. His employee. His computer, and his subscription to whatever databases Althea had legally used.

Her hacking? It was at least his non-discouragement that allowed that as well.

As always, Althea's office appeared to contain more computer gear than creature comforts. The chair I sat in, facing her electronics-laden desk, was small but sturdy.

Althea sat, too, and simply stared at me at first. I gazed right back. This lovely lady was a grandma? That concept always took me aback. She was slim and curvy and pretty. I could only hope that when I reached my fifties, middle age would be as generous with me as it had been with her.

But that, fortunately, remained a decade and a half away.

Which didn't sound so far off after all. . . . Yikes!

"Okay, tell me all about it," Althea finally commenced our conversation.

"Lunch? It was pleasant. We can clearly remain friends, even though there's nothing romantic"—or sexual, but I wasn't about to discuss that—"left between us."

"Mmm-hmm." Althea's affirmative sound managed to seem skeptical. "We'll see. Okay, you've fulfilled your end of this bargain. I'll tell you what I found out on Dante De-Francisco's background. And, let me tell you, I used some of my most intense computer skills to try dig up more."

In other, less subtle, words, she'd done some hacking.

"So what did you learn?"

She handed me printouts of some partly redacted computer pages—where anything that could identify the source was neatly obscured. At the same time, she explained, "I didn't get much on Mr. DeFrancisco's early life— childhood, I mean. But once he came of age, he joined the Marines and got into a supersecret covert special ops division. He worked with K-9s, and one dog apparently saved his life overseas. When DeFrancisco got out of the military, he brought the dog along—some special dispensation allowed him to adopt the animal. That experience apparently led to his love of pets, and he supposedly vowed to do everything in his power to make sure they were well cared for, no matter where they were, who owned them—or who got in his way."

"That sounds like some sort of PR that his company

HotPets would feed to the media," I suggested, not quite scornfully. But it seemed too slick to be true.

Althea shook her head. "There's no official story in any of their media releases. Lots of unrelated Web sites extol his virtues for his support of pet rescue organizations like HotRescues and his wildlife sanctuary, HotWildlife. He got an undergraduate degree in biology at the Illinois Institute of Technology and an MBA at Harvard. He was apparently well into his twenties when he headed into higher education, so he could have had a short but sweet military career first."

"And he made his money how?" I couldn't help asking.

Althea's smile was cynical. "Ah, there's the question. Nothing I discovered made that absolutely clear. The party line at his company was that he started working at a pet food manufacturer's, decided he could improve on it, and started his own small shop." Close enough to what he'd told me. "People loved what he offered to their pets and bought lots, he expanded his enterprise, and the rest was supposedly history."

"And you don't buy that?"

"Do you?"

My turn to smile. "I've bought a bunch of dog food and fun toys for Lexie at HotPets. So, yes, on some level, I buy it."

But when I left Althea and the Hubbard Security offices a short while later, I was still wondering where the heck Dante DeFrancisco really came from . . . and how he'd become so filthy—or spotlessly—rich.

MY MIND CONTINUED to spin as I got in the car to head toward the San Fernando Valley and my law office. Dante's past seemed interesting enough . . . if any of it was true. His present was absolutely fascinating. The guy's wealth apparently rivaled that of the country's richest moguls. And he'd made it all in a way that I could really relate to: supplying special treats to pets.

His future? Well, if all went well, it should still include *Animal Auditions*. Mine, too. Did that mean his future and mine would somehow merge?

In my dreams.

Or maybe, if my general luck with men remained in place, in my nightmares.

Okay. Enough. I had to focus on what was absolutely important to me: my pet-sitting, my law career, and now my affiliation with *Animal Auditions*.

As I started out, I recalled I might be able to address in tandem a couple of important issues relating both to my law practice and *Animal Auditions*—by meeting with the two remaining reality show judges. I might get some helpful feedback about Princess's separation anxiety . . . and learn Matilda Hollins's and Eliza Post's perspectives on the slaying of Sebastian Czykovski.

Using my cell, I called both again, but reached only Eliza. I'd hoped to set up a meeting with each in the next couple of days, but Eliza had a window of opportunity only that afternoon. So, instead of heading over the hill toward the Valley, I directed the rental car toward the studio where her radio show on pets was recorded.

It was located in the so-called Miracle Mile area around the middle of Wilshire Boulevard. When I reached the address Eliza gave me, a short, squat office building sat there. I wasn't certain where I expected a radio station to be located—maybe on top of a mountain, surrounded by old-fashioned antennas.

In any event, I located the station's facilities on the fourth floor. KVLA wasn't one of the city's most popular stations, but I'd listened to it now and then. It aired an eclectic mix of talk shows and soft rock. Plus, its Web site was wonderful, full of information about the talent and celebs showcased onair, as well as programs easily accessed and enjoyed even in the absence of a radio or portable player.

A young guy who talked as if rehearsing to be an on-air personality—or maybe he *was* an on-air personality unknown to me—ushered me down a long hall, past a glassed-in studio where a guy wearing earphones talked into a microphone about baseball.

"Are you one of Eliza's guests?" my escort asked after we'd started down another hall. His gaze inquired who the heck Kendra Ballantyne really was, and did she deserve to be interviewed onair by one of the station's primo person-alities?

"I'm a pet-sitter," I replied, as if that explained every-thing.

"I see. And do you have some interesting experiences to describe to our listeners?"

He sounded less than enthusiastic about my subject, so I decided to say something shocking, just for fun. "Maybe, if you consider having some of my clients petnapped, and having to go many miles to find them. Or maybe finding some of my clients' owners' corpses is a tad more exciting. Or—hey, I think we're here."

The sign on the door said "Eliza Post, The Perfect Pet Show Host." I gave the guy a smile filled with absolute in-nocence, while he leveled on me a gaze that suggested he either didn't believe a word—though all of it was true—or he considered me the devil incarnate.

"Thanks." I turned the doorknob and strolled in.

Eliza sat behind a table strewn with pet paraphernalia: a huge bone-shaped plastic container filled with giant doggy biscuits, woven nylon leashes, several six-packs of canned cat food, and countless stuffed animals, from rats to smiling snails.

"Kendra, hi," she said in her soft British accent. "Please come in."

"Thanks." After placing rawhide dog chews on the floor, I took the seat I'd removed them from. It had a metal frame, and its back and seat were of leopard-patterned fabric.

I hadn't paid a lot of attention to Eliza's appearance at the *Animal Auditions* filmings. She had sat at the judges' table but had been dwarfed in importance by Sebastian's irritating gibes.

She appeared a decade older than me, which made her mid-forties. Although I hadn't noticed glasses on her before, she now sported rimless ones. Perhaps she wore contacts oncamera, but presumably her appearance mattered less here on the radio. Her hair was long, brown, and pulled back into a pretty clip.

"As I told you on the phone," I began, "I'm trying to find some answers for a law client whose dog has severe separation anxiety." Which was absolutely the truth, but not the entirety. I also wanted to subtly quiz Eliza about her opinion of Sebastian Czykovski, and how he died.

And whether she might have had a hand in it.

"I suspect you'd have more luck getting information from Matilda Hollins than me," she said. "She's the pet shrink."

"Have you interviewed people on your show who might be able to help?"

"Sure . . . and one was Matilda." We both laughed.

Then Eliza said, "If you've ever listened to my show, you know I attempt to find people who work with animals in all different ways. It's hard to find the right interviewees for the radio and Internet, although at least on the Web I'm able to post segments that show the pets we talk about in action. That's why I bring on people like the heads of rescue organizations and those who train service animals . . . not to mention people who own birds who say crazy things on the air, and controversial sorts who want people to stop treating their pets like family."

"That," I said fervently, "will never happen."

"No, but it generates a whole lot of caller interest and Web site feedback."

"Then you encourage controversy?" I asked it mildly, but inside eagerly awaited her answer. If she said yes, then she probably appreciated Sebastian and his nastiness. If she said no, then perhaps she wouldn't want to be in the presence of someone so contentious. But would she kill him?

"I encourage whatever brings in advertising revenue, since that's how my success is judged. Same thing on *Animal Auditions*, isn't it?" She didn't wait for my response. "I might have added a nasty edge to the judging there, if you hadn't brought in that really controversial Sebastian. I interviewed him on my show last year, by the way. The guy had a real reputation in the dog agility community as a hard-nosed, difficult-to-please judge. Plus, he had guts. And a mouth that generated a lot of interest in my show, as it turned out. Can't say that I liked him, but I'll sure miss him. So will *Animal Auditions*, unless you find someone else who's the same, only different. I've already taken a role there as somewhat of a peacekeeper, so it can't be me.

But I'm ready to help you find someone else, if you'd like. I like that show, and my own audience has increased over the last couple of weeks."

I now surmised Eliza Post had nothing to do with Sebastian's death. Unless, of course, this was an act designed to convince me of exactly that.

Call me cynical, but I'd learned, as a murder magnet, never to completely believe anything anyone said in the interest of exonerating him- or herself.

"Thanks for the offer," I said. "I'll mention it to Charlotte and the others who are scrambling to replace Sebastian." Like Dante.

Dante. Another interesting query sprang to my lips.

"I have to admit that I didn't listen much to your show until lately," I said with an expression on my face that I hoped appeared half hangdog. "Have you ever had our executive producer, Dante DeFrancisco, on it? With his interest in animals and sales of pet products, I'll bet he'd be a natural."

"I'd bet so, too," she said sharply. "But the guy's people claim he likes staying in the background. Doesn't want to be interviewed or appear in any kind of medium, not radio or the Internet. They offered others from his home office, but I turned them down. I want the real thing."

Interesting. The guy was well known in the pet industry. Didn't hide his backing of *Animal Auditions*. Even sat in the audience . . . during filming? I'd have to check some of the footage that had been shot.

But he wouldn't allow Corina to interview him oncamera, either. Was he hiding something—like himself? If so, why?

"Maybe he's shy," I said with a small shrug.

"More likely, he's *sly*," Eliza said. "Like a fox."

This meeting was generating a whole lot more questions than answers, other than taking some suspicion in Sebastian's death off Eliza.

"Could be," I said noncommittally. Time to change the subject. "Anyway, if you think of any of your guests who might have ideas about canine separation anxiety, please let me know." I reached into my purse and pulled out one of my Yurick law firm business cards. My interest in this was more legal than pet-sitting. "And certainly tell Charlotte if you have ideas for a replacement judge. I need to run. Thanks for your time."

As I drove back toward the San Fernando Valley, my mind whirled. Had I eliminated one suspect in Sebastian's death? Could be. But I'd learned nothing to help me fix the problems of poor Princess and her shrieking separation anxiety. Maybe I should have suggested Eliza's recording her as a radio guest.

And now I wondered even more about Dante DeFrancisco. He certainly didn't strike me as a shy guy.

I knew he didn't want to be seen on TV, and now I'd learned he also didn't want to be heard on the Web or the radio.

Why?

Chapter Eleven

I PONDERED THAT darned Dante and his devotion both to helping pets and to staying, somewhat, out of the limelight. In fact, I thought of little else on my way to Doggy Indulgence Day Resort to pick up my dearest canine friend, and to see my dearest human one.

Lexie gave me one of her most wonderfully exuberant greetings nearly the instant I stepped through the door, but my other buddy didn't even say hi.

That could have been because I didn't see him in the chaos of the facility filled with canines and their caretakers.

I asked his employee Kiki where he was. "He's not here." She dipped her head so her bleached hair all but obscured the little bichon in her arms.

"I figured. Do you know where he is?" If he'd just gone down the street to Starbucks, I'd catch up with him there.

"Yes," was her curt response, and her blue eyes sneaked a sly glance toward me.

"Okay, let's play Twenty Questions. Is Darryl out for

just a short while?" I didn't want to make the question compound, like, did he leave for the day instead. That might be too complicated for this irritating person to comprehend.

"Yes. And rather than prolonging this sillyness"—I felt my eyebrows elevate toward my hairline. "Prolonging" seemed too sophisticated a word for Kiki even to grasp, let alone use correctly in a sentence. Maybe she'd read it in a script somewhere. —"I don't know where he is. But I know who he's with." Her smile grew a lot more snide, but I bit anyway.

"Okay, then. Who's he with?" By this time, I'd lifted Lexie into my arms, and she squirmed to get down and resume playing with her pup peers. But I wanted to leave as soon as I'd learned what I was after. Which now consisted of satisfying my curiosity about Darryl's companion. I suspected, judging by Kiki's demeanor, that he was with his new girlfriend. And I was dying to learn who it was.

"His new girlfriend," Kiki confirmed, and for once I joined in her grin.

"Great," I said. "Who is she?"

"If he wanted you to know, he'd tell you himself." She squatted to put the wiggly bichon on the floor.

I swallowed a stinging retort and said sweetly, "Is there a reason for him to keep it a secret?" Like, was she a serial killer? Or seriously ugly? Or an animal hater? He'd know that any of those would lower her in my estimation, although the ugly one was the most acceptable.

"Of course there is." Kiki rose and shot a look up and down my bod as if assessing whether I was worthy of this conversation. I held my tongue between my teeth so as not to say something insulting . . . this time. Antagonizing her wouldn't get me answers.

"Please, Kiki, tell me who it is." If that didn't stir her, I'd add a pretty please with sugar, spice, and everything nice.

"Can't," she responded brusquely. "I promised him."

"But—" I began.

She waved a manicured hand to shush me. "But I didn't promise not to give you a hint. It's a big one—and the only one: You know her. Now, I need to get back to work. Have a good day." She reached toward me in a manner that made me want to step back. I thought for an instant she was going to shove me out of her way. Instead, she gave Lexie a quick and gentle caress on the head. "See you soon, Lex, my friend." And then she turned her back and hurried to the area of the room where the canines were cavorting, playing tug-of-war.

Leaving me there, staring at her back . . . and wondering. Darryl's new girlfriend was someone I knew? I knew a lot of people, and approximately half were of the female persuasion.

Who was she?

I FOUND MYSELF refereeing another game of tug-of-war a short while later. One of my former ADR clients and now longtime pet-sitting customer, Fran Korwald, remained out of town, and her pug, Piglet, seemed even more lonesome than usual in her absence that evening. I'd brought Lexie inside while I tended to Piglet's dinner—and wondered what this small, chunky dog who'd been named as if he were a potbelly would do if he actually was in the company of his namesakes. He was way smaller than the piggies who were *Animal Auditions* contestants, and he'd drawn Lexie into a game with a two-looped rubber toy. Both were pulling and growling and looking adorable. I watched for a long while, letting them have their fun till I really had to interrupt to take Lexie to our next client's.

Eventually, our evening's duties—hard to call them that when they were so darned fun—were over. With Lexie in the backseat of the rental car, I headed home.

When we reached the wrought iron fence outside our Hollywood Hills abode, I reached for the button attached to the visor to open the outside gate—and stopped. In the light of the early August evening, I observed two playful canines gallivanting on the lawn outside my rented-out house. One, unsurprisingly, was Beggar, Rachel and Russ's lovely and loving Irish setter.

The other was a lithe and lively German shepherd. One that certainly resembled Dante's dog, Wagner. Couldn't be, though . . . could it?

I knew the truth as soon as I pulled inside the gate. Sitting on the steps beside the garage, the ones that led up to my second-story apartment, was Dante.

Why? Even more important, how had he gotten inside our super security gate? I'd had Jeff Hubbard upgrade the system after a murder had taken place in the large house a while back—one in which ferrets owned by Charlotte La-Verne's former guyfriend had been sorta suspects. So had Charlotte.

Dante maneuvered toward the driver's door as I parked. Lexie started leaping around inside the car, she was so excited to see him. "Cool it," I told her—even though, somewhere inside, I was leaping around in a similar fashion.

As Dante, gentleman that he was, opened the door for me, I immediately demanded, "How did you get through the gate?"

"Rachel let us in before she ran off to pet-sit. She thought you'd be here earlier than this, but Wagner was having so much fun with Beggar, the time went fast." Unasked was the implied question "Where the hell have you been, and why did it take so long?"

I didn't respond to the undercurrent and instead said, "Got it. Next question: Why—"

"Are we here? That's obvious, isn't it? Waiting for you."

"That's half an answer. Why—"

"Are we waiting for you? I have things to discuss with you about *Animal Auditions.* I've already run some ideas about a new judge by Charlotte and Rachel, and wanted your input."

Was that merely a magnanimous gesture—to give me a supposed say in something so important? Maybe not. I was, after all, also on the production staff of the show, even if not one whose deep pockets determined if the show would go on.

But had Dante already had a new judge up his sleeve—even before he disposed of Sebastian?

Okay, I assumed a lot here, but despite my initial inclination toward innocence, I really hadn't ruled Dante out as an upper echelon suspect. More likely that he dunnit than Detective Ned Noralles, after all.

Dante was still speaking. "How about if we leave the dogs here and go out to dinner to discuss it? Have you eaten yet?"

At least he asked without presuming I'd do anything for an evening out with him, even pretend I was hungry. "No.

I was going to grab something here." I pondered his invitation. And his presence. Oh, what the hell?

And why the hell were my insides now doing additional flip-flops at the idea that I'd spend another hour or two in Dante's presence?

"Fine. Wagner's eaten, so why don't I watch him here while you feed Lexie, and then we'll put them both inside and go."

I hesitated. "Lexie's great with other dogs, and it looks like Wagner is, too, but he *is* a German shepherd. They can be aggressive, especially without human supervision." I'd studied different breeds as part of my pet-sitting profession, although I'd never had a purebred shepherd as a customer.

"He'll be fine with Lexie. I doubt she'll try to go alpha on him, and even if she does, he's well trained. He attacks only when I tell him to."

Startled, I stared into Dante's gorgeous face, only to find him looking at me sincerely. "But he does attack sometimes?"

"Only during training exercises. I thought it would be good for him to learn such things."

Then maybe some of what Althea had found on Dante as a former special ops operative who worked with K-9s was true. Well, heck, Althea was good enough at what she did for me to be certain that all she discovered *was* true.

Was Wagner one of Dante's former K-9 partners? And was his training sufficient for me to feel secure that he wouldn't attack Lexie?

"They haven't been around one another enough for me to be comfortable leaving them alone together," I said firmly, so Dante wouldn't dare to argue. If he did, I'd simply refuse dinner.

But he got my message. "Okay, let's take them along and find someplace with outdoor dining facilities, like last time."

"Sounds good," I said.

WE ATE OUTSIDE an informal sandwich shop along Ventura Boulevard. I probably shouldn't have worried about the dogs not getting along alone. They were becoming close friends, sniffing at each other occasionally, and engaging in joint begging when food was about.

And Dante and me? How close friends were we becoming? Anybody's guess.

The eating area wasn't extremely busy, a good thing. Traffic slipped by along the boulevard, and I speared forkfuls of a pretty decent chicken Caesar salad.

"So," Dante said after a sip of dark beer, "Charlotte and I have been mulling over replacement judges. We've brought Rachel into the discussions, too, and even our host, Rick Longley."

And did you dispose of that undear departed judge who's being replaced? But I didn't ask. "Who are the suggestions so far?"

He took a bite of a smoked turkey panini, which also made my mouth water—not for the food, but for the hungry yet satisfied look on Dante's face as he bit into it. "One's Charley Sherman," he said after he stopped chewing, "if he'll do it."

My eyes opened wide. "Charley? But I enlisted him as a producer."

"He's stayed behind the scenes. And he won't have biases about who wins. And as a former trainer for Hennessey Studios who occasionally got oncamera, he'd be a natural."

I'd met Charley a while back when his wife, Connie,

and he had become law clients because of a claim against a Santa Barbara resort that failed to deliver a fun time as promised. I'd helped resolve that, and we had become friends.

"I like that idea," I said. "If he'll go for it. Who else have you thought of?"

"There's an old buddy of mine who might work. Maybe you've heard of him—Brody Avilla."

"Brody Avilla's a friend of yours?" Despite being a longtime Hollywood resident who sometimes saw stars in the supermarket, I was impressed. The guy was—or at least he used to be—an actor in all sorts of action features, ones in which he always triumphed over evil and won the girl. Kinda like the old westerns, but not all his shows were set in the past.

"We've known each other a long time. The fact he starred in a remake of *Rin Tin Tin* and another film about the Iditarod race made me think of him. He likes animals, and people associate him with them."

"I don't think I've seen him in anything for a while," I blurted. A dumb thing to say. Lots of Hollywood sorts lost favor with fans eventually, especially as they aged. Women more than men, though. And Brody Avilla was definitely all man.

"He's been busy with . . . other things," Dante said, in a tone suggesting he wasn't about to elucidate those things for me.

"But you think he'd be interested in something like this TV show?"

"He's coming to our studio tomorrow to audition," Dante said with a self-satisfied grin. "Charley Sherman, too."

"Wow. I'll be there. It'd be great for Charley to become a judge." I inserted the last somewhat defensively as I caught Dante's raised-brow expression that suggested I was just like every other lust-filled fan of Brody's. Which, maybe, I was, although I'd no intention of admitting it. Especially to a man with whom I felt a lot more realistically lustful. "So how did you meet Brody Avilla?" I asked.

"We worked together a long time ago."

"You were in the film industry?"

"No, he and I . . . well, let's just say our friendship precedes our current successful careers." Dante took a decisive bite of panini that suggested he'd elaborate no further.

At least this gave me something to Google tonight. Learning about Brody's early days could give me greater insight into Dante's. Maybe they'd both worked in special ops with K-9s, as Althea had unearthed about Dante. That would mean Brody's similar film roles had come naturally.

In the meantime, this discussion had reminded me of some mystery surrounding Dante's past. And perhaps his present. "What about you?" I asked. "You'd be an ideal judge for *Animal Auditions*. Your background with pets is perfect."

"That's exactly it. I like to stay in the background." His tone invited no argument. Which resolved not a scintilla of the suspicions in my mind. He didn't want Corina to interview him oncamera. He didn't want to be oncamera on his own TV show, except hidden as a member of the audience. He didn't even want his voice heard over the radio. Why?

We didn't discuss *Animal Auditions* and plausible judges any further. Our topics gravitated naturally to the area in which we both shared a deep and delighted interest: pets. Dante described new products that HotPets was starting to stock, more wholesome food and fun-filled toys. Which got us both speaking more to our own delighted dogs, who assumed they were about to receive treats from the table. We were both judicious about amounts, at least.

At last we were finished eating. It was time for Dante to drive us home in his silver Mercedes. He'd come sans chauffeur tonight. As he pulled up to the gate, he said, "When we were talking about judges, both Charlotte and Rachel let me know what a wonderful landlady you are. That led into a discussion about why you're renting out the main house on property you own. Now that you're a successful attorney again, plus a pet-sitter, wouldn't you like to resume living in that"—he pointed toward my property's main abode that I now adored from afar—"than that?" He pointed toward my home-sweet-garage apartment.

"Someday," I said with a shrug. I wasn't about to get into a discussion of my still dismal finances with this megamillionaire. I got along just fine, of course, but couldn't swing living well if I again started paying my home loan without assistance via rent payments. I loved the way I now practiced law, but it was a fraction as lucrative as being an associate with a major law firm had been. Sure, I supplemented it with pet-sitting income. And although I'd already refinanced my mortgage, I still felt a whole lot more comfortable financially this way than I would by modifying my lifestyle by kicking out Rachel and her rent-paying dad, Russ.

If only I wasn't so concerned about financing a new car . . .

"How about if I become your lender?" Dante's dark eyes looked earnestly into mine. "I'll pay off your loan and we'll work out payment terms."

I blinked, blindsided. This guy could buy TV shows and pet empires . . . and he thought he could also buy me?

Okay, Kendra, something inside warned. *Could be the guy is just trying to be nice.*

But even "nice" didn't trump "controlling."

I needed to stay on his good side for the sake of *Animal Auditions*, and of my friends and acquaintances who had put so much into it. That meant I couldn't kick him where it hurt and shriek accusations at him.

Besides, that really would be overreacting.

Instead, I said in what I hoped was a reasonable tone, "Thanks, Dante, but I don't think that's a good idea. I'm fine where I am."

He gave a short laugh. "You're looking for ulterior motives where there aren't any, Kendra. I admire your independence. And I can counter any arguments you might have against this suggestion. Think about it. It'll stay on the table."

He leaned over as if intending to adjust something on his amazing computerized dashboard, but instead stroked the back of my neck as his head bent toward mine.

Well, hell. It would be awfully ungracious to beat a hasty retreat, and so I allowed the man to give me a good-night kiss.

In fact, I found myself participating. Heatedly.

And in yet another one after Dante and Wagner accompanied Lexie and me up the stairway to our apartment.

"Good night, Kendra," Dante said in a low, sexy tone that all but elicited an invitation from me to come in. Better yet, a shove into my apartment and onto the kitchen floor for uncensored, flaming sex.

Instead, I said softly, "Good night, Dante." And then Lexie and I fled inside.

THAT NIGHT, AS it neared my bedtime, my cell phone rang. Dante? My heart started to race till I picked up the phone. It wasn't his phone number, or even Jeff's.

It didn't look familiar. I nevertheless answered.

"Kendra, it's Ned Noralles. My sister . . . well, my detective friends"—he spat the word like an epithet—"are even more stupid than I ever was when butting heads with you on a murder case. They're zeroing in on Nita, of all people. No way could she have done it. My sister and I need some legal advice. Can you help?"

Chapter Twelve

OKAY, SO I'M not a criminal attorney. Never have been, never wanted to be, and besides, I know a wonderfully wise and winning criminal law expert I have used myself when I've had to—Esther Ickes. Of course I'd referred Ned and Nita to her.

She had a court appearance scheduled for the next morning, so I found myself with Ned at the North Hollywood police station bright and early. I wasn't exactly representing him. I was there as a friend, and as Esther's temporary surrogate. And if I had to give him legal advice . . . well, I'd do it judiciously.

He'd dressed as if on duty, in a dark suit. He somewhat mirrored his counterpart, Detective Howard Wherlon, who had shown us into a glassed-in room and motioned us to sit on the chairs around the table. Howard's suit was his habitual gray. "Turning yourself in, Ned?" he asked with a smile that was an eerie change from his usually glum expression.

"Nope. I'm here conducting my own investigation, since you obviously won't resolve this case without my taking charge."

"Don't count on that, Noralles," spoke a voice from the doorway. Detective Vickie Schwinglan sashayed into the small room and lowered herself into the chair at the head of the table. "Besides, you've lawyered up." She aimed a vicious half-nod in my direction. "Which, as you know, tells investigating detectives a whole hell of a lot this soon in a case."

"Good thing you're not judge and jury." I stared daggers into her snide pale eyes. "They're supposed to weigh genuine evidence before rendering judgment and not make inferences based on what they want to believe—or ignore a person's constitutional right to counsel."

"You think that's how it really works?" The shake of her head didn't dislodge even a single hair from her tortoiseshell clip. "I didn't think you were so naive, Kendra."

At least she wasn't reminding me she'd told me to stay out of this investigation altogether. But, hey, I was arguably here in official attorney capacity.

"Maybe I'd like to be a little ingenuous," I retorted. "But I know as much as anyone that our judicial system is far from perfect. And with cops who turn on their own without the slightest proof, I can't help thinking there's something really wrong in this room." I turned my head so my glare next fell on Wherlon.

"Enough," Ned commanded. "We're all on the same side, even if some of us don't know it." I smiled into my lap at his dig that was gentler than mine. "I know I can't be officially involved in this investigation since I have an obvious bias. But how you could ever even consider my sister . . . ? That makes even less sense than wrongly accusing me."

Whoa, I thought. Was he protesting so much because he, too, wondered whether Nita could be the killer? Somehow, my gut told me to consider this further . . . later. I only hoped the detectives didn't start thinking similarly.

"If we share information," Ned continued, "we'll solve Sebastian's murder faster than if we all go our separate ways. Agreed?"

"What would you like to tell us, Ned?" Vickie asked, much too sweetly.

"I'll give you what I've got if you'll do the same," he replied.

"Do you have anything?" Howard demanded.

Ned turned to face him. "Do you?" he countered. "Besides hope, that is." Ned looked at me. "Howard and I were partners, as you know. We aren't any longer, and not just because of this case. We aren't the best of buddies these days, though that's still no reason to try to pin a murder on me."

"What happened?" I asked.

"Oh, just some backstabbing." Wherlon's voice had grown hard, and so had his glare. "But I agree that's not relevant here. As one of us, though, Ned, you know that obstruction of justice is a crime. If you know anything about this case, you need to tell us."

"And I will," Ned said agreeably. "But the condition is that you share anything helpful with me, too."

Detective Schwinglan slammed her hands on the table and stood. "We're just going in circles. Detective Noralles, you know we don't share information with civilians—and before you say anything"—Ned had also risen and now faced her—"until you're fully cleared, if you are, we're not telling you anything regarding yourself or your sister. On the other hand, if you withhold information vital to this case, not only will your suspension become permanent, but we'll also make sure you're prosecuted for obstruction of justice. Do I make myself clear?"

Ned now faced her. He wasn't a whole lot taller than the willowy bitch, but she managed to appear on his level. And absolutely uncowed by his obvious anger.

"Yeah, you're clear, all right. Clear"—he obviously swallowed his intended epithet—"clear cop, all the way through. So, let's go, Kendra, and hand these . . . professionals"— his tone suggested they were anything but—"the resolution of this case on a silver platter. Soon. See ya." He stomped out.

I looked from one to the other. Both appeared furious. Which made me grin. "It's times like this," I said to neither in particular, "that I'm glad I've become a murder magnet." Not true, of course, but they didn't need to know that. "I'll take even greater pleasure in solving this one and rubbing it in your faces because of the way you're treating your own colleague." Before they could remind me of their prior warnings, I followed Ned's lead and added, "See ya . . . soon." Then I, too, was gone.

Ned was waiting for me in the small parking lot. He appeared absolutely steamed. "Those damned . . . Never mind. We need to do something, Kendra. Fast." He appeared to wilt before my eyes. "I know how these things go. I always attempted never to stomp on the wrong suspect, but when evidence seems to point in one direction, that's the way you go. They obviously think it's pointing toward Nita or me. I can see Vickie Schwinglan coming after me like this. She's really hard-nosed. But Howard? Sure, I didn't give him the best rating when he was up for a promotion, but that was right around when his girlfriend dumped him and he was too preoccupied to do a good job."

"He had a girlfriend?" I knew I sounded amazed, but I didn't exactly consider Howard Wherlon dating material.

"Yeah. I never met her, but I heard she was okay. Then something happened that he never talked about, but I gathered she died. Or nearly died, then left him. Whatever, she was gone."

She probably wised up and realized what a snail Wherlon was.

"Anyway," Ned continued, "I'm too close to this to conduct a perfect investigation. You'll still help, won't you?"

"Sure," I said. "But I really want you to meet with Esther Ickes. You need a real criminal attorney, and you've seen in the past that she's the best. Nita needs an attorney, too." I considered how to suggest this. "She sounded even angrier than you that day, and there were lots of witnesses."

"You, too, Kendra? Nita's innocent. Period."

But I did think this devoted brother did protest too much.

"Got it," I said. "Meantime—"

"What?"

"We're doing another test *Animal Auditions* show this afternoon to conduct—what else?—an audition, this time for a replacement judge. If you happen to appear at the studio to watch, maybe you'll see something or someone that'll give you ideas for where to search for additional evidence."

"See you later," he said, a small smile returning to his face. "And thanks, Kendra. I mean it." I was only a little surprised when he bent down and gave me a soft kiss on my cheek.

AFTER CHECKING IN at my law office to be sure nothing dire would occur if I didn't appear that day, I headed toward nearby Studio City and Doggy Indulgence Day Resort.

Darryl was there. My long, lanky pal greeted me nearly as effusively as Lexie usually did when I entered. "Kendra, glad to see you—although you usually don't come here this time of day."

I quickly looked around for someone who could be his new and secret lady friend. Someone I knew. . . . Was her presence why he brought up my unexpected appearance? But all I saw was his regular staff and a bunch of contented canines.

"I'm off to another test filming for *Animal Auditions*," I told him, "and this time I want Lexie to have the pleasure of participating."

"Another dog scenario?"

I nodded. "Wanna come?"

"Wish I could, but I've got too much going on here." Everything appeared under control, but this was his business. Perfect care of its patrons was absolutely vital.

"Okay. I'll let you know how it goes." I took Lexie's leash as she eagerly wagged her long, furry tail. She appeared surprised to see me, too, and perhaps delighted about it. "Oh," I said as I started toward the door, "say hello to her for me."

His initially puzzled expression turned suddenly horrified. "To who?" he asked, much too casually.

"Your girlfriend. Who's also my friend, right?"

"Who told you . . . ?"

"Aha!" I sang triumphantly—not that I'd won much of anything. "I surmised as much, thanks to all your secrecy." Only then did I dare darting a glance toward the inimitable Kiki, who watched this exchange with daggers darting from her eyes toward my vulnerable throat. Much as I didn't like her, I wouldn't give her away to her boss and possibly deprive her of her job. She was an excellent caretaker of the dogs in her charge, no matter what else she might be.

"You know a lot of people, Kendra," Darryl said smugly. "Have you figured out which of them I'm seeing?"

"Possibly, but I'll confirm it with her first." With that, I turned my back and led Lexie out the door.

Let Darryl stew on that for a while. He deserved to worry after keeping me in the dark over so important an identity.

I LED LEXIE inside the back building at SFV Studios. As soon as we entered, I heard a lot of barks. Wasn't this audition supposed to be a demonstration of ideal doggy training?

In this instance, there wouldn't be a series of shows like in our usual *Animal Auditions* scenarios, nor would there be a weekly narrowing down of contestants till we wound up with a winner.

No, this time, the winner would be our new judge— although the doggies who did best could be invited to participate in a genuine *Animal Auditions* production.

As Lexie and I entered the sound stage, I understood

what had excited all our day's participants. A whole bunch of dogs and their owners had formed a circle around the two contenders for the open judgeship, and each seemed to vie for everyone's attention. To my utter amazement, one of those with a dog on a leash was Corina Carey, the assertive reporter. A cameraman stood on the sidelines, filming her. Her energetic pup was an adorable Puli—a medium-size black bundle of fur that looked like moving dreadlocks.

Charley Sherman, the former trainer for Hennessey Studios who resembled the Pillsbury Doughboy, appeared to conduct a canine orchestra with his arms waving in the air. And of course his unmusical band would bark in response, since instead of a baton he waved a huge bone.

As if not to be outdone, his rival, whom I recognized from movies such as the *Rin Tin Tin* remake, was likewise brandishing a bone, pretending to gnaw on it. Brody Avilla was a muscular man with a gorgeous square jaw and an understated acting style that drove female audience members mad.

The heartfelt, hungry woofing that surrounded the men was definitely deafening. And both of them shouted as well.

"Vote for me, all of you," Charley barked in a strong voice for a seventy-year-old.

"I'm the one," countered Brody, in a much deeper and stronger tone that seemed to brook no resistance—at least to those of the human persuasion. I had to assume that dogs, too, wouldn't be inclined to oppose him.

Lexie leaped at the end of her leash, obviously eager to join the fray. I restrained her, even as I couldn't help laughing aloud at the absurd excitement of the situation.

The audience seemed to be composed of people I'd seen

around the studio before. This event wouldn't be aired on TV, but was just for judge selection. Even so, Charlotte LaVerne seemed to be in charge. She stomped to the middle of the floor—although not where the doggy teasing took place—and clapped loudly. "Okay, let's get down to business, shall we?"

She was followed by our official show host, Rick Longley, as well as by Rachel, dressed in a snazzy outfit as if this was the real thing.

Rick spoke into his microphone. The former weatherman looked fully at home in front of the camera, a huge smile gracing his model-perfect face. "It's time for our owners to take lessons from our trainer, Corbin Hayhurst." He waved toward the side of the stage, and Corbin stepped forward. Rachel led the audience in applause.

The would-be judges dutifully exited center stage and took their places at the table reserved for them. Matilda Hollins and Eliza Post already sat there. I'd sidebar Matilda later to set up a time to talk to her about doggy separation anxiety from a veterinary psychologist's position—and ask my own questions about Sebastian's demise.

Chubby Corbin, in jeans and an *Animal Auditions* T-shirt, had the canines line up with their owners. What the hell? Lexie and I joined them. This wasn't for real, and we'd get a kick out of it. We edged in beside Corina. She had dressed for the occasion in a shocking pink shirt over casual beige slacks.

"Fancy seeing you here," she said with a smile.

"Ditto. How'd you learn about the judge's audition today?"

She inclined her head to one side. "A hunky bird told me." I saw Dante enter from stage right with Wagner. They must have just arrived. Otherwise, I would absolutely have noticed them. He caught my eye and gave me a huge grin that I took as a challenge. He looked a whole heck of a lot better than Corbin, in tight jeans and a plain navy T-shirt.

"Dante called you?" I asked Corina in surprise. He'd seemed inclined not to encourage the avid reporter.

"On condition that I not interview him."

"Got it." Obviously, he wanted to remain on Corina's good side but still stay offcamera.

What was he really hiding?

No time to ponder that puzzle just then. "Introduce me to your pup," I told Corina. "You know Lexie, of course."

As the two dogs sniffed each other with interest, she said, "This is ZsaZsa. I thought that was an appropriate name for a Hungarian sheepdog. She's really smart. She'll show up all the other dogs today."

"Hmmph," I said to her as I knelt and muttered to Lexie, "You've got to forget all the times I let you get away with not listening."

Rick Longley walked down the line, introducing handlers and dogs. Some had been there before. One other I especially noticed was an adorable fuzzy beige pup with floppy ears, whose name was Mooch. I gathered that she might be a schnauzer, from her soulful brown eyes and fluffy mustache, but she also seemed somewhat like a terri-poo mix. I'd seen her doing an excellent job while the judges played. She clearly could dance on her hind legs like a pro when a bone was held above her head.

The scenario for that afternoon was relatively simple. The dogs were to pretend to participate in Doggy Olympics. They would compete in a canine version of softball.

Corbin Hayhurst of Show Biz Beasts made the instructions easy. He would roll the ball, and the dogs, one at a time, were to catch it and carry it to an improvised base, where Corbin himself headed. The winners would tag him out.

Each pup and owner were given time to train, and then to test their abilities. "Come on, Lexie," I urged her as she followed the ball, then scooped it up in her eager mouth.

She didn't seem inclined to carry it to where Corbin waited to be tagged out, so I encouraged her by tugging on her leash. She finally got the message . . . sort of. She dropped the ball at Corbin's feet and stood wagging her tail, waiting to be petted.

"Close enough," I said to her with a sigh. She surely wouldn't be champion of this competition.

Mooch did a much better job, playing chase as if she did it all the time. So did ZsaZsa.

And, unsurprisingly, Wagner performed like a pro.

Then it was time for the actual contest to begin. I went through the same scenario with Lexie, but she seemed more inclined to seek attention than to play doggy softball.

The judges were then called on to comment. Which caused me to cringe in anticipation.

Okay, so Sebastian wasn't around any longer. But even so . . .

Matilda, psychologist that she was, said, "Lexie's certainly a sweet dog, but doesn't seem cut out to be an Olympic athlete."

Eliza said simply, "I'd consider this a C-minus performance."

Then it was time for those who were here to audition. Charley Sherman said, "You're one in a million, Lexie, even if this isn't your best game." I wanted to hug him.

Brody Avilla was a lot less tactful, yet I thought he did a good job, too. "Okay, Lexie. You're a young dog, so I'm sure we can teach you some new tricks—although this game isn't one of them. Maybe you'd be better in our audience, cheering your fellow dogs on."

Of course Wagner was perfect when told to perform. The judges rated him commensurately. Mooch, too, was one of the premier performers among the pups.

But it was up to Dante, Charlotte, Rick, and Rachel to help decide whether Brody or Charley would be chosen to continue with the show. They'd discuss it soon.

When all dogs' performances had been done and dissected, I heaved a sigh of relief. It might be a good thing that Dante would be occupied with judging the judges. I wouldn't need to talk to him just then.

So why did I feel so bad that we wouldn't get to chat?

I was gathering Lexie to go when my eyes connected with one of the audience members'. He was attempting to maneuver around all the others who were streaming onto the stage.

I froze, even as I wanted to flee. But I really wasn't afraid of him.

And it would be a good thing for me to find out why the heck he was here.

In a moment, he'd caught up with me. He bent and patted Lexie. And then he stood up and smiled.

"Hello, Kendra," he said.

"Hi, Jeff," I responded as casually as I could. "What brings you here?"

"You, of course. We need to talk."

Chapter Thirteen

"I DON'T THINK SO," I said, even as traitorous Lexie, who didn't understand the ephemeral nature of human relationships, leaped up on Jeff's leg. They'd been buddies for a while and might remain that way, notwithstanding my recently acquired almost-aversion to the man I'd nearly moved in with.

"It's about that guy Dante," Jeff hissed into my ear as he stopped petting Lexie and grabbed my arm.

Okay, I admit it. He'd attracted my attention. I started to walk to the side of the stage area with him.

But suddenly we weren't all alone in the milling crowd. Possible judge Brody Avilla had joined us.

"You're Kendra Ballantyne, aren't you?" he asked. "I heard that *Animal Auditions* was your idea, conceived to help the Hayhursts resolve a legal problem."

"That's about it." I studied his movie-star handsome face to determine whether he was criticizing or complimenting me for my ingenuity.

"I love it," he said enthusiastically. "And I really hope I'm chosen to be the new judge."

Jeff shifted beside me in impatience. So what? Recruiting the right replacement judge was important to _Animal Auditions_, and that show was absolutely important to me. Jeff could wait if he wanted. Or leave, if he didn't. It was all the same to me.

"I hate to profit by someone else's misfortune," Brody continued, his husky voice raised to be heard above the excited crowd murmurs around us. "I heard about Sebastian Czykovski's death on the news, of course. Do you have any idea what happened to him?"

I stared for an instant. "He was murdered," I said, incredulous that anyone connected with this show, even newly so, wouldn't know that.

Brody's smile seemed indulgent. "I figured. But what I wondered was whether you had any ideas about who killed him. I've heard you have a knack for solving murders."

"Oh." I felt my features soften. "You could say that, though I can think of better hooks for my reputation. I'm a lawyer. And a pet-sitter. And—" Oh, hell. Was my babbling a semblance of flirtation with this film star? If so, I figured I'd better cease floundering.

"So who's the front-runner among your suspects?" he asked.

"I'd like to hear that, too." Jeff had stood aside but he hadn't left. Now, he interjected himself into the conversation.

"Sorry." I stared from one man to the other. I'd thought Jeff was here as a follow-up to our lunch, as an attempt to stay on my good side. Brody was here because he wanted to be our show's newest judge. But was their nosiness about my suspicions of suspects more than idle curiosity?

Of course, Jeff snooped as a profession. He was a P.I. as well as a security systems specialist. Trying to find out whodunit was probably second nature to him.

And Brody would surely have an interest in who offed the guy he hoped to replace on the show. He'd need to know if the role came with hazardous strings attached—or whether Sebastian's killing resulted from that particular man's making enemies.

"I haven't come to any conclusions except certainty that neither Ned Noralles nor his sister, Nita, is guilty," I opined, "no matter what ill-conceived tree his brethren detectives may be barking up."

"Clearly the wrong one." Brody nodded knowingly.

"Then we're all in agreement," Jeff said.

On this issue at least, although I felt certain there were lots of others on which we wouldn't see eye to eye.

Lexie started straining on her leash, and I looked in the direction she pulled. Dante was coming toward us with Wagner, untethered, at his side. "So you've now met Kendra," he said to Brody. He maneuvered himself in a manner that appeared to sever Jeff from the conversation, as if the P.I. wasn't even present. Did he know who Jeff was?

I decided to be polite and introduce them, as Lexie and Wagner acted pleased to see one another again. "You two obviously know one another," I said to Dante and Brody. "I'd like you both to meet Jeff Hubbard." I moved to include him in the group. "He was my first pet-sitting client, and he's also a private investigator and security expert. Maybe he can help figure out who killed Sebastian so this show can go on with no further stigma attached."

"Assuming no one connected with it was the killer." Jeff's stare landed on Dante.

Uh-oh. The fiery glare that passed between them could have been explosive had there been even a hint of tinder in the air.

"Do you have any idea who might have done it, Jeff?" Brody asked calmly, stepping between Jeff and Dante as if he stopped arguments often. He had to maneuver around the two sitting dogs, and he patted each playfully on the head. "Of course, they haven't arrested either Noralles, but I understand from Kendra that they may be leaning that way. Is it possible the police are right this time?"

"No way," Jeff said.

"Of course not," I added. "Ned Noralles is a cop himself. He respects the law. If he hated Sebastian enough to kill him—which I doubt—I'd see him conducting an investigation and finding something on the guy so he could arrest him. And I certainly don't see his sister, Nita, killing Sebastian just because he trashed her poor pig Sty Guy's performance on *Animal Auditions*."

"Right," Jeff said with a decisive nod. The way he smiled happily at me . . . was he actually here to try to clear Ned? They hadn't exactly been friends for quite a few years, but lately their mutual hatred had mellowed. An interesting thought struck me: Had Ned hired Jeff?

"Well, hello, all of you," gushed a female voice as ZsaZsa the Puli started sniffing Lexie and Wagner. They stood to invite her into their doggy circle.

Too bad Jeff's Akita, Odin, wasn't here, too. This could be a pup party. Did Brody also own a dog?

Corina joined us, her cameraman all but glued to her back. "This was fun," she continued. "ZsaZsa and I would like to really compete sometime soon. In the meantime, has a decision been reached about which of the two delightful gentlemen will become the new judge? I could state pros and cons for both of them oncamera, but think either would make a wonderful addition to the show."

"That's the main reason I came over here," Dante said, "although I got a little sidetracked." His expression hardened just a little as he aimed a glance in Jeff's direction, then eased up again. "I wanted to tell Brody that he's in." Brody responded with a huge grin. "Fortunately, we producers didn't have to make the difficult decision. Charley Sherman has conceded, mostly because, even though he said he had fun, he felt he'd bring more to the show if he remained a trainer and kept coming up with scenarios to use in each round of episodes." Dante's smile looked almost smug. Obviously, this was how he wanted things. Had he convinced Charley to back out graciously?

I supposed it didn't matter. Dear Charley would still stay connected with the show, probably in a way that made most sense, given his perfect training background.

And Brody as replacement judge? Looking at him on-screen would undoubtedly attract a lot of female viewers. Since he was an actor, he could play the role of ill-tempered judge if asked to, as well as if he truly despised performances of some animal contestants. That, too, could appeal to viewers.

All seemed well on the set of *Animal Auditions* . . . now. But I caught the complacent look that passed briefly between Dante and Brody. Both appeared pleased.

Was there something buried between them that they hadn't yet revealed? Something that would affect our show?

If so, I sure hoped I could dig it out.

A WHILE LATER, we'd cleared out the stage and the gang had started to depart.

"We've got the next pig filming tomorrow," Charlotte said to the band of judges congregating near the door. "You're all set for it?" Her eyes were on Brody.

"Of course. Looking forward to it. And if there's anything you lovely ladies can give as pointers in advance, I'd be delighted." He looked at Matilda and Eliza, who all but fluttered beneath his flirtatious glance.

No doubt about which judge would be in charge on the show in the future. Was that good or bad? Guess we'd find out.

The three of them decided to go out to dinner together—and didn't invite us. No matter. I was tired and had pet-sitting duties to tend to anyway.

Jeff fell into step beside me as Lexie and I headed out of the building. "Can I come over tonight? I'll bring Odin and Thai food. We can talk about the Sebastian situation—and how best to clear Ned and Nita."

"The last part of that sounds good." It might be especially good to have a sounding board regarding my suspicion that Ned wasn't absolutely certain his sister was innocent. And so did his bringing Odin. I'd spent a lot of time with Jeff's dear Akita, especially when Jeff had apparently disappeared. But since Jeff was no longer in my life, neither, unfortunately, was Odin. And I couldn't trust my suspicions to him any longer. "I'll talk to you in daylight now, though. And no Thai as part of the bargain."

"Kendra—"

Whatever he intended to say, Dante's appearance with Wagner squelched it. We were in the parking lot by now.

"I think we're way ahead," Dante said, apparently speaking to me and shunning Jeff. "Brody will make a much better judge than Sebastian." I didn't attempt to hide the suspicion from my expression, and he added, "We'd have done fine with him, of course, if he hadn't died. And I definitely feel sorry about how we lost him. Just in case, Mr. Hubbard, you suspect I'm the killer, the answer is an emphatic no." He planted himself dead in front of Jeff and stared him straight in the face.

Both men's hands curled instinctively into fists. I had to laugh, though, when Wagner was the one to ease the tension. He nosed his way between them and gave a big, healthy bark, as if to warn them that if either attacked, so would he.

Of course, I suspected Jeff would get the short end of that confrontation. So did he, since he turned to me and said, "I'll be in touch, Kendra, to talk over that matter of importance I mentioned."

"Fine," I said. "Have a good evening, Jeff. And give Odin a big hug for me."

He zoomed off in—what else? He'd lost his Escalade in a flood canal, and had replaced it with a new one. It was black and shiny and newer than the last.

I watched him drive off, Lexie sitting on the pavement at my side. And then Dante said, "I'll see you later, Kendra." He didn't wait for any response from me, as he and Wagner headed for his sleek, silver Mercedes.

And I sighed as Lexie and I hied ourselves to our ugly little rental car. It was absolutely time to replace it. And I now thought I knew exactly what I wanted.

All I had to do was to figure out a way to pay for it.

CALLING MY OFFICE on my way to my first pet-sitting stop, I learned that my presence had hardly been missed.

"No emergencies today, Kendra," Borden assured me. "How were things on your animal show?"

"Interesting," I told him. "It's going well. You should come to a taping with me soon."

"I'd love it."

I promised to be in bright and, for me, early tomorrow morning. It would be Friday, my last official law practice day of the week, although I always brought stuff home on weekends when necessary.

Nothing especially eventful occurred with any of my afternoon's animal charges. Of course Lexie and I took our time visiting and entertaining each, as well as feeding them. And after I entered each visit in my pet-sitting journal, we headed home.

I guess I shouldn't have been surprised at seeing a silver Mercedes parked at the side of my driveway, on the garage side of the wrought iron gate. But Rachel was undoubtedly at home, and she'd have let Dante in, though I'd chided her slightly the last time.

This time, I'd be more forceful. Maybe.

Once again, Dante sat on the top step to my apartment along with Wagner.

"We just saw each other this afternoon," I reminded him. "Is my company so addictive that you couldn't wait to call and set up another time to get together?" I was jesting, of course. And I certainly had no intention of suggesting that he ask me for a date. Even though I hoped he would.

"Yes," he said, so seriously that I stopped climbing the stairs to stare. His face appeared utterly solemn. Which somehow made him seem all the sexier, even more than some of those winsome smiles he sometimes focused on me.

Or maybe this man would look sexy even with a ferocious frown creasing his gorgeous face.

"Well, come inside." I maneuvered around Wagner.

"Give me time to say something nasty enough to make you want to run away."

"That won't happen, Kendra." This time he did level one of those killer smiles on me. And I do mean level. He'd stood, and bent down just enough to plant one soft yet super scorching kiss on my lips. "I'm cooking dinner for you tonight."

"Wh-what?" That kiss had obviously messed up my mind. "You cook?"

"Gourmet," he asserted, gesturing grandly toward the rear of the small porch outside my apartment door. Several plastic bags from Gelson's, an upscale supermarket chain, were aligned there. "I hope you like things a little spicy. I'm going to make my famous chicken and sausage jambalaya for you."

"I love spice," I said truthfully as my mind momentarily lighted on the Thai foods I'd often shared with Jeff. Pad thai has a definite kick. And somehow it had acted as an aphrodisiac. . . .

Well, that had nothing to do with the spiciness of the food. And I had no intention of jumping into bed with Dante.

Even though the thought made my blood start to simmer . . . along with the water that started to boil to make the jambalaya's rice.

As he began sautéing the ingredients, his back was toward me. Not a good time to start a fascinating conversation, since I couldn't see his face. He could be smirking as he shot fibs at me, and I'd never know.

Even so, I needed to talk. "You never told me how you knew Brody before—only that you worked together once. Where was that?"

"Nowhere around here." Dante's tone was so casual he

might have been describing his recipe. Or not. If he was truly a gourmet cook, his recipe might be even more of a secret.

"I didn't literally mean what location. What did you do together?"

He turned to face me, his expression as heated as the pan on top of the stove. "Did anyone ever tell you that you ask too many questions?"

"That's what good lawyers do." My voice came out in a throaty croak, especially when I realized I could not draw my eyes away from his.

"And you're most definitely a good lawyer. I'll bet you're good at everything you do." Talk about huskiness sounding sexy. . . .

"So I've been told."

He had to maneuver around our hounds, who lay on the floor between us, imbibing the luscious aromas from the jambalaya ingredients. Suddenly, I found myself in Dante's arms.

"Prove it," he whispered.

Our kiss was long and absolutely lusty. I thought what I heard was my skin sizzling . . . until I realized the sound came from the stove. I reluctantly pulled away. "Dante—"

"Yes, I know. Dinner is served."

What? He wasn't going to suggest turning down the heat—under the food? Hurrying off to the bedroom?

Instead, he did as he'd said: served our dinner. It was luscious. And spiced with the taste of what else could have been. Might still be, once we were done eating.

Only, then he said, looking me straight in the face with his deep, dark, delicious eyes, "I want you, Kendra." The words made me shiver all over. "I think you know that."

"Er . . . really?" My voice squeaked, and he laughed as my insides did a combined volcanic eruption and earthquake of nerves.

"When we make love—and we will," he said, "I want you to have anticipated it even more than the way I'm already obsessing over the idea."

Hell, I already was . . . well, if not anticipating, at least obsessing. I suspected that making love with Dante could be addictive, and might be the most foolish thing I'd ever do. *If* I ever did it. The man was way out of my league, in terms of power and finances. And there was still so much about him I didn't know. . . .

"Talk about having an ego," I blurted. "What makes you think—"

"I understand that who you are involves asking questions," he interrupted. "Maybe because you want to make sure your friend Ned Noralles isn't falsely accused of killing Sebastian. Just understand that I've taken steps to ensure that even if I'm considered a suspect, I won't be arrested for the murder."

That made me blink. "What did you—?"

"Let's just say I've got a perfect alibi," he said. Yeah, right. If he did, why didn't he use it before? And just like that, he'd distracted me from sex to murder investigation. "All I have to do is ensure it works. For now . . . well, let's both look forward to the time in the future when we'll make love together, shall we?"

Which knocked me off balance all over again.

"In your dreams," I said. And my own, although I merely scowled at his sexy smile.

Lexie and I trailed Wagner and Dante down the steps a short while later. He was leaving. He'd also left me a lot of delicious leftovers, so, like it or not, I'd be thinking of him even more over the next few nights as I savored his food . . . and the—maybe—unwanted memory of this night.

"What an ego," I said to Lexie for the hundredth time as we entered the apartment after she'd had her evening evacuation outing. The place was filled with the spicy aroma of recently cooked jambalaya. And with memories of sexy suggestions that still got me all steamy—and steamed up—inside.

As I sat down on my sofa, about to turn on the TV news to move my mind away from Dante, my cell phone rang. Was it Dante, calling to say good night? No. The number on my caller ID wasn't familiar.

"Kendra, this is Matilda Hollins." The female *Animal Auditions* judge whom I hadn't yet interviewed.

"Hi, Matilda," I said. "When can we get together to talk? I'm sure a veterinary psychologist like you has lots of ideas I can pass along to my law client whose dog has separation anxiety."

"Please come to my office at eleven o'clock tomorrow morning. There's something about Sebastian I want to discuss with you."

"Sure," I said, wondering if I'd get any sleep that night while I considered what she had in mind.

I needn't have worried that anticipating my meeting with Matilda would keep me awake that night. Of course it did.

But so did my rehashing in my head of what Dante had said. Stuff that neither my mind nor my body could discard.

The thing I realized was that, with all Dante had said about his alibi, he'd never once said he was not guilty. In fact, he'd seemed to talk all around that most important statement of all.

So now my thoughts kept racing around all those I considered suspects . . . and Dante DeFrancisco was quickly hurtling toward the top of the list.

Chapter Fourteen

NEXT MORNING, I asked Lexie, as soon as we rose, if she was ready for another fun day at Doggy Indulgence. She wagged her tail excitedly, so what could I do?

Even though Darryl gave me a good rate for Lexie's frequent stays at his facility, the cost was adding up. I should slow it down . . . soon. But Lexie and her well-being—especially now that she didn't have the daily company of Odin—absolutely came first.

Better yet, I needed to stop squandering money on rental fees and buy a new car, but that meant incurring the additional long-term commitment of an auto loan.

In any event, I was pleased to see that Darryl was signing in doggy visitors that day. "Lexie's joining us again?" he said as soon as he saw us. "Excellent!"

"I thought so," I agreed. "So . . . when will I hear who your new ladylove is?"

"You never stop, do you, Kendra?" My tall friend was

obviously irritated as he stared at me over his specs. "What makes you think it's your business?"

That hurt. Of course it was my business. We were buddies. Buddies shared important bits of info like who they were seeing seriously. At least I did, with Darryl.

"Never mind," I muttered. I bent to cuddle Lexie. At least she loved me. Only, after giving my cheek a lick, she dashed off to her favorite Doggy Indulgence play area where a few other pups were already relaxing on human-type sofas. She grabbed a nylon bone and started settling down on a seat.

"See ya," I called to neither of them in particular as I stomped out the door alone and in a snit, ready to give whoever I saw next a hard time.

That happened to be a profusion of pet-sitting clients. Since they needed human attention and affection, it made no sense for me to act anything but adoring. Which was absolutely how I felt about each of them—even if my caring for them did nothing to soothe my injured psyche.

Nor could I take my bad mood out on the effervescent and adorable Mignon when I reached the Yurick firm. Instead, I slammed my office door shut and started revising a miserable motion to dismiss that I had already begun drafting for a contracts case—an elder law matter I'd taken on for Borden.

As if I could concentrate.

Thus, I was pleased when ten-thirty rolled around. Time to keep my appointment with Matilda Hollins.

Her office was in Eagle Rock, a moderately nice residential area with some commercial parts that seemed to be undergoing significant redevelopment. I therefore had to navigate my way around several partially closed streets before I could figure out where to park as well as how to get into her two-story office building. Down below was a veterinary clinic, and her practice was located upstairs.

I sat down in her waiting area but didn't have to amuse myself long with her selection of animal-care magazines. A middle-aged lady leading a prancing Chihuahua left with tears in her eyes, and Matilda followed her into the ante-room.

"Hi, Kendra," she said cheerfully, as if oblivious to the sorrowful state of the person who had just left. "Come on in."

Matilda was maybe mid-forties, dressed more profes-sionally here at her place of practice than she'd been at our TV show. There, she seemed to favor flashy pantsuits with glittery blouses. Here, she wore a conservative blue suit with a skirt.

"I don't want you to breach any confidentiality," I said as I settled onto a nondescript beige sofa in her office. "But what was going on with the woman who just left with the Chihuahua? The dog looked happy enough, but the lady looked miserable."

Matilda's face was round, her short, bleached hair form-ing a starchy cap around it. When she pursed her lips, wrin-kles formed around them like pleats. "I can't get into details, of course, but sometimes people act like their pets are their kids."

"Mmm-hmmm," I said, waiting for the punch line.

"They're animals," she said in apparent exasperation, sitting down beside her perfectly clear desk. "They need to be taught rules. That's why *Animal Auditions* is such a good idea. The contestants are trained in scenarios that make sense for their kind."

Uh-oh. For a veterinary psychologist, Matilda seemed

much too vehement about treating pets like animals instead of family. If ever Lexie needed psychoanalysis, I'd find someone more simpatico to treat her. But of course my pup was absolutely well adjusted.

More important at this moment, would I get any practical suggestions about how to deal with poor Princess's separation anxiety? Well, I'd just have to see.

Since that was one reason I'd come, I started there. "I have a law client," I began, "whose Brittany spaniel cries pitifully outside each time she's left home alone. They've tried closing her doggy door, but then she has accidents in the house and is still heard outside. They've tried a trainer and other advisers already. Do you have any suggestions?"

Her possibilities ranged from harsh punishment, to leaving around puzzle kinds of toys like treat-filled rubber balls that required some time to empty and eat the contents, to not leaving the pup on her own. Then there were the high-tech ideas, like placing microphones and cameras with the pup, and scolding severely when the wailing began. Our discussion went on for ten excruciating minutes before she understood I wasn't hearing what I'd hoped for and wanted to move on.

"So what are your thoughts about *Animal Auditions*?" I asked. "You mentioned when we spoke yesterday that you had some ideas about what happened to Sebastian."

Matilda sat back in her desk chair, and her round face suddenly seemed frozen in frustration. "I wish that man had never been chosen as a judge for the show in the first place—even though I should have respected him. Or at least appreciated him. He sent several dog patients to me—dogs who would never have required psychological counseling at all, if it wasn't for him."

"What do you mean?" I asked.

"Do you know anything about Sebastian's background?" Matilda studied me as if determining my suitability to be given additional knowledge.

"A little," I said. "He was involved in agility training, right?"

She nodded. "First and foremost, he is . . . er, was . . . a trainer himself, plus a judge well known in his field, primarily agility matches. He knew his stuff there. He also was just as critical as he was at *Animal Auditions*. He reduced many a dog to frustration and exhaustion, and many owners to tears."

I kept my silence, recalling Matilda's patient who'd departed as I'd arrived.

"But because of his expertise," she continued, "he was greatly admired. That's probably how Charlotte found him for the show—recommendations from agility folks who knew him by reputation. Plus, he was a nice-looking man. And he certainly could treat people well—and even animals, too—if he chose to."

Oddly, Matilda's expression grew suddenly dreamy, and her taut lips relaxed into a soft smile.

"So you sometimes saw Sebastian socially?" I surmised.

The hard look returned to her face, and she glared at me as if in chastisement. "For a short while, yes, since I wanted to get to know the man whose harsh treatment at agility trials sent so many new patients to me. He could be charming. When he wanted to, he turned on all the charisma you could imagine. But I saw through it. After a few dinners at which he seemed really sweet, I started asking him cogent questions about why he judged animals so harshly. 'Because I love to see them, and their owners, squirm and try to please me,' he said. I realized that's what he wanted from me. Not necessarily the squirming, but when I stopped trying to anticipate what he wanted from me and started acting myself, he let his real self shine through, too. And his true character was . . . let's just say he wasn't a very nice person."

So Matilda had dumped him. Or that's what she seemed to be saying.

What if it went the other way, though, and she had, over time, stuck her own spin on it? When they were put in close contact with one another at the *Animal Auditions* judging table, had that made her edgy enough to want to teach him the ultimate lesson?

And there was something else. Something I recalled from just before Sebastian was killed and Ned lost his cool after his critiques of Porker and Sty Guy.

"So you're not sorry that Sebastian isn't an *Animal Auditions* judge any longer," I stated instead of asking.

"Not particularly, though if you're asking if I killed him, the answer is 'of course not.' I neither liked nor disliked him by then. And even if I'd hated him, killing him that way was much too harsh. I'd have had more fun humiliating him on the show." The way she smiled then almost made me shudder. And I believed she was serious. She'd adore humiliating Sebastian, or anyone else who got in her way.

Me included.

Even so, I wasn't through. "Thanks for your insight," I said insincerely. "I'll definitely take your suggestions for separation anxiety into consideration while giving legal counsel to my client. And . . . well, I assume you'd tell the police if you had any thoughts about who killed Sebastian. And as an animal psychologist, I'm sure your ideas would have a lot of credibility. Care to share any possibilities with me?"

Of course she did—but without knowing any details. "I wasn't there, of course, but I heard that someone punched Sebastian out after he criticized his dog at one agility trial. Maybe there were more, too. I wouldn't be surprised."

Neither would I, but that wasn't as helpful as I'd hoped.

And then I had to ask what had been eating at me ever since I'd heard Matilda's comment a couple of days ago. "You know," I said, as casually as I could muster, "I've been a little curious about why, when Ned Noralles threatened to dig something up on Sebastian and the other judges, you said that you didn't want them to snoop around in *your* business. I'd love to know why."

She smiled a cryptic, psychologist's smile and said, "I'll just bet you would, dear."

My return smile was somewhat snide. "I suppose I could mention that to some of the cops I know, in case they'd want to dig further."

Her expression grew hard. "There were accusations against my professionalism a while back," she growled. "Entirely false, but the authorities could jump on them and make untrue assumptions about my ethics. Not that they would lead to my murdering anyone, but I'd hate for the whole thing to get sticky again." Her glare suggested that she'd be glad to stick something up me if I dared to mention this.

I wasn't about to reveal that I'd gone through something similar. Of course I'd been innocent, and that had ultimately been proven.

"But you know what?" she continued. "That was the past. Right now, I don't think the police would care one way or the other if they heard about those terrible things that were untrue in the first place. In fact, if you mention this to the detectives investigating Sebastian's death, I think they'd be more likely to come down hard on you for obstructing justice or whatever they call it, since you'd get them to waste time on a suspect they'd know fast couldn't have hurt a fly." She beamed brightly, the picture of psychological innocence.

But as I said my goodbyes and thanks to Matilda for her time, I couldn't help wondering. Whether or not she was innocent of those claims against her, what if Sebastian had learned about them and held them over her, in the context of her judging the show or otherwise? Even if she'd had no social motive to kill the man, she might have had a professional one.

She had no fear of the police digging into her background, so I should probably assume she was innocent.

Even so . . . I couldn't help pondering the phrase that dissected the word "assume": to make an ass out of u and me.

I didn't consider myself, murder magnet that I was, the rear end of any kind of equine.

And my mind kept inquiring: Was Matilda the murderer?

Chapter Fifteen

BACK AT MY law office that afternoon, I had a heck of a time concentrating on anything attorneyish. Which made me wonder if I should just go home. It was Friday. Maybe what I needed was a long weekend to get my head on straight—without thinking about doggy separation anxiety, *Animal Auditions*, Sebastian Czykovski's murder . . . and Dante DeFrancisco.

As if that was possible. As it turned out, I stayed involved with all of the above.

Still, instead of fleeing, I sought out our senior partner, Borden. Unsurprisingly, he was in his office. Seated behind his neat antique desk, he looked up immediately as I entered, and smiled. His aloha shirt today was bright pink with golden posies. "Come in, Kendra," he said happily. "We haven't talked for a while. Have you solved that man Sebastian's murder yet?"

"Not yet," I said, as if it was a foregone conclusion that

I'd ultimately figure out whodunit again. "Any ideas?" I slid into one of his ornate client chairs.

He waved his hands at me as though warding off an ancient curse. "I love the idea of your *Animal Auditions* show," he said, "and I'll bet your ratings are sky-high now, with this additional thing for your audience to consider. But solving mysteries is your thing, not mine. Although . . ."

" 'Although' . . . ?" I prompted, hoping for an insightful idea. Instead, he mentioned a problem more pertinent to him.

"I probably shouldn't bring this up since you already have so much on your mind, but Geraldine Glass popped in this morning and mentioned that her clients, the Jeongs, had called her. They're really concerned about their own mystery—well, dilemma, really: the fuss their neighbors are making over their dog's noise while they're away. They asked Geraldine to talk to you about it. Since you weren't here, she spoke to me."

I forbore from rolling my eyes. Geraldine was the attorney who'd referred the Jeongs to me in the first place. "I'm sorry, Borden," I said, "that you got stuck in the middle of this. I'll let Geraldine know I've been working on it, but the legal issues are really just a part of this whole sad situation. You know I'll defend our clients vigorously, and their pup, Princess, too, if the threatened lawsuit is filed. Better yet, I want to learn what attorney is representing their grumpy neighbors and try some animal dispute resolution. For now, I'm researching doggy separation anxiety. I even spoke with a veterinary psychologist of some repute about it this morning." Absolutely true, even if it was utterly false that I felt I'd gleaned anything remotely useful from Matilda Hollins.

I withdrew from Borden's office, then peeked into Elaine Aames's to say hi to her and Gigi, the Blue and Gold Macaw. Then I stopped at Geraldine's, but she was the one absent this afternoon—maybe a good thing. I soon sat behind my messy desk and moved things out of my way so I could lean on it as I talked to the Jeongs. I reached Treena right away in New York City, where they'd ended up on their prolonged business trip.

"I understand you've expressed concern about how your matter is being handled here," I began in a stern yet friendly tone. "I'd be glad to discuss it with you directly."

The silence lasted for a few seconds, and I was sure Geraldine would get another earful. Instead of defensiveness or criticism, though, I heard a soggy sigh. "Sorry, Kendra," Treena said. "I didn't mean to make trouble for you, but we heard from our neighbors again. It's not only that they've told their lawyer to go ahead and file the lawsuit; I feel so awful that poor Princess cries so much and is so sad while we're gone. If only we could just come home and be with her more, but we're both involved in lining up investment possibilities for our electronics business, and that takes time."

"I understand," I said. "And I'm trying some nontraditional ways to research your problem, although of course I'll deal with any legal action on your behalf. A veterinary psychologist I've spoken with suggested giving Princess some additional training in the future, but that won't help now—and I'm not absolutely convinced that it's the way to go."

"Me neither—especially not after the stuff we already tried—but thanks for checking. My neighbors correspond with me by e-mail, and I've told both them and my housesitter to contact you, okay?"

"Not your neighbors, if they're represented by counsel," I said. "But I'd love to hear from their lawyer. Give me the sitter's number, though, and I'll see if she can stay home longer hours. If not, I could check with some of my pet-sitting friends to see if they could back her up. But I don't want to intrude on your relationship with your sitter."

"Anything that will help," Treena cried. "I don't suppose you could just stay at our house. . . ."

"Not full-time," I said. "And I suspect that might be what's needed. I know of a great doggy day resort, though. It's reasonably priced but not really cheap. Would you like me to take Princess there for a few days?"

"Next week? Absolutely. Our sitter should be around most of the weekend, and tomorrow's Saturday."

"Fine." I wondered how I'd fit the additional doggy transport into my already difficult schedule. But I'd give it a try . . . while still looking into how to keep poor Princess from crying her puppy heart out while alone.

ONCE AGAIN I thought how welcome the weekend would be, starting tomorrow. But though I'd wanted a much-needed break from all that was squeezing my brain, I got a call in my car late Friday from Charlotte LaVerne. I listened on the hands-free phone.

"It's the oddest thing, Kendra," she said. "Sebastian's next-of-kin is a nephew, and he said that the instructions in his uncle's will insist he's to be cremated and his ashes spread on some agility field in New England, where he's originally from. And there's to be no memorial service for him."

Damn. There went my idea of observing everyone who showed up to mourn—or gloat. Who else had it in for him besides disgruntled show contestants . . . or Dante? People he worked with, those he'd judged in agility contests or elsewhere? Well, I'd check out as many as I could find, via Google, Althea, or whoever.

Even so, I heard myself grump, "Dante promised a big send-off for him."

"He told me that, too, but he'll honor Sebastian's wishes."

I bet Dante regretted it. Less chance for a big HotPets promo that way.

"We'll dedicate some shows to Sebastian," Charlotte continued, "but I don't think we can do more. Anyway, since everything went well today and we now have a replacement judge, we've decided to get together for an all-hands production meeting tomorrow morning at ten, to plan where we're going. The main SFV Studios facility has been released back to us, so we're having it there. Can you come?"

I glanced in my rearview mirror at Lexie, whom I'd just picked up at Darryl's. She regarded me quizzically, and I had to ask, "Will any animals be there?"

"No training or tryouts, but pets are permitted, if you'd like to bring Lexie."

"Great! Who else is coming? I could carpool with Rachel and Beggar."

"Good. See you then."

As soon as I got home after completing my pet-sitting agenda, I called Annie, the Jeongs' doggy-sitter. She confirmed she had no classes that weekend and intended to keep Princess with her constantly. That would prevent the pup from disturbing the neighbors in the short run, and I told Annie about my intent to take Princess to Darryl's on Monday.

"I need to warn you," she said, "I have some late classes

and study group sessions next week that I can't miss. Is your doggy day care open late?"

"No," I told her, "but I'll work something out either myself or with one of my other pet-sitter contacts."

Still, this was only a stopgap fix, I figured. The Jeongs wouldn't be home for another week. I'd try to talk to their neighbors' lawyer. But even if I somehow made the legal situation go away this time, it wouldn't solve the long-term dilemma of Princess's lonesome anguish.

That night, my phone didn't ring—except once, when Avvie Milton called to inquire about upcoming piggy scenarios on *Animal Auditions*. I told her I'd be back in touch after tomorrow, when I had better information.

No calls from Jeff—a good thing. Or from Dante . . . maybe not so good, at least for my psyche. But much better for my own long-term dilemma over my absurd attraction to the man.

Next morning, my pet-sitting went like clockwork— time-consuming yet utterly fun as I checked on my charges, walked and fed them as required.

Later, Rachel seemed in a good mood as I drove us both to the studio. All four of us, in fact. Lexie and Beggar camped in the backseat of the small car, sometimes sniffing out the slightly open windows, and other times sniffing at each other.

"What's this meeting really about?" I asked Rachel.

"Coordination, I think." My pretty, young assistant was all grins as she sat in the passenger seat. Today, since she wasn't to go öncamera, she wore a bright green T-shirt that said *Animal Auditions* over tight jeans.

I'd dressed a little less casually: my gold, silky shirt tucked into cream-colored slacks. No telling who'd be there. . . .

"We want to schedule the final potbellied pig sessions and start creating more scenarios for dogs," Rachel continued. "Get started filming them. Figure out which will air when on the Nature Network. Like that."

Sounded fine to me.

When we arrived, Dante was already there, with Wagner. Everyone else on our staff was present, too—almost. Only two of our judges joined us. Matilda was absent.

That wasn't necessarily a major issue, except that Charlotte seemed to be flitting around in some kind of panic.

"She left me a strange message," Charlotte said to me as we pulled chairs into a circle for our conclave. "Something about needing time to herself to determine how to deal with Sebastian's death and the problems it created. That's partly what we're all doing here today. But when I tried to return her call and tell her, I only got voice mail, and she hasn't called back. What should we do?" Her voice rose into a pitiful wail that reminded me a little of the pup Princess. But Charlotte's had little to do with separation—unless she was that attached to Matilda, which I doubted. It had everything to do with anxiety. She was our guru of reality shows, and the reality of this one was becoming all too unnerving.

I didn't intend to raise Charlotte's hopes unnecessarily, so I excused myself as if to head to the restroom—leaving Lexie cavorting with Wagner and Beggar. I saw Dante watch from the corner of his gorgeous brown eyes and immediately raised my chin. I wasn't embarrassed by the call of nature—especially since this exit wasn't caused by one. Instead, it was a call of another kind—to Matilda. But I, too, got only her voice mail. I left an upbeat message requesting that she call me back. And then I did head for the ladies' loo, since the suggestion had, in fact, instigated what came naturally.

When I returned to the meeting, stuff had apparently gone on in my absence, which was fine with me.

"Okay, are we agreed on this schedule?" Dante demanded, apparently having assumed at least temporary control.

Everyone concurred. I was informed that our next pot-bellied pig filming would occur on Monday, when it would have been scheduled anyway had Sebastian not died. It would be dedicated to him, whether or not that was written in his will.

I agreed to call my main media contact, Corina, to invite her to attend our Monday session. She'd also be officially invited to participate in our next canine training scenario with her Puli, ZsaZsa, who'd put on a pretty good performance during our session to choose our replacement judge.

Eliza was designated to impart our upcoming schedule to Matilda. "I'll suggest that the three of us, including Brody, get together an hour ahead of filming to coordinate how we interact." She glanced at our newest judge, who gave a nod. She'd worn her glasses, but otherwise looked as good as if we'd been scheduled to shoot a show today. The way she smiled at Brody suggested she had ulterior motives for dressing up.

Now, why would anyone do that? I refused to look down at my own nice outfit or wonder whether Dante had noticed. . . .

No matter if it was how I dressed or something more substantial, I got a dinner invitation from Dante. I considered saying I'd check my schedule, but decided that would sound too contrived. Instead, I agreed.

He invited Brody to join us, which was fine with me. I anticipated that Dante would come to pick me up, but instead he said he'd meet us at a nice restaurant in Beverly Hills. "We'll eat inside," he said, "so, unfortunately, no dogs allowed."

I hid my initial disgruntlement that quickly dissipated. This obviously wasn't a date. But why did Dante want to dine with Brody and me?

I agreed to meet them both at seven. Which meant I had to hurry to return Rachel, Beggar, and Lexie to our Hollywood Hills home, then accomplish my evening's pet-sitting visits early. That would give me time to dress and primp before dinner.

But as I backed my car out of my driveway, my cell phone rang. The caller's number was Matilda's.

"Hi, Matilda," I said heartily. "You missed an interesting meeting today, but I'm sure Eliza will fill you in."

"She left a message." Matilda's voice sounded strained.

"Is everything all right?" I asked.

"Sure," she said, although I was certain she lied. "Someone ran into my car today and I couldn't drive it."

But she hadn't returned either Charlotte's or my call to let us know—not until now.

"Are you okay?" I asked. "You weren't in it, were you?"

"No. It was parked. A hit-and-run."

"Oh, my. Are you insured?"

"Sure," she repeated, then stayed oddly quiet.

"Well, just so you know, your next judging will be on Monday. A continuation of the potbellied pig scenario. I hope the timing is all right with you. It's the time we'd already planned for."

"It should be fine."

This didn't sound like the outspoken and self-assured

veterinary shrink I'd spoken with only a couple of days earlier.

"Matilda, is everything okay with you?" I asked. "I mean, I know you're upset about your car. But you'll still be able to act as one of our judges, won't you?"

"Of course," she said curtly. "Wouldn't dream of backing out. I'll see you then."

But as I hung up, I felt absolutely certain something was wrong with Matilda.

I could only hope that, whatever it was, it did not affect her role on *Animal Auditions*. The loss of one judge had been one judge too many.

Chapter Sixteen

THE RITZY RESTAURANT where we were to meet had valet parking. Of course.

Even so, I sought a spot on the street. I used to do that with my beloved Beamer so no careless cowboy who'd lassoed a parking job could carom it into another car. I didn't care so much whether my rental car got another ding—except that I'd be liable for it. Mostly, it was my obstinacy that dictated I do that on this night. Dante had decided that I'd drive here. I would decide how to handle it.

The Italian *ristorante* was on a busy street, behind an elegant facade. It was late enough that I didn't have to feed the meter, and I strode from my car straight inside. No sign of Dante or Brody . . . till I mentioned to the high-chinned, dark-suited maître d' that I was meeting two men. "Ah, yes, Ms. Ballantyne?" He grinned at my confirming but pseudo-blasé nod. I wasn't about to convey that I was impressed in the least by his personal greeting. "Follow me."

I saw my two dinner companions at a table in a corner.

Their heads were bowed and they seemed to be engrossed in a chat I was about to interrupt. Unless, of course, they included me in their inner circle of conversation.

Dante glanced in my direction as I approached. He immediately ceased talking, and stood. So did Brody. The maître d' pulled out my chair, and I levered my butt into it gracefully.

I'd dressed for the occasion in slinky gray slacks with a sequined, sleeveless top beneath a silver-trimmed black jacket. I'd glanced into the mirror in the visor before exiting my car to ensure that my shoulder-length hair appeared neat as it framed my face, and that my makeup was enhanced, but not overdone, for the evening. Beautiful, no—but absolutely acceptable. And I basked in what appeared to be the appreciation of both men.

Each wore a dark suit, but neither resembled the other in the least. Dante seemed all smoldering Italian: olive skin, dark hair, eyes deeper than the richest dark chocolate.

Okay, so I was smitten by the guy. I admit it.

But Brody was no slouch in the looks department. How could he be, when he was movie-star handsome? His jaw was even firmer than Dante's, his cheekbones so prominent they practically pierced the skin beneath his golden eyes. His hair was a light brown, thick and wavy.

Both guys greeted me with such effusion that I almost blushed—and I'm not the blushing kind.

"Kendra, delighted you could join us." Dante motioned over a suited waiter who set a wineglass before me with a flourish, then lifted a Chianti bottle from the table and poured me a substantial serving. Dante and Brody lifted their already filled glasses, and we toasted each other and *Animal Auditions*.

The white-clad table was set with elegant dishware surrounded by sparkling silver. A small vase in the center held one red rose. I felt like a fairytale princess surrounded by two princes, each appearing to vie for my attention.

Wow.

I ordered a salad with, of course, Italian dressing and a delicious-sounding chicken and pasta dish. The waiter dashed off to see to our order. We were far from alone, since the place was crowded, but our corner seemed somewhat private.

"Okay," Dante said after a sip of wine. "Here it is, Kendra."

I smiled. Damn, but the guy was sexy. And there was more to it: I really liked him. Unwise, sure. He probably had a slew of women waiting to be beckoned by one of his slender, well-groomed fingers. But there was electricity between us. And . . . well, I genuinely had a sense that, somehow, we communicated, both verbally and non. I waited eagerly for him to continue.

"I know you have a reputation for solving murders," he said, "but I want you to leave Sebastian's to us."

Communication? Man, had I been mistaken! I stared. His dark eyes seemed absolutely commanding, as if he wasn't used to anyone contradicting anything he said.

But I simply smiled sardonically. "And you're ordering this because . . . ?"

"For your own safety." Brody was the one to respond. He appeared earnest, his brown brows knit as if he gave a damn. Even so . . .

"Are you threatening me?" I demanded, sending my glare from one to the other.

"Not at all," Dante said quite calmly. "The danger isn't

from us, but since we don't know who killed Sebastian and why—"

"That's it exactly," I said. "And assuming it wasn't either of you"—I stared only at Dante. Brody hadn't had anything to do with the show or, to my knowledge, with Sebastian at the time of his demise—"there's no reason to assume that whoever killed him will have anything against me."

"Do you consider me a suspect, Kendra?" Dante's tone seemed somewhat amused. "And what would my motive be?"

Our salads were delivered just then. Our waiter offered us freshly ground pepper, which I declined, and grated Parmesan cheese, which I accepted. When he'd again ceased his hovering, we began once more.

I responded to the pending question. "I don't know you well, Dante, but your reputation of being, well . . . let's say powerful . . . precedes you. Sebastian alive was possibly a good pick for our production, since home audiences love nasty reality show judges. But even the nastiest, other than Sebastian, often come across with some redeeming qualities. Sebastian didn't. And Sebastian dead brings in more viewers because of curiosity—about the show itself, and how it'll survive without him . . . and, of course, who might have killed him."

"Granted," Dante said. "And that's my motive because . . . ?"

"Because you're backing the show," Brody interjected, and I nodded my agreement. "The more it makes, the more you make." His smile was filled with irony as he stated exactly the point I'd been about to make about Dante's possible motive. "Kendra, the thing is—" He looked at Dante as if asking permission. For what?

Dante gave a slight nod, which surprised me.

Especially when Brody made his big revelation. "I can't elaborate for reasons of security, but let's just say that Dante and I have experience unraveling mysteries, too."

"Really?" Interesting. "How, when, and where?" I asked. "Not to mention why." Corina the reporter would be proud of me.

But Brody's response remained oblique. "I've done some preliminary checking, and have reason to believe this isn't a situation where an amateur ought to be involved. Even one as skilled as you at solving homicides." His expression suggested that he was more than a little impressed, and I smiled modestly at him, even as my mind churned.

"And a film star who plays at being a hero would be better at it?" I asked.

"Enough," Dante said softly.

Brody glanced toward him with a shrug that suggested submission, even as his grin widened. "Well, what do you know?" he asked rhetorically. "I never thought I'd see the day."

"What day?" I demanded. But whatever the hell they were talking about was now clearly between these two men only. They stared expressively at one another before both looked back at me.

"Today." Dante suddenly appeared more relaxed as he lifted a forkful of salad to his mouth. "Today is the day you'll back off a bit in the Sebastian matter." He seemed to hesitate, then added almost through gritted teeth, "Please."

I laughed. "Look," I told them both, "you better believe I never set out to be a murder magnet. But I seem to be one anyway. And although it doesn't make complete sense to enumerate our respective reasons to get this solved fast, I'll do it anyway. Dante, you have a big financial interest."

Not to mention the remaining possibility that he was a serious suspect. "It's unclear whether that interest will be helped or harmed by determining who killed Sebastian."

He gave a small and somehow sexy nod of acquiescence.

"Brody, I'm not sure what your interest in solving the murder is." I studied him carefully, wondering about what he had more than hinted at before. Something about security prohibiting him from giving more details. What kind of security? Security for the show?

National security?

I was really letting my imagination run wild . . . wasn't I?

"Curiosity," Brody responded. "And self-preservation. The man was my predecessor judge, after all."

"So tell me this," I said. "Why is an actor more qualified than an attorney to investigate a killing on an amateur basis?"

"Depends on the actor," Brody said. "Some have past lives that may mean they're not quite amateurs."

"Some like you?" I glanced at Brody, whose expression had become absolutely blank. Dante's seemed more open, so I addressed my next inquiry to him. "Dante, you told me you knew each other previously. Did Brody work for you in some security capacity before he went into showbiz?" I remembered my speculation that they'd been in military special ops together, since Althea had unearthed that tidbit about Dante's past. That might make sense in this context.

"As a litigator, you should be wary of compound questions," Dante responded silkily, which absolutely irked me. But when I attempted to qualify my queries, all either would admit to was knowing the other before.

"Where?" I demanded again. "And how?"

"Compound again," Dante said, and as our dinner was served, I got no further.

I pondered my position as I took a delicious bite of chicken tetrazzini to die for. As I did in court, I queued up the questions I intended to ask. Was Brody's prior relationship with Dante, whatever it was, a reason to add him to my suspect list?

But before I could start my inquiry, Dante's hand slinked across the table and took one of mine.

"I'm not being officious here, Kendra," he lied softly. "The thing is, I really care about you. Don't want you to be hurt, if I can prevent it. Let's just say that Brody and I go back a long way. We were in the military together and have a history of doing things in the interest of our country." Aha! I'd been right! As far as it went . . . "We learned a lot that can be translated to solving situations like this. And I really want to do that. For me, sure. But also for you. I know you have things at stake—your interest in the show, and in helping your friend Ned. Will you let me take care of this for you, Kendra?"

Well, hell. I'd grown teary-eyed, an emotional reaction I rejected . . . almost. I responded, "Thank you, Dante. But let's all work on it together."

I saw irritation shadow his face, but to his credit he didn't argue. Neither did Brody.

I almost started to relax as the three of us talked about all kinds of things during the remainder of our meal. Much revolved around pets—unsurprising as to Dante, whose thriving business empire was animal-related.

With only a little urging, he regaled us with tales of wild animals whose lives were saved by HotWildife, the rescue organization he funded, and visited often, just north of L.A.

"It's really something," Brody agreed.

"You'll have to come and see it with me soon, Kendra," Dante offered, and I jumped at the possibility. Of course he'd offered a visit there to Corina Carey, too.

Then there were the movie experiences Brody shared with us. I had the impression that the high jinks surrounding the evolution of a hit film were even more enjoyable than the film itself, even to its famous stars.

"I don't have anything lined up for a few more months," Brody said to us, "but you're both invited, whenever I do, to come watch us film. I won't schedule anything that could conflict with *Animal Auditions*."

All too soon, we were finished eating. Though each of us eschewed dessert, we sat around for a while with our coffee. And then it was time to go.

Why wasn't I surprised when Dante apologized for not accompanying me to dinner? Or when he insisted on following me home? Maybe it was simply delight at his ongoing attentiveness.

When we reached my wrought iron gate, I left it open long enough for his Mercedes to trail my rental up the drive. I invited him in for a nightcap.

Lexie was excited to see us, and Dante joined us on a brief and productive doggy walk on my narrow, hilly street.

"Will Wagner be okay alone this long?" I asked.

"He'll be fine. My personal assistant will have let him out in the yard several times by now."

I nodded, unsurprised that Dante had full-time help. I was curious about what kind of mansion he must live in, especially as we sat in my small, nondescript living room, sipping an okay but not especially elegant wine. Lexie lay snoring slightly on the floor near where I'd curled my feet up under me on my sectional sofa. Dante watched me with an enigmatic expression so sexy I wanted to jump his bones.

Okay. Eventually, the inevitable happened. Can't say who moved first, but I was soon in Dante's heated embrace. His kisses were indescribable, his touches electric . . . and his suggestion that we move to my bedroom absolutely appropriate.

Our lovemaking was every bit as extraordinary as everything else about Dante DeFrancisco.

Much later, as I lay bare beneath my sheets, my breathing heavy and my body hot, Dante nuzzled my neck. "I really care about you, Kendra," he said.

"Ditto, Dante," I responded lazily.

"So you'll back off a bit on your investigation of what happened to Sebastian?"

My whole body suddenly chilled. "Over your dead body," I said.

Chapter Seventeen

IT WASN'T EXACTLY easy having a disagreement like this with a guy with whom I'd just made love. Especially one with whom I'd exchanged sentiments about caring for one another. If I'd been clad, I'd have jumped out of bed and harped at him with my hands on my hips. I considered it anyway, but figured I'd look a bit bizarre. Besides, both of us might wind up distracted, and the inevitable could happen again.

So, instead, I stayed snuggled close as we sniped at one another. Talk about a bizarre way to quarrel. . . .

"I promised to help Ned Noralles," I reminded Dante irritably, attempting to ignore his nearby warmth.

"You could always let the police handle their own business." Dante sounded not at all sympathetic, and a lot like the cops who'd also pointedly warned me off. I didn't know where Dante had rested his hands, but happily—or unhappily—they weren't on me.

"They may already think they have a suitable suspect.

Two. Ned and Nita. But I disagree." I didn't mention that I wondered whether Ned suspected his sister. *I* didn't . . . did I?

"For what it's worth, I disagree, too. But Brody will look into it. Back off, Kendra, and let us handle it."

"And he's qualified because of some mysterious connection you two had in the past?"

"Exactly."

"And you expect that's enough to convince me to rely on you and back off."

"You got it."

"I got nothing, Dante. Except maybe a headache."

He started to gently massage my temples, and I began nearly to purr as contentedly as some of my feline pet-sitting charges.

He was attempting to distract me. And almost succeeding.

"That feels good," I allowed. "But it doesn't change anything."

He stopped stroking, which made me feel bereft all over again. He backed away from me in my queen-size bed. "Has anyone ever told you how difficult you can be?" he demanded.

"Often," I said with a smug smile.

He laughed. And then grew so solemn that I blinked as I watched the sudden sorrow in his eyes.

"I was serious when I told you that I care for you, Kendra. That's not something I say to women easily. In fact . . . it's been a long time since I've said it to anyone. I lost the last woman I said it to. In a way that made me think I'd never say it again. And to know that someone I feel about this way is throwing herself into a potentially dangerous situation just because it's there—"

"I'll be careful, Dante. I always am, you know."

"I know that too often you find yourself a 'murder magnet.' Apt expression, by the way. But do you know any genuine self-defense tactics? Have you ever been trained in authentic investigation techniques? So far you've been lucky. But . . . I don't want you to be hurt."

I nearly melted with emotion. He actually did seem to care. And I was filled with curiosity about the mysterious woman whom Dante had cared about and lost. "Tell me about the lady you referred to."

He smiled sadly, reached out and pulled me against him. "Maybe someday." His kiss wasn't the fuel of passion that we'd shared previously, but more of a fond farewell. Sure enough, he untangled himself from my embrace and sheets, and stood.

I was filled with a combo of sexual admiration and sorrow. He started to get dressed. "Sorry I can't stay the night," he said. "I have commitments first thing in the morning, so I need to go. If I stay here, I won't get any sleep."

I didn't consider contradicting that. He was right. Of course, I wouldn't sleep whether he stayed or left, so his staying seemed smarter from my perspective.

"Tomorrow's Sunday," I reminded him. But I didn't really believe that in megamoguldom like his, he could relax on weekends.

"I know," he said. "But I have commitments."

I didn't attempt to dissuade him. Genuine business commitments or not, he had the right to exit when he pleased. Just as I had the right to do whatever *I* pleased, including investigate murders.

I did, however, stand up and seek out a robe. I could at least see him to the door. Plus, I'd need to ensure he could drive out my gate, since I'd no intention of handing over one of the automatic controls. Of course all the motion woke Lexie, and she bounded from one of us to the other, demanding explanation. Better yet, a treat.

She got neither, not then.

"Promise me one thing, Kendra," Dante said as we reached my apartment door.

"What's that?" I inquired noncommittally.

"If you won't keep your lovely nose out of looking into what happened to Sebastian, then you'll at least stay in touch with me. Preferably close touch. If I can offer any suggestions, any help at all, I want to be there for you."

He bent down, kissed me, and was gone before I could rustle up a clever retort. So all I whispered was "Thanks."

AS WITH DANTE, despite its being Sunday, it was a work-day for me. The pet-sitting, at least. And although I groaned when my alarm went off at six, I dragged myself out of bed—trying hard not to stare at the spot where he'd been only hours before.

I realized immediately that, during the catnaps I'd managed that night, I must have dreamed about Dante, since images of him floated rampantly about my mind, and not all of them resulted from our wonderful evening. Or even from the times I'd seen him before, or *Animal Auditions*.

"I'm really interested in him, Lexie," I said as I prepared to take my Cavalier for her morning outside constitutional. She wagged her long, furry tail in sympathy, and we both went down the steps.

I continued my partly one-sided conversation, alternately chastising Dante both for his absence and for his attempt to control me when he had absolutely no right—and feeling ecstatic that he gave a damn enough to tell me what to do. Consistent? Not hardly. But my state of mind kept skipping from one opinion to the other.

"Enough," I finally said as Lexie and I piled into my rental car. I needed the company and intended to take her along on my pet-sitting assignments.

Which reminded me of my promise for tomorrow. I'd have to go pick up Princess, all the way out by Thousand Oaks, and bring her to Darryl's day resort. Fine. I had a plan. But it was only a partial solution. I'd promised the Jeongs, and their pet-sitter Annie, that I'd find someone to be with Princess in the evening, after Darryl closed and before Annie returned from her late classes.

From my large purse I pulled my address book, in which I'd put all the information about my fellow sitters who belonged to the Pet-Sitters Club of Southern California, and scanned the entries. And as we sat in our driveway, I began making calls.

Tracy Owens, the PSCSC president, thought she still owed me since I'd done her a favor a few months ago. Plus, we'd become good friends who occasionally got together for fun. "I'm sorry, Kendra," she told me. "I'm so booked up that I can't stay even a few hours around Thousand Oaks tonight. Maybe another time."

Lilia Zieglar, the club's oldest member, simply didn't want to do the long freeway drive, especially since at least one way would be in the dark. I didn't immediately reach Frieda Shoreman, an elegant pet-sitter who'd once intended to be a movie star. But Wanda Villareal answered her phone right away.

"Oh, Kendra," she said, sounding a smidgen out of breath. "I've been meaning to call you."

"Really? To schedule a play date?" She owned a Cavalier, too, a pretty Blenheim—red-and-white—boy named Basil.

"Sure. Let's do it soon. But what's on your mind now?"

I explained my predicament and the promise I'd made about Princess. "Would you have time during a couple of evenings this week to help out?"

"For you? Absolutely. Give me the particulars."

Which I did, including how to get hold of both the Jeongs, since she'd be visiting their home as well as their pup, and the sitter Annie, who'd have to work out getting Wanda inside. "I'll let Darryl Nestler know you're picking Princess up, starting tomorrow. He owns the Doggy Indulgence Day Resort in Studio City. Nice guy."

"I'm sure," she said.

"Thanks a lot, Wanda," I finished, then hung up.

And wondered exactly why I had the impression that Wanda had sounded grateful to *me*. Was her pet-sitting business in trouble? I'd have to find out if she needed additional help.

THE REST OF my morning—pet-sitting, then taking Lexie to a premier dog park in the Hollywood Hills—all went fine. But even as I observed Lexie romping with other off-leash attendees, and exchanged greetings with their owners, my mind continued to spin around all that had happened the night before.

Dante. Desire. Caring . . . a lot.

And irritation at his controlling nature.

We stayed for three-quarters of an hour. Lexie seemed worn out by the time I decided we'd both had enough.

We'd already gotten home when I got a call on my cell from an unfamiliar number.

"Kendra?" shouted a high-pitch squeal. "I shouldn't be calling you, but I figure you'll know what to do. This is

Dr. Hollins. Matilda." Suddenly, she stopped talking. Said nothing at all.

To fill the silence, I prompted, "You know about our next *Animal Auditions* taping tomorrow?"

"Yes. Yes, of course," she said, much more softly—a good thing, since my ears were already ringing. "I'm not calling about that. Kendra—I need your help. I think. I—Never mind. Forget I even called." She hung up.

And when I tried phoning her again, she didn't respond. I left her a message.

Curious, I tried her again ten minutes later. She still didn't answer, and I left yet another message.

What was going on with her?

I'd ask her tomorrow at the taping.

Assuming she showed up.

Chapter Eighteen

THAT EVENING, AFTER I again finished my perfectly fun
pet-sitting rounds, I sat on my sofa with Lexie on my lap—
remembering with whom I'd been the last time I'd simply
sat here.

Actually, it hadn't been so simple . . .

That's when my cell phone sang.

I smiled, certain that karma was in control again. It
would be Dante calling me. To apologize. To let me know
he'd been wrong to attempt to tell me what to do.

Or, more likely, to check up on me, to make sure I
wasn't disobeying his final order to keep him informed.

If he'd called me every time I'd thought of him that day,
I'd never have been off the phone. . . . And I'd have been
even more confused—and irritated—than I was now.

But it wasn't his number in my caller ID. It was Jeff
Hubbard's.

I took a deep, bracing breath before I answered. No

sense avoiding him. But neither did I have to pretend I'd been waiting for *his* call.

"Hello, Jeff," I said in a not entirely unwelcoming tone. After all, a plan was brewing in my mind, and I might need his cooperation.

"Hi, Kendra. How've you been? I've been thinking about you. I've been looking further into Sebastian Czykovski's murder to help Ned, but need more than I've found so far to clear him." Nita, too? But I didn't inquire. "What's new? Are you pursuing anything I should follow up on? Or do you need Althea's input?"

Of course I'd cooperate with him—to a point. It wouldn't hurt for me to have a P.I. I could still call on.

And wouldn't that just piss Dante off?

"Attorneys always avoid compound or multiple questions." I grinned sardonically but invisibly at Jeff, recollecting one of Dante's criticisms designed to knock me off balance. "But no new direction to point you in, unfortunately, or Althea, either—not yet, at least. Have you spoken with Ned recently?"

"He sounds okay," Jeff said. "That's one reason I called. He's coming to your potbellied pig taping tomorrow. I told him it wasn't wise, but he figured Nita and he would look guiltier if they stayed away. He convinced me, but what do you think?"

Jeff Hubbard, excellent P.I. and security expert, actually asked me for an opinion? Wow! Was the sky about to fall?

Or did he think they all needed an attorney's point of view?

"There's definite merit in that," I told him. "If I were the lawyer representing the Noralles siblings, I'd stress that acting normal was absolutely a good thing."

"Got it. I agree."

"And do you happen to be professionally representing them as a P.I.?" I finally asked.

"Sure am," he confirmed. "Look, are you available for dinner tomorrow night after your taping? I'd like to strategize with you about how best to look into things. For Ned."

I considered the invitation. Dante would be at the *Animal Auditions* filming. Just because we'd made marvelous love last night didn't mean I would leap into a monogamous relationship with the man—especially since he hadn't asked, and possibly had used sex to bribe me to see things his way. Well, it wouldn't work.

Even if I wouldn't mind the sex part again . . .

But, hell, I wasn't the sort of woman who got off on making men miserable. If I said yes to dinner with Jeff, I'd be leading him on. And possibly turning Dante off, an even bigger issue, from my current perspective.

"I'm busy then, Jeff," I said softly. "But maybe we could get together over coffee soon to brainstorm our strategies. I'd love to get the cops steered in a different direction from Ned, Nita, and their piggies."

"Oh. Okay. We'll talk about a time tomorrow."

He sounded sad, which made me sorry. Partly because I didn't intend to hurt him the way he'd recently hurt me. But also because I continued to need his help. Or at least Althea's. We still had contacts in common—some we both cared about.

"How's Odin?" I asked. Jeff's sweet Akita had become a special friend to Lexie and me.

"He's okay. I take him for more walks these days. And I've found another doggy day care center a little closer to me than Darryl's, so I don't have to leave him alone for long periods. And—well, I have a trip coming up in a few weeks. Maybe you could still pet-sit for me." He sounded wistful and unsure of my response, so I quickly assured him I'd gladly watch Odin again.

As long as his owner wasn't around.

"So . . ." I said, since he didn't seem inclined to hang up, "from the way you phrased your question, it sounded like you've come up with at least a little in Ned's and Nita's defense. What have you got?"

"That's something we should talk about in person," he said, sounding utterly reasonable—and absolutely aggravating. "See ya tomorrow." He hung up, leaving me glaring at my phone.

NEXT MORNING, LEXIE and I left bright and early to pick up Princess. Fortunately, she wasn't crying when I arrived, though she seemed excited to see us.

I had no fun at all fitting both dogs into the backseat of my little rental car. But I was committed to staying a pet-sitter. I needed the ability to carry canines and other animals all over, if necessary. My dear old Beamer hadn't been ideal, but it had been big enough to work with—unlike this small sedan.

It was way past time for me to pick out a new car. And face the fact that I'd have to go miserably into debt to buy one. I could choose a used one, of course. But if I was going to go for it, I was really going to go for it.

"What do you think, Lexie? Princess?" I asked the pups in the backseat. Their response was absolute interest, waggy tails, but no commitment to my making a choice.

I soon deposited the dogs at Darryl's for a day of fun. He wasn't available when I arrived, so I had no opportunity to push him further about who he was seeing.

Fortunately, most of my pet-sitting pals were as cooperative as usual. Not Stromboli, though. The sweet shepherd mix scooted his butt along the sidewalk as we headed home after our otherwise ordinary outing. "I need to tell your mama," I told him as he rolled his eyes at me and panted. "You might need to be wormed or have your glands cleaned, so get ready for a vet visit."

Stromboli's owner, Dana Maroni, was due back in a few days. I had her phone number and let her know about this situation—not that it was a medical emergency, but she'd need to deal with it.

"Ugh," she said into my cell phone as Stromboli and I started back into his house. "Thanks for letting me know. I guess."

I grinned. "That's what a pet-sitter's for."

Their next-door neighbor, Maribelle Openheim, popped her head out her door. She was a friend of mine, and so was Meph, her wiry terrier. Once I'd gotten Stromboli fed and settled down, I visited briefly with Maribelle, then headed for my law office.

Using my hands-free gadget in the car, I phoned Matilda Hollins. Twice. She didn't respond or call back. Well, I'd see her that afternoon at the *Animal Auditions* taping. I hoped.

And then I thought again about the whole Sebastian situation. Jeff's officially acting as a P.I. to help Ned and Nita didn't matter. Neither did Dante's attempts to get me to back off. Till the situation was resolved, I had to help the Noralles siblings. I'd promised.

But without a true memorial service for Sebastian, I

was somewhat at a loss about who, besides the obvious possibilities connected with *Animal Auditions*, might have had it in for him. I needed to come up with a proactive plan—one that would land me additional suspects. If I didn't, Dante might decide I'd tacitly agreed to follow his initial orders.

And that was something I definitely wouldn't do.

I FIELDED A couple of legal emergencies that morning, one of which required a quick trip to court—Van Nuys, fortunately, and not downtown, which was farther away.

I finally escaped and headed for SFV Studios. Sure, I was in my producer role. But just because I intended to look for likely suspects away from *Animal Auditions* didn't mean I wouldn't continue to keep my eyes and ears open here.

In fact . . . well, I'm a listophile. A listaholic. Before I exited my car and went inside, I grabbed a pad of paper and started listing questions I needed answers to before I could get a better handle on who might have had it in for Sebastian.

And with a call to Althea later, maybe I'd be able to aim my investigation in more productive directions.

I finally entered the building and went into the big soundstage area where porcine chaos was already in progress. The official piggy activities hadn't yet started, but our animal stars were being exhorted by their owners to do excellent jobs in today's scenting scenarios. Once again, the pigs were to pretend to be on the job as investigators smelling out contraband such as illicit drugs—in the form of some soapy stuff that really didn't reek too badly, and also wasn't actually illegal.

Okay, I admit it: I was fast becoming a pigaphile. I loved the porkers. They were utterly smart and personable, chuffing and oinking their little hearts out while attempting to ascertain what was going on around them. Most were chubby, and all waddled around their owners as if to assure they'd obey any command. Their broad and inquisitive snouts alternately were raised into the air to check its scents, then lowered toward the floor.

As I took it all in, I slunk up to the nearest pigs and knelt to hug their bristly and chunky carcasses. "Hi, guys," I said, and received some satisfying grunts in exchange.

As I stood again, I looked beyond the crowd, toward where the audience sat. Once again, we hosted visiting cops, including detectives Howard Wherlon and Vickie Schwinglan. I assumed they were here watching us like hawks as they continued to conduct their official investigation into Sebastian's demise, not just to cheer on Ned and Nita, nor Porker or Sty Guy.

With their resources, I'd be spending my investigative time elsewhere, questioning others in Sebastian's life about why his death had occurred.

Well, heck, I could still do that. Would do that. Soon. But I felt frustrated for now. I needed to do something more to reach a resolution. Today, the best I could do was ponder possibilities, as I watched the people and pigs who'd been around here before Sebastian was killed.

Dante stood on the sidelines beyond where the cameras would point, Wagner sitting at attention at his side. The human of those two seemed to sense when I walked in and smiled sexily straight at me. I gave Dante a large smile right back and immediately looked away. If he wanted more than attempting to manipulate me, he'd have to ask.

I let my gaze wander from person to person. Charlotte

was there in her producer's capacity, taking charge of everything. Our hosts—my assistant Rachel and weatherman-on-hiatus Rick Longley—stood together, reviewing paperwork that I assumed contained their "ad-lib" lines. Trainers Charley Sherman and Corbin Hayhurst each worked with a couple of pigs and their people—Corbin's people included Nita and Ned Noralles.

But my attention was quickly riveted on the table below our bleachers. That's where the judges were to sit. And all three were there.

Eliza Post appeared composed as she initially assessed the competitors. No glasses on her today, and her makeup appeared perfect. She'd smoothed her long brown hair around her shoulders and appeared somewhat younger than the mid-forties I'd estimated before. Maybe someday I'd ask . . . as I assessed her more closely as a murder suspect.

Matilda Hollins was there, too. That relieved me, after my earlier doubts. On the other hand, she seemed somehow to have aged into her fifties since the last time I'd seen her. Yes, she was there—with reading glasses, perched on her nose, emphasizing the roundness of her cheeks. Her short hair underscored her wrinkles. Looked like the makeup gurus here hadn't been extremely successful.

What was going on with her?

Of course, compared with the handsome Brody Avilla, neither lady judge could stand up. He stood in their center, also watching the goings-on along the soundstage.

I glanced at my cell phone to see the hour. We were to start taping in twenty minutes. That gave me a little time.

I edged up to Dante, who unobtrusively touched the small of my back. I liked the way it felt, but not the possessiveness it might have meant.

Especially since I saw Jeff Hubbard come through the soundstage door.

"What's he doing here?" Dante asked irritably.

"Backstopping me," I said too sweetly. "Looking for something to help Ned and Nita."

"Then let *him* do it, Kendra," Dante commanded. I shrugged as I edged past him, obviously intending to ignore his words.

Besides, there was someone I wanted to talk to right away. Maybe there was one person here with some answers—or at least she was causing me questions.

Matilda didn't seem pleased to see me approach the judges' table. She glanced around, as if seeking a spot for asylum.

Brody must have gotten the drift of what I was up to, and moved to block her way. "Hi, Kendra," he said smoothly. "I enjoyed our dinner last night."

Which statement got me stares from both Matilda and Eliza. "Strictly business, unfortunately," I said with a shrug.

Eliza laughed. Matilda still seemed to search for a way out—and I wasn't about to give it to her.

I directed my attention back to Brody. "Since you've started with us, I don't suppose you've gotten any sense of someone who's angry with our judges, have you? I mean, I want you all to stay safe and healthy, but I'm still hoping to figure out what happened to Sebastian. Since you've taken over his spot, I'm most concerned about you."

Not entirely true. After all the innuendoes about his prior mysterious affiliations with Dante, I had a definite sense that Brody wasn't just another pretty face. He could take care of himself, and then some.

"Thanks," he said. "But if I get any hint of danger, I'll

go to the police right away. I've played law enforcement officers in some of my films, and have a healthy respect for what they do. How about you ladies? You're not feeling spooked, are you? Whatever happened to Sebastian, surely it wasn't a result of being a judge here . . . was it?"

Eliza smiled again. "Not to my knowledge. But I'll be the first to warn both of you if I feel at all concerned."

We all looked expectantly at Matilda, who stayed quiet.

"Did you get my phone messages?" I asked, deciding not to push her about her odd call to *me*. For now.

"Yes, and I'm sorry I didn't get a chance to call you back," she said, her expression hinting of sourness. "To fit in this taping this afternoon, my calendar became quite a mess, and there were pet patients I just had to see. No time for the phone."

Not even on Sunday? I wanted to ask, but forbore.

"No problem," I told her. "As long as everything's okay."

"Of course it is," she said with a pseudo smile that seemed to turn her round face into a jack-o'-lantern lookalike.

"And you're not feeling in any danger being a judge for this show, despite what happened to Sebastian?" That question blessedly came from Brody, who was backing me up on this inquiry.

"Absolutely not," Matilda responded emphatically. But her attention seemed solely on the paperwork on the table in front of her, and not on any of the people, such as Brody or me.

Was she lying? I had the distinct impression she was.

At that moment, at least, I didn't see her as Sebastian's killer, any more than Ned. Or Nita. Of course, I could be absolutely wrong.

Was she simply afraid that what had happened to Sebastian could happen to her? I could certainly understand that.

But she was a psychologist—even though an animal shrink. I'd try to get her to talk about it soon.

And hopefully I'd get her to feel a lot better once I figured out who'd harmed her fellow judge.

Chapter Nineteen

BUT MURDER WASN'T on my mind as soon as the cameras started rolling. The piggy fest rocked!

All our remaining contestants appeared to be excellent sniffers. I was highly impressed when most discovered the hidden treasures that, if genuine instead of well-placed props, could have been terrorist equipment beneath the audience bleachers, hidden in judges' notebooks, and in pockets of other pig owners. Everyone seemed to enjoy the scenario filmed for showing on the Nature Network that night, especially the porcine participants.

Even those in the audience whose inclusion oncamera might not have been anticipated acted like good sports—cops included. That surprised me. But detectives Wherlon and Schwinglan were apparently animal lovers even if they suspected the worst in all people.

At the top of our bleachers, I saw Corina Carey taking notes. She hadn't brought her camera guy—possibly a good thing, especially since our *Animal Auditions* company held all rights to whatever went on here. But on the other hand, a reporter—even a sleazy one—had the legal okay, as fair use, to record snippets of our show for a newscast. And the extra piggy publicity could actually be good for us.

Of course, she was likely most interested because of Sebastian's murder—something I absolutely understood.

Standing on the sidelines, I continued to take in the pig scenarios as I studied the people in attendance. After each entry came the time I'd come to dread before, when Sebastian was judging and cruelly criticized our contestants. Sure, some pigs were obvious showstoppers, others were average, and a couple were clearly out of it. But all deserved to be treated with at least some respect.

Eliza was critical in her evaluation, sure, but managed concurrent kindness. Brody was our unknown, and he tended to jest, even as he took jabs at the smart, scenting swine. Nervous Matilda was mostly uncharacteristically mellow, although she managed verbal swipes at some of our contestants—especially Porker and Sty Guy. Clearly Ned and Nita weren't pleased with that, but both sucked it up and acted accepting, at least for the camera.

Afterward, we all milled in the middle of the sound stage. The judges had done as directed and met for an hour before the show to determine how to coordinate their responses—not necessarily in agreement, but at least somewhat sympatico, instead of à la Sebastian. They'd chosen their favorite piggy performers during the taping, but it would be up to the TV audience to phone in when the show was aired later and decide which sows or boars would be booted off next week.

"I have a feeling we'd better put Judge Hollins in protective custody," Detective Wherlon said to me, loud enough for everyone to hear.

Dante and Jeff were both standing near me. All three of us turned toward the cop. "Why?" I asked—glad that Corina Carey appeared to be interviewing contestants across the stage. No need for her to include this in her story about the show.

"She dared to criticize the Noralles pigs," Detective Schwinglan said, as if in concert with Howard Wherlon. The two glanced at each other and grinned almost maliciously. In unison, they turned toward the pig guardians in question. Ned and Nita stood nearby with some other contestants, all making a fuss over each other's pets. With them was Rick Longley, smiling and chattering amiably, as a TV host should.

Judging from the sour expression on Ned's face, he'd heard the detectives' every word. He didn't deign to comment, though. He also appeared to be holding Nita's arm—and she looked royally peeved.

Was her temper the reason Ned suspected his sister? Maybe his instincts were correct. . . . Or not.

As I started to turn back toward the two detectives, considering giving them a tongue-lashing for their nastiness, I noticed Matilda Hollins standing at the periphery of the crowd. She'd gone decidedly gray.

Had she, too, heard Howard Wherlon's inappropriate comment?

Was she in fact scared enough to consider protective custody? If so, why would she think herself especially at risk?

I edged in her direction, but she immediately bolted.

"You've spoken with her, haven't you, Kendra?" Dante demanded softly.

"Not as much as I'd like," I said. "I'll try to learn more from her later."

Dante's eyes bored into mine as if he was about to issue another edict, but his expression softened resignedly. "Just keep me in the loop, okay?"

He sounded so concerned that I almost relented in my determination to do things my way. But I dropped that idea immediately.

Ned approached us, notwithstanding the nearby presence of his former cohorts—and the way his sister leveled irritated glares in his direction as she stayed with the piggies. I soon gathered it was Jeff that Ned wanted to speak with. But he didn't insist on solitude. A good thing, since Rick Longley sauntered behind him.

"Those guys aren't joking around." Ned nodded toward Howard and Vickie. "They're insisting that both Nita and I go in again tomorrow for further interrogation. I've called your attorney friend Esther Ickes to ask her availability."

"Wow, are you really a suspect?" Rick asked. "They've talked to me, too." The guy acted too innocent—and interested—to be for real. And was that a speculative and suspicious gleam in his eye, or was I simply hoping to broaden my suspect list?

Even so, I studied him as he sidled away. I'd look into his background a little more, just in case.

Meantime, Brody Avilla had joined us, obviously also tuned into the prior conversation. "Why you?" he asked, as inquisitively and innocently as if he was simply the movie star and judge he appeared to be.

"Wishful thinking on my fellow detectives' part," Ned said with a shrug. "I'm better at this than they are, so why not get in their digs while they can—till the real killer is ID'd?" Like . . . your sister?

"Which is where I come in." Jeff also joined us.

"You're on the case?" Dante inquired.

"Sure am." Jeff's tone held a note of belligerence, as if he anticipated Dante's disapproval. But I knew why our *Animal Auditions* backer was asking while obviously knowing the answer. His sidelong glance at me suggested I was right.

He wanted to point out again to me that a pro—a real P.I.—was investigating the murder on behalf of the same suspects I wanted to help. So why should I interfere, especially at my possible peril?

Because I wanted to. Because I'd all but promised Ned. Because I'd sometimes proven myself better at badgering out killers than the professionals did.

And mostly because I wasn't about to buckle under to Dante DeFrancisco's issuance of orders. Okay, I liked the guy. A lot.

But he wasn't the boss of me.

And so I said, "Like I've said, Jeff, I'm glad you're on it. Two heads are better than one, though, so I'll keep digging to see what else I can learn about Sebastian's enemies. I'll give you what I find, as long as I can continue to use Althea as a resource."

"You got it," Jeff said, looking particularly pleased as he aimed a small smile in Dante's direction.

"Four heads are even better than two," Brody broke in before said Mr. DeFrancisco could say something nasty. "Dante's a good sounding board, and I like to butt in, now and then, when I'm not wanted." His big grin was intended to be disarming. And it was . . . to some extent.

I still wanted more details about the backgrounds of Dante and Brody. But I certainly wasn't going to get my answers now.

I was, however, the center of attention as both Jeff and Dante walked me to my car. Fortunately, Ned and Nita distracted Jeff with questions on how his inquiry on their behalf was progressing.

"That guy still wants you, Kendra," Dante observed with obvious displeasure as he stood beside me. *As do I*, his heated gaze asserted.

"We're just friends," I responded with a sadistic smile.

"Could be. In any event, have a good evening."

But would I, when I'd obviously be spending it alone?

ALL THE BETTER for digging into my murder inquiries, I recognized a short while later.

Which meant reliance on some of my usual sources. One in particular: Althea. I called her on my short journey from the soundstage to Doggy Indulgence Day Resort.

"Jeff sounded pretty pleased this afternoon when he called," Althea said. "He told me to continue to cooperate with you if you asked for information. You interested in some of the additional data I found about Sebastian? Jeff will look into it, too, but there are a couple of people he now thinks you'd be better questioning—Sebastian's ex-wife, for one."

"Really?" Sounded like Jeff was going all out to impress me. Which made me smile. But didn't make me think I'd let him back into my life for anything but investigating.

I pulled to the side of the road and grabbed the list of stuff to look into concerning Sebastian's murder that I'd already started. Althea gave me the data I needed to contact Sebastian's ex, and I gave her some additional things to look into for me, mostly about Sebastian's dog agility training academy and his reputation as an agility judge. I also requested a little background check on Nita Noralles and Rick Longley, just in case.

"Thanks, Althea," I told her. "I owe you. As usual."

"What you owe me is to stay on Jeff's good side. I know better than to warn you against getting too close to Dante DeFrancisco, but . . . well, I haven't completed my own kind of research into his background, Kendra, but I'm getting discouraged. Sure, he's ruthless at times, when it suits him, but I haven't found anything too awful. And I've found oodles of stuff on how he started from nothing but a love for animals, built a magnificent empire selling pet-related products, and expends tremendous amounts endowing pet shelters and wildlife rescue organizations."

"Right," I said, expecting her, with the repetitious buildup, to say something nasty about the guy.

"Don't you get it now?" she exploded in obvious exasperation. "You did before. This is all PR hokum. It may be true. In fact, it most likely is. But Dante DeFrancisco's life appears to have begun when he was in his twenties or so, in the military. I've found nothing on his childhood, where he went to college, or anything else about how he really started out."

A sudden insight started tugging at my brain synapses. "Did Jeff give you a request similar to mine—but tell you to make sure to find out lots of awful stuff about Dante?"

Althea's hesitation shouted her response. Jeff, suspecting I had a romantic interest in Dante, would want to discredit the guy in my eyes, maybe so I'd come running back to him.

Not gonna happen, even if Dante was as disreputable as Jeff wanted him to be.

Even so, I remained intrigued. And damned curious. And if anyone could get answers, it would be Althea.

"Can I give you a similar track to follow without your spilling it to Jeff?" I asked. "I hate to put you in that position, though, so if you have any qualms—"

"No, it's okay, Kendra," she told me. "Jeff said I should do any research you wanted. He wants me to give him any new results on Mr. DeFrancisco, but he also said he figured you'd tell me not to do that—and he agreed even before the question was asked."

"Really?"

Jeff was actually being reasonable. He must really want me to return to him. Which made me feel flattered. But still not inclined to bolt back into his arms.

"Yes," Althea said.

"Okay, then." Still, I felt a clarification was in order. "But, Althea, if at any time you feel you can't keep a confidentiality promise to me, tell me before you continue with any research assignment I give you."

"Will do."

That was when I asked her to search deeper into her magical Web sites—in other words, hack into secret government stuff—to dig out more about the way Dante's path crossed Brody Avilla's somewhere in the military. And more . . . before.

BEFORE COMPLETING MY regular rounds, I picked up Princess and Lexie at Darryl's Doggy Indulgence, and drove all the way almost to Thousand Oaks. I confirmed first that Wanda Villareal, my friend from the Pet-Sitters Club of Southern California, would meet us there.

She was sitting in her car, awaiting our arrival. She gave me a hug in greeting, then fussed over her new friend Princess, who leaped around, then settled down to lick Wanda's face.

Wanda was a petite person who favored flowing, gauzy tops. The one she wore today over blue jeans was lime green. Her face was pretty, her huge brown eyes enhanced with green shadow, and her mouth was turned up in a radiant smile. "Great to see you, Kendra," she said. "And thanks for the referral. My pet-sitting practice is doing well, but I like to broaden my horizons."

"Princess's people will be thrilled you're here," I told her. I was, too. If only I could converse in Barklish with Princess to reassure her when she was alone . . . but since I couldn't, ensuring she had constant company was the best alternative for now. "The Jeongs are at wits' end trying to keep Princess from crying out and disturbing the neighbors. She's got the world's worst case of separation anxiety."

"Not on my watch, she won't." Wanda's smile grew even broader. "You just brought her from Doggy Indulgence?"

I nodded. "I think she had a good time there."

"At our daytime competition's?" Wanda was teasing . . . wasn't she? "Doggy day care's a good thing, though," she finished.

"And Doggy Indulgence is the best," I added.

"Could be. Anyway, I've arranged to have my Basil visit his breeder some evenings this week while I come out here, but I miss him. Come here, Lexie. I need a Cavalier hug."

When Lexie had completed licking Wanda's cheeks, we located the set of keys Annie, the live-in sitter, had stashed for us, and Lexie and I left Wanda and Princess to their evening together till Annie returned.

We were on the freeway, on our way home, when my cell phone rang. I used the hands-free gadgetry to answer, hoping it was Dante.

It wasn't. In fact, it was difficult to hear exactly who it was, thanks to the loud siren shrieking in the background.

"Kendra?" shouted a voice—female, I figured. That was soon confirmed. "This is Matilda Hollins. I . . . I don't want to call the police. Not yet. But I thought you, as a lawyer and investigator . . . well, could you come to my house right away? I think someone has broken in."

Chapter Twenty

As I'd somewhat anticipated, Dr. Matilda Hollins lived in Eagle Rock, the same area as her office was located—the easier to deal with emergencies. What I hadn't expected was her home's almost Victorian look—not huge, yet turreted and somewhat ornate, set off the street behind a decorative metal fence. Though it was turning twilight, I could still appreciate the pretty green lawn with a walk lined with low bushes. Charming, as befit a shrink whose practice was entirely veterinary. A Dr. Doolittle kind of feel to it.

After parking, I looked around. And listened. No sound of a security system's siren, at least not now. I heard a couple of dogs barking nearby. No other cars drove by along this side street near Eagle Rock Boulevard. All appeared serene—except for Lexie leaping around the car in excitement because we'd stopped. She obviously hoped for a walk. At least there was no sign of the break-in that had terrified Matilda, but I'd be careful—especially with Lexie along.

I exited the car, my pup's leash in my hand, and slowly opened the gate.

As we inched up the walk while I looked around and listened, the front door opened and Matilda emerged. She was alone. Lexie lunged in her direction as a black cat scooted behind her in the doorway. I held Lexie's leash taut and she settled down while remaining alert.

Matilda's smile appeared forced. All color had drained from her round face, which looked nearly as pale as her bleached blonde hair. She wore a nice yellow shirt tucked into navy slacks, not as dressy as oncamera but not especially casual for an evening at home. Of course, she might have worn this outfit to her office and not had a chance to change upon arriving home to find her security alarm screaming.

"Kendra, thanks for coming." She stopped in front of us on the walkway. "I apologize, though. Guess I keep panicking after what happened to Sebastian. I've been on edge, which isn't surprising. But I checked inside, and everything's fine. I might just have set the alarm this morning without making sure all doors were firmly closed. My kitty, Midnight, may have pushed one open and set off the alarm."

Sounded possible.

But I still felt there'd been more behind Matilda's previous panic and otherwise odd behavior than was warranted by an accidental tripping of an alarm.

"Is your system hooked up to a security company?" I asked. "Did anyone call to make sure you're all right?"

Her shrug told the story before her words. "I have only an alarm," she said. "The neighbors around here are nice, and would call 911 if they thought the alarm wasn't a false one."

I slowly scanned the neighborhood. Couldn't tell if anyone was home—or if they'd choose to get involved if they were. I supposed I had to take Matilda at her word.

"Then you didn't call the police yourself?" I asked. She certainly had sounded terrified when she'd called me. I pulled my cell phone from my purse. "It wouldn't hurt even after the fact, in case there's something you've over-looked."

"No need to bother them," she said somewhat stiffly.

"Then you don't think a fan of *Animal Auditions* tried to break into the house of one of our nicest judges for a souvenir?" I kept my tone light, but the small amount of color still in her complexion drained away. Or maybe that was partly because daylight had continued to wane and streetlights had gone on behind me, washing out Matilda's hue even more.

"Of course not," she said, "although I've half expected someone to show up at my front gate with a trained dog or other pet to try an end run to get on the show." She was obviously attempting a joke, so I played along.

"Well, I happen to have brought my brilliant dog, Lexie," I said. "Lexie, sit." My adorable Cavalier actually obeyed. Guess she'd given up attempting to see Matilda's cat inside the house.

Matilda laughed. "I hope to see her around the set. But, seriously, Kendra, I apologize again for calling you; I'm fine. So's my home. No need to worry about this anymore. I'll see you at the next filming—our first official dog scenario on Friday, right?"

"That's my understanding," I agreed.

"Thanks for coming so quickly to my rescue. Good night, Lexie." Matilda knelt to give my pup a pat. "Good night, Kendra." No pat for me, thank heavens—just a half wave. And then she hurried into the house.

Leaving me standing there and wondering why she hadn't invited me in, even for a minute.

Was there something she hadn't wanted me to see?

LEXIE AND I stopped for fast food on the way home. For me—not her. Even if I dined at times on stuff that could clog my arteries, I wouldn't do that to my dearest companion. She would get specially prepared dog food when we got home.

Although I'd inevitably save a taste for her. . . .

After we made our way along the drive-thru line, my cell phone sang. I shoved the button for my hands'-free gadget and said hello.

"Kendra? It's Esther."

"So Ned's been in contact again? I knew he felt uncomfortable as a potential suspect, and his former colleagues were on his case again at our filming today."

"They want Nita and him to come in for further interrogation tomorrow," Esther said. "Anything useful you can tell me—like your opinion on who's really guilty here?"

"I wish," I said as I pulled my car onto our street and headed up the hill. "But it's really silly to consider Ned a suspect. Nita, too." I hoped. "What's their motivation? Revenge for on-air ridicule of their pet pigs?"

"People have killed for less, as you know, Kendra," Esther said softly. "I'll defend them with all I've got, although of course I'll warn them that if their interests start diverging, I'll need to withdraw from representing at least one of them. Since you think they're innocent, that goes a long way in convincing me, too. Not that it entirely matters. I'd have taken their case even if I thought them guilty; even the worst rats deserve a good defense."

"Their pets are pigs," I teased her, "not rats."

"Got it."

I thought for a second how to phrase what I wanted to say. "Regarding diverging interests—you might want to confirm that neither truly suspects the other."

After a contemplative pause, Esther inquired, "You think that's the case?"

"Unlikely," I said, "but it's something to consider."

I soon said goodbye and pushed the button to open our front gate. I touched base with Rachel about the day's pet-sitting. Tomorrow's, too. The outside lights were on, so Lexie and Beggar got in their last rambunctious romp of the evening. And then I went inside, wanting to veg out before bed.

When I checked my e-mail, I'd gotten one from Althea, with attachments. She hadn't yet researched all the new people I'd requested, but she'd sent some interesting info on Sebastian Czykovski and his known friends and foes— at least known to her after her computer research both licit and illicit. They included not only agility cronies, but also his ex-wife.

And what was absolutely interesting was that said ex happened to be a store manager.

At a HotPets.

"CONSIDER THE SOURCE," I said to Lexie a short while later.

She was paying utter attention to me, her sweet black nose on my lap, and her fuzzy black-and-white tail wagging wildly.

Not because she was fascinated by my fractured logic. No, I'd fed her a doggy food dinner and was now engulfing my own hamburger and fries. That left Lexie in the role of abject and adorable beggar.

I didn't intend to encourage bad habits like begging at the table. But I ate while sitting on my living room sofa, TV news on in the background. She was begging on the floor. I saved some choice but teensy morsels for her, awful human that I am.

But I also allowed my mind to wander. Jeff Hubbard knew of Dante DeFrancisco's involvement with *Animal Auditions*. He knew how important that show was to me. He knew that Dante was of importance, too. He'd encouraged me to use his greatest information resource, Althea. Could he have planted this data for her to dig out?

Hell, that was a stretch. Jeff's alleged intention, that is. I could verify the truth easily enough.

And even assuming Sebastian's ex was employed by Dante, that still didn't mean she killed the guy. Or conspired with her boss to do so.

As I finished eating and continued pondering, my cell phone rang. I checked caller ID.

It was Dante.

"Hi," I answered much too perkily.

"What's wrong, Kendra?" he asked, obviously recognizing something off in my tone.

I tucked my feet underneath me, attempting to convince myself to be casual. "Nothing," I lied. Well, fibbed. There really wasn't anything wrong, was there?

"Okay, let's assume that's correct. What's going on that causes that too-cute tone in your voice?"

"Well . . . I just found out some interesting information." I wondered all of a sudden why the media hadn't picked up on it. This connection wouldn't exactly be confidential—would it?

"Which is . . . ?"

"Sebastian Czykovski's ex-wife—"

"Is a manager at a HotPets," he finished. "I only recently learned the connection."

"How?" I asked, sure it wasn't the same way I had. And was he lying anyway? How long had he known? Had he tried to hide it? Why?

"Long story." Which he obviously wasn't going to reveal. "Let's just say that Brody has his sources." Oh. Did he hack, too? "And, yes, I've met her, but I don't know her well. I have staff members who choose and manage the managers." Dante gave a huge sigh into the phone. "I still wish you'd back off and let other people look into this, Kendra," he said. "Even more, I wish I was with you right now, looking into your gorgeous blue eyes while I try again to convince you. But that would be futile. So, I'm convinced we need to work together on this." I'd opened my mouth to insert a comment, but he didn't stop long enough for me to interrupt. "Here's what we'll do. I'll make some calls tonight, then get in touch with you first thing tomorrow to tell you the time."

"Time for what?"

"For you to join me at the Long Beach HotPets store to meet the former Mrs. Sebastian Czykovski."

Chapter Twenty-one

When I hung up, my heart rate hammered in anticipation of meeting Sebastian's ex, not to mention a personalized visit to a HotPets—oh, yeah, and seeing Dante.

It was nearly ten o'clock. That was the time the Jeongs' live-in pet-sitter was due home, so Wanda could leave Princess's company for the evening and go home to her Cavalier, Basil.

With Lexie on my lap as I sat on the sofa, I called Wanda's cell. "It worked out fine, Kendra," she told me. "I had a good time with that sweet Princess. I'll bring Basil and do it again a couple more evenings this week when Annie will be late."

"Did you meet the nasty neighbor?" I inquired.

"Once, briefly, when I walked Princess just before dark. The woman made a point to come out and say something snide about Princess's shrieking. She mentioned that a conversation between her attorney and the Jeongs' is long overdue. Better yet, a court appearance. I tried to get her talking, involved in a nice, neighborly conversation, and she almost bit—but then she started complaining again. I wanted to say something especially nasty, but I held my tongue—this time. Anyhow, good night, Kendra. And now that I know where Princess lives, I'll be glad to pick her up at Doggy Indulgence on the evenings I'll be watching her, if you can bring her in the mornings."

"Excellent!" I said. "Do you know where Doggy Indulgence is?"

"Sure. Annie will be home tomorrow evening, and she has a friend looking in on Princess during the day, so our next round of Princess-pampering isn't till Wednesday. Talk to you then."

IT WAS TUESDAY, early afternoon. I'd driven down the Long Beach Freeway to the HotPets where I was to join Dante in a discussion with Sebastian Czykovski's ex-wife.

Just before I left, I'd finally gotten a return call from the attorney representing the Jeongs' nasty neighbors. The guy sounded as crazy as his clients, making all sorts of damage claims he intended to insert into the complaint he was drafting. Unless, of course, we came up with the perfect solution to placate those *poor people who kept losing sleep because of that awful, shrieking dog*—his description, not mine.

We agreed on a time to meet the following week. I was even cordial enough to capitulate when he suggested his office as the site. And I all but slammed down the phone. That was adding insult to Princess's injurious loneliness. The Jeongs would be back the end of next week, but even if I could get this obviously litigation-minded lawyer to lay off now, it would at best be a temporary solution.

I'd suggest that my clients find Princess a beautiful boarding situation next time they left town—despite their earlier assertions that she became utterly depressed at such locales. But the problem also occurred when they were in the area but out of their house. Perpetual pet-sitters? Maybe. At least there were probably acceptable doggy day care facilities closer to them than Darryl's.

Enough of that for now. I opened the door to my rental car that I was determined would leave my life soon, and looked at the exterior of this HotPets.

It sat in a nice urban strip mall, surrounded by complementary stores: a supermarket that catered more to people; a drugstore; a couple of fast-food restaurants.

HotPets seemed the second hugest, after the grocery store. It had several entrances, including one especially for the adjoining grooming facility.

Some people left just as I was entering, one holding a beautiful boxer's leash, and the other hugging a Yorkie. I wished I hadn't left Lexie at Darryl's. She would have adored this outing.

Inside, I discovered that Dante hadn't made that mistake. Wagner sat obediently beside him, no leash reminding him that he needed to be on his best behavior. Of course, the owner could get away with breaking the leash rule posted at the door.

Dante stood near the row of check stands, speaking earnestly with a short woman with medium brown, curly hair who regarded him as if he was a god.

Well, hell, most women looked at Dante that way. Even so, I suspected that this one was the store manager, wanting to earn brownie points with the company's CEO.

Not to mention flirt with one darkly handsome dude.

As I approached, he seemed to sense me even though he

faced the other way. He turned and shot me the sexiest welcoming smile I'd ever seen. Which reminded me of our previous bedroom encounter. And made me wonder when I'd get more.

Cool it, Kendra. I wasn't here to pant over Dante. I was on a mission to help Ned Noralles by soliciting information on murder suspects.

"Hi, Dante," I said, then turned to the woman he was with. "I'm Kendra Ballantyne. Are you the store manager?" No need to belt her immediately with belligerent innuendoes or accusations. After all, she might have parted quite amicably from Sebastian and have had absolutely no motive to dispose of her ex. I'd heard of a few marriages that dissolved that way.

Very few.

"Hi, Kendra," she said in an utterly friendly voice. She was dressed professionally in a pantsuit and incredibly skinny stiletto heels. "How can I make your shopping experience at HotPets outstanding?"

She was really buttering up the boss by behaving that way. But I decided to disabuse her of her impression that I was a customer with a complaint.

"I love these stores," I said warmly and truthfully, darting a sidelong glance at Dante. "Especially the ones closer to my home in the San Fernando Valley. I'm not here to complain. Or shop. Did Dante tell you? We want to talk to you about your ex-husband, Sebastian Czykovski."

I'd kept my voice relatively low, but wasn't surprised to see her blanch and glance around to ensure no one had heard.

"How on earth did you find that out? I've kept it secret." The hiss in her voice sounded almost feral. Frightened. "Come into my office. Please."

Without waiting to see if we agreed, she turned and stalked in those high heels to the rear of the crowded store. Dante took his place behind me as we followed, and I felt his fingers touch my shoulders as if to steer me through the people, products, and pets filling the aisles between shelves filled with the greatest of pet delights.

Or maybe just to make physical contact with me. Which I didn't exactly mind.

And Wagner? As always, that brilliant German shepherd stayed close to his master's side.

The woman led us into a bright hallway beyond a door that closed automatically behind us. She entered the farthest office and stood at its entrance, glowering until we, too, came inside. Then she slammed the door.

"Okay," she said. "Now, answer my question. How did you learn I was once married to Sebastian?" She motioned Dante and me to uncomfortable-looking seats lining one wall of the room and yanked another to face us, placing her back to her messy desk. Wagner lay down at Dante's feet.

"I'm an attorney who's assisting one of the alleged suspects in Sebastian's untimely death," I said, my statement full of euphemisms. "I'm trying to find out all I can about him before he joined the *Animal Auditions* show as a judge, which is when I met him." I didn't directly address her inquiry, and I wasn't about to inform her that I was good buddies with a computer hacker. And Dante's knowledge of her background was from an entirely different source, perhaps even her employment records.

The woman shook her head. "Mr. DeFrancisco, I tried so hard. You know me as Flossie Murray, my maiden name. I started with HotPets right after my divorce, seven years ago. Before that, I worked for one of your competitors. When I interviewed to become assistant manager here, I expressly requested that my résumé and application information be kept confidential."

"As far as I know it was, Flossie," Dante said soothingly. "We didn't use it to find you. And our sources are confidential, too. If it's any consolation, we won't tell the media. Or any police detectives, either, unless we're asked directly." He aimed a confirming look at me, and I nodded. "We can't lie, of course—at least not to the authorities."

"I understand," she agreed. "They already know, anyway. I've been questioned by a detective looking into Sebastian's death, a lady cop." Most likely Vickie Schwinglan. "She was nice enough, said she wouldn't reveal anything I said unless it became necessary in the investigation, or the conviction of a suspect they ultimately arrested. I tried so hard." She sighed. "After we divorced, I took my maiden name back immediately and changed all my identification and credit cards."

"Did you ever speak with Sebastian afterward?" I wanted to lead her gently into other areas.

"Not often, but occasionally at agility trials. I was a trainer, and so was he. We both loved to enter our dogs. We fell in love at agility trials a long time ago. He was so sweet at first. Then he became a judge. That's when everything changed."

"How?" Dante asked.

"It was like he'd been waiting to ascend the throne, to become king. Or a god. See, in agility, the judge determines the path the dogs will take, how high the jumps will be, which side they'll enter tunnels, how complicated it all is—within certain parameters, of course. Sebastian had enjoyed it when his dogs—mostly medium-size guys like Sheltie mixes—were entrants. He did really well. One of his best dogs, Slick, even got as far as his MACH title—the best there is, Master Agility Champion. That's one reason he was asked to become a judge. After that, he wanted revenge, I guess, for every slight he or any of his dogs ever suffered, and he took it out on many of the contestants— definitely the slowest and worst, but sometimes even the best. I hated seeing that, hearing how badly he was hurting some of our closest friends. When he started bringing some of that egotism home, lording it over me and the dogs I was training . . . well, I had enough. I started despising him. I divorced him and wanted him entirely out of my life."

"That's why you changed your name," I said with sympathy. "But did you also give up agility trials? You'd still have seen him at some of those."

"Exactly. For a while, I stopped going, missed them terribly. Then I went back but was able to avoid his judging the trials I had my dogs run in. The organizers understood—conflict of interest and all that."

"And that was—what, seven years ago?"

"Our divorce was. I rejoined agility about two years ago. Did well, although I had to start some young dogs who were fairly green. One's doing great, though—enough to aspire to MACH someday."

"But Sebastian wasn't ever your judge when you returned?" Dante asked.

"No. I pitied the contestants he did judge, though. He seemed to purposely hold them up on the five-second pause table—that's where, in the middle of all that running around, the dogs are supposed to sit obediently still before going on. If they stay longer than five seconds, they have a much harder time making up for it. See, contestants start out with one hundred points, and some are subtracted for every fault. Plus, they're given a time limit for getting through the course. Judges raise their hands to signal to the scorekeepers when points are to be taken off for things done wrong. Sebastian seemed to have his favorites right from the beginning—a no-no for judges, who, like those in court, are supposed to be impartial. He was really hard sometimes on those he didn't like. Some wound up really upset. In tears. And I heard that one even attempted suicide."

"How awful!" I cried, while wondering why anyone would take anything Sebastian had said so seriously. On the other hand, I knew how seriously some people took the results of different kinds of dog shows they entered.

"I don't know whether it's just a rumor or true," Flossie backpedaled. "There are trials at a park in Anaheim this weekend. You could go there and ask around, if you'd like. Oh, by the way, like the detective asked, I had no motive to kill him. Not after all that time. But back then . . . well, if I'd been inclined to revenge, I'd have considered doing something awful." She shook her head. "I shouldn't be afraid now. But in situations like this, people always suspect the spouse—or former spouse. I tried so hard to put Sebastian and all he stood for behind me. But now he's caught up with me again." She sighed and attempted a sardonic grin. "I could kill him for that."

"ARE YOU CROSSING her off your suspect list?" Dante asked as we exited Flossie's office. "She's pretty low on mine."

"Same with me, though she could simply be giving lip service to how long ago her dislike of Sebastian occurred."

We soon stood near one another in an aisle, with Wagner

nearby—sniffing the air as if sampling all the marvelous stuff in the store.

"And you're going to those agility trials in Anaheim this weekend that she mentioned, aren't you?" he asked.

"What do you think?"

"I think we could go together. Compare notes, and all that."

"Sure." At least he wasn't telling me, again, to butt out.

"You're heading back to L.A. now?" he asked.

"Yes. You?"

He nodded. "Don't suppose you'd want to join me for dinner, would you?"

Dante DeFrancisco, sounding somewhat unsure of himself? That was something new.

"Why not?" I said.

"Great. I'll be at your place at seven—with all the makings for dinner. I'll cook again."

I MADE ONE stop on my way home—at a car dealership in Long Beach. I needed to get my head and arms around the concept of going further into debt for that new car I had to buy.

The prices here weren't worse than what I saw in L.A. No better, either. It was time, though. I was tired of this tiresome little rental.

Tomorrow was Wednesday. The next *Animal Auditions* taping was Friday. I had no court appearances this week. Maybe by Thursday I'd have a new car.

And a heck of a new damned debt.

My phone rang as I neared downtown L.A. on the Long Beach Freeway. I recognized Ned Noralles' number.

"Hi, Ned," I said with a smile. "I talked to Esther last night, and—"

"Yeah, thanks. Good thing, too. Those fools I work with have just arrested Nita, and I'm on my way to kick their asses."

Chapter Twenty-two

I CALLED JEFF, Dante, and Darryl as I sped to the North Hollywood station of the LAPD.

Jeff was outraged. "I'm up in Santa Barbara on a security stakeout for another client," he said. "I'll be back early this evening, but can't get there now to look into things for Ned. You're going?"

"Yes. I'll let you know what I find out."

"Good. I'll owe you."

"Make it another round of Althea's excellent work," I requested, and he agreed.

Darryl promised to take good care of Lexie as long as I needed him to, and to turn Princess over to Wanda Villareal, whom he recalled from some Pet-Sitters Club of Southern California meetings to which he'd accompanied me.

To Dante, I explained the situation. "I may be late for dinner," I said. "I'll keep you advised."

"I get it. And I don't suppose it would do me any good

to attempt to get you to back off now, for your own safety."

"No," I said into the air, thanks to my hands-free phone. "It wouldn't. And surely you don't think that Ned and Nita are going to harm me."

"No, but if you find a way to get them off, whoever is attempting to frame them isn't going to be your best friend."

As we hung up, I thought that over. For about three seconds. Yes, Dante was right. But like it or not, as a murder magnet I'd found myself with enemies who killed more than once in the last bunch of months. Did I know how to take care of myself? Maybe. Would fear of reprisals force me to back off?

Hadn't yet. Why start now?

I reached the North Hollywood station around four in the afternoon. I recognized the bright red Jaguar belonging to Esther Ickes sitting in the small parking lot. I squeezed into a space nearby, wondering if the SUV I was zeroing in on to buy would be as easy to park as this rental. Was I getting cold feet?

Nope, just making a mental observation.

I hurried inside the familiar police station—and stopped. Ned Noralles, dressed in jeans and a T-shirt, loomed over Esther in one corner, near the rack of brochures offering advice to citizens on a multiplicity of topics. It was far from the desk where cops greeted entrants, and even farther from the door to the station's inner sanctum. Esther's silver hair was flawlessly styled as always, and her sweet, lined face seemed screwed up in anger. She was as impeccably dressed as if she had just come from court. Maybe she had.

I approached quickly, wondering if I'd need to referee or find Ned other representation.

"Are you nuts?" were the whispered words I heard issuing from Esther's lips as I drew close.

"You're my lawyer," Ned responded, sounding equally enraged. "I hired you. Now, do as I say."

They appeared to have reached an impasse, both standing with arms crossed and expressions filled with fury. Time for intervention from an opportune outside source: me.

"Hi!" I said brightly, my voice not nearly as soft as either of theirs. I lowered it immediately. "Okay, you two. What's going on?"

"Detective Noralles is a very nice man," Esther hissed. "Too nice. You see, his sister is now—"

"In custody. Like I said, they're arresting her for that jerk Sebastian's murder." Ned's fists were clenched and he appeared ready to strike almost anything or anyone within range.

But certainly not two lady lawyers who only wanted to help him—I hoped.

"I'm so sorry," I said, touching him gently on his bare arm. He flinched as if I had socked him.

Then he looked down at me, bleakness radiating from his dark brown eyes. I hadn't realized that African Americans could grow so pale, but there was a grayness behind his otherwise dark skin. I wanted to give him a huge hug, but held off. He clearly didn't want any contact.

"I've been trying to talk Ned out of making matters worse," Esther whispered. "Client confidentiality prevents me from telling you the stupid thing he wants to do, but—"

"Hell, I'll tell her," Ned interrupted. "I'll confess to the killing. If either of us did it, it's me, not Nita."

"Oh, Ned," I said, "don't let your emotions erase your common sense. You've been a cop long enough to know she'd still be held as an accessory." I looked toward Esther for confirmation. She nodded for a second, then froze. I looked in the direction of her gaze and saw Detective Howard Wherlon emerge from the door to the bowels of the station.

He immediately came over to us. "You ready to add anything to your statement, Noralles?" he demanded.

Flames seemed to shoot from Ned's eyes.

"I think you've spoken with my client enough today," Esther said quite calmly. "Are you intending to arrest him? If not, we're going to leave."

"Nope, he's free to go. For now."

"And you'll let me know before you attempt to interrogate Ms. Noralles any further. Right, Detective?"

Howard didn't appear happy about it, but he nodded. "She's lawyered up, so we'll do it all by the book."

Esther and I stood on each side of Ned and urged him out of the station.

The three of us stood outside on the sidewalk, its pavement decorated with fake fingerprints.

"What happened?" I asked. "Did Nita say something in her interrogation that sounded like a confession?"

"No way," Ned insisted a little too loudly.

"No," Esther agreed. "But they obtained another warrant and searched her home, then showed her something they found there while they questioned her. A harness just like the one they say strangled Sebastian. One designed for potbellied pigs."

"I gather there isn't a whole lot of variety in those harnesses," I said. "Aren't nearly all of them nylon, sometimes in bright colors? That's essentially what Avvie Milton has, and what I saw on the set of *Animal Auditions*."

"Yes, but there was something different about this one," Esther said. "Most manufacturers make them so they don't have to be pulled over the pigs' heads, since that apparently makes them upset sometimes. A lot of them have side or top buckles. The kind that killed Sebastian was a different design, handwoven by a pig fancier who lives in Ohio, with similar straps but snaps instead of buckles, and decorated with leather inserts. They're relatively rare, since the designer doesn't mass-produce them."

"And Nita happened to own one, too?"

Esther shrugged, suggesting client confidentiality.

"She didn't," Ned exploded, then quieted down again. "Those fools seem to think that finding a similar harness is enough evidence to haul her in on a murder rap."

"Do you have one for Porker?" I asked.

"No. I go for the standard nylon kind—bright yellow."

"Where did Nita get the one that looks like the murder weapon?"

"That's just it," Ned said. "She didn't. She loves Sty Guy but spends money on him for good food and toys and all. No silly designer harness for him. Whoever killed that jerk Sebastian must have planted it at Nita's place, to frame her. But would my fellow detectives believe that?"

"Apparently not," I surmised, and Esther nodded.

"My sister suspected of murder? Ridiculous!" Ned nearly shouted. "They should check out who bought that stupid harness." He sounded serious now. Maybe I'd been mistaken when I'd thought he suspected his sister could have done it. Either that, or he was rallying to her defense no matter what.

In any event, I suspected the detectives were looking into the harness's source. It was something I'd also suggest that Jeff look into . . . or maybe I'd do it myself. Either way, I'd first ask Althea to seek it out online.

And Dante? If he didn't personally have knowledge of this particular pet supply, he surely had employees who did.

"Meantime, I'll do anything I have to, to get her out of there," Ned said.

"Like get yourself thrown in jail, too?" I asked. "That's just stupid."

"And I can't represent both of you," Esther said. "Your interests are clearly diverging."

"Which one will you hang on to?" I asked. The wise thing, given her disagreement with this client, would be to dump him and continue to represent his probably saner sister.

Saner but guiltier?

"I want you," Ned said, his tone much more subdued than it had been. "But I also want someone really great for Nita. Any ideas, Kendra?"

I reminded him that I'd gotten a referral to an excellent local criminal lawyer named Martin Skull when my dear friend Darryl had been a not-too-serious suspect when I'd been accused of a couple of murders.

"Good choice," Esther said. "I'll contact him, and we'll work out who'll represent who." She glared at Ned. "Either way, you'd better behave and take some sound legal advice, or you'll have to find a different attorney to take your abuse."

"Got it." He hung his head as if he actually did finally see some sense.

"I'll take you home now, Ned," Esther said gently. "And you'll be able to care for both pigs? They'll need you."

"Yes," Ned responded, his voice so soft I could hardly hear him. "Are you in touch with Jeff, Kendra?"

I nodded. "He'll be back this evening. I'm sure he'll contact you."

"Thanks," Ned said. "To both of you."

I DID MY pet-sitting stuff rather emotionally that evening. A little faster than I should have, sure. I couldn't help feeling somewhat distracted, considering all that Ned and his sister Nita were going through.

Could one or the other have killed Sebastian? Why? Because he was an S.O.B. of a nasty judge on a TV reality show? Not hardly. A cop like Ned wouldn't be that sensitive, and although I didn't really know Nita, I doubted she would, either—even though I'd seen a hint of a temper.

Who, then? Sebastian's ex? Unlikely, after all this time and her successful escape from his life . . . unless she was hiding something, which was entirely conceivable.

Or was it one of our other contestants, either a pig owner or dog owner? Seemed as unlikely as one of the Noralles siblings, but I'd keep it in mind.

I supposed it could even be one of my buddies who'd helped put together the show. Charlotte? Unlikely, but she really threw herself into the success of our reality show venture. If she thought Sebastian was going to spoil it . . . ?

Same went for my other co-producers: Charley Sherman, the animal trainer, and Shareen or Corbin Hayhurst of ShowBiz Beasts. One of them? Nah . . . I hoped.

My mind quickly glossed over Rachel, my young and eager assistant. But what about her co-host, Rick Longley? What if the former weatherman didn't want to undergo any more thunderstorms and considered Sebastian Czykovski a major threat to his TV future? Nah . . . I didn't think so. Still . . . I'd have to urge Althea to unearth the worst on him.

And what about Matilda Hollins? She'd seemed upset lately, and why not? Her fellow judge had been offed . . . by her? Sure, she was a shrink—of the veterinary persuasion. In my experience, people who became psychologists often had mental issues of their own.

Or could it have been our other original judge, Eliza Post? I hoped not. I'd much rather the killer be someone unrelated to the show whom Sebastian had pissed off somewhere along the line. That seemed feasible. But who? Most likely, I hadn't even met the murderer. It was probably someone connected with Sebastian's other life as a dog trainer and agility judge. That was something I would certainly look into. Fast.

When I finally arrived home, I wasn't in the least surprised to find Dante's Mercedes parked inside the gate. His dog, Wagner, and Lexie both greeted me at my own door, tails wagging.

"So Rachel let you in again?" I entered my kitchen, following my nose as it filled with luscious spicy aromas.

"Of course." Dante came close and took me into his arms. His smile was suggestive as he kissed me but good. Really good. And I had a feeling I knew what he intended for dessert.

We walked the dogs along my narrow, twisting street while the savory pot roast in my oven finished cooking. Night was drawing near, but since this was still summer, there was enough light for us to see and be seen. Wagner and Lexie were engrossed in smelling the outside world and doing what doggies do on walks, leaving the humans to talk.

I filled Dante in on what was going on with Ned and Nita, ending with "As the country's, maybe the world's, most successful pet entrepreneur, what do you know about potbellied pig harnesses that are handwoven in Ohio?"

He laughed. "I've got purchasing managers who'll know a lot more than I do. But, believe me, I'll find out."

We soon headed home. Dinner was, of course, delicious, although it was interrupted by a phone call from Jeff. "I'm at Ned's now," he told me. "Fill me in on what you know."

"Ned has a lot more info than I do," I said, "although I'm conducting my own research into the type of pig harness that seems to have gotten Nita into trouble."

"I'll just bet you are," Jeff growled. He must have figured out the source from which I was gathering information. "You'll keep me informed?"

"As long as you do the same. Althea, too."

"You got it. Oh, and tell your friend DeFrancisco that I asked about him," Jeff said as he hung up.

I took a big swig of the delicious wine Dante had brought before I conveyed that message.

"Too bad your buddy Hubbard had nothing to do with Sebastian while he was alive," Dante said. "I'd love to be able to put together a case against him as a killer. But I guess he's been there, done that, the last time you looked into someone's untimely demise."

"Exactly," I said. "And that sounds familiar. I'd bet he's hoping to prove you're the one who did away with Sebastian." An excellent segue, or so I thought. I smiled innocently at Dante, expecting his vehement denial. Or at least an incredulous laugh that I would even suggest such an amazing thing.

He did neither. Instead, he took a sip of wine and stared thoughtfully into the goblet.

Could Dante genuinely be guilty? I certainly hated that idea . . . especially since I was sure that suspicion wasn't enough to keep me out of bed with him that night.

Turned out I was right.

Wagner and he stayed until morning. I didn't sleep well, even when I wasn't otherwise occupied. My mind kept turning over all the suspects in Sebastian's murder.

And as I lay there listening to his deep breathing, I realized I simply couldn't rule out the reputedly ruthless Dante.

Chapter Twenty-three

"WHAT ARE YOUR plans today?" Dante asked as we stood outside our respective cars in my driveway.

I'd already conferred with Rachel who would do what in our pet-sitting that morning, so I was good to go. She was discreet enough not to inquire about the extra car in the driveway.

Now, Lexie was in my rental car, blocked in the backseat as always. We needed to go pick up Princess, which would make that rear area awfully crowded.

"Pet-sitting first, as always. While I'm on the road, I'll check on Ned and Nita via Esther, to see how that situation's going. After that . . . I'm going to buy a car," I asserted impulsively. And then, more subdued, "I think."

"Really? What kind?"

I told him how I'd loved the Escape. I didn't tell him my fears about affording it. I'd manage, even if Lexie and I had to reduce our food intake for a while. Or she wound up visiting Darryl's fewer days despite our excellent discount.

"Sounds good," he said. "Would you like me to—"

"I'd like you to call me later." I stopped any follow-up with a kiss. I wasn't certain what he'd been about to say, but I had no doubt he intended, somehow, to attempt to assert control.

We parted ways—Wagner with Dante and Lexie with me. I immediately had a sense of loss. And supreme sexual tension. I'd had a wonderful night with Dante, but it wasn't only sex I saw in that man.

As long as he wasn't giving me orders—ostensibly for my own good—I found him a great guy with a wry sense of humor that occasionally snuck through, combined with compassion and an incredible amount of intelligence. Over a brief breakfast, we'd brainstormed about our mutual Sebastian murder investigation, and he'd said he would share with me some stuff he knew Brody Avilla was unearthing . . . later.

I still wondered about Brody's investigative credentials, and hoped Althea would unearth something soon. In any event, I appreciated Dante's cooperation. Maybe we genuinely would work together to learn who'd killed Sebastian.

Unless, of course, his promises were simply a ploy to get me searching in a direction other than directly beside me.

After my morning animal activities, I headed to my law office, where my silver-haired boss, Borden, was his usual sweet self, inquiring again, almost as I stepped in the door, how *Animal Auditions* was doing—and whether I'd figured out yet who'd killed its nastiest initial judge.

"Still working on it," I said, and he smiled. So did Mignon, the receptionist, who sat behind him, eavesdropping.

"Knowing you, you'll get it solved before too long," Borden said. "I heard on the news that the police think one of their own, or at least his sister, is the guilty party. Do you agree?"

"Remember Detective Ned Noralles?" I inquired obliquely.

"He's the cop you've butted heads with before. I thought so. Are you hoping he did it? Nope, I can see otherwise in your expression. Well, good luck on a speedy solution. Any law matters I should keep my eye on while you're partly unavailable?"

"I think I have everything under control," I said. "In fact, I'm taking this afternoon off. Finally buying a car . . . I hope."

"Really? That's great. If you need a loan, or an advance on your salary or partner's share, let me know."

"Thanks, Borden." I gave the guy a hug right over today's yellow aloha shirt. "You're a dear. And I'll take you up on it only if I have to."

I had calls to make on a couple of Borden's senior citizen clients whose cases I was handling, and a response to a motion in another matter to draft. I left a message for the Jeongs' attorney, but he still—again—wasn't available. Lunchtime soon arrived, and I had things under control well enough to leave.

I'd already checked the local Ford dealers online to see their respective inventories of Escapes. I'd made one of my inevitable lists of those I was most interested in, and headed for a dealership on the other side of the hill from the San Fernando Valley first—in Hollywood.

I drove to the back and stepped into the lot—where I found the car I was looking for. It was shining ice blue, and it was loaded.

When the sales guy spotted me and sauntered over, I

was ready. I let him convince me to take a drive, which was lots of fun, since this car had a GPS system, and all the info about whether it was in gas or hybrid mode showed up on the screen. But I stayed unconvinced, at least externally. Somewhat internally, too. I wanted everything on this one, though it cost a lot more than the basic, stripped-down hybrid—which itself wasn't cheap.

I nonchalantly told the guy to give me the best price he could, especially since I hadn't a trade-in after the demise of my once-beloved Beamer. I told him to throw in a screen accessory to keep dogs I drove with in the backseat for their safety. Since I'd need to finance it, he could play games with the figures that way, giving me the supposed best interest rate and payment schedule.

Imagine how surprised I was to find that the bottom line was well within the payment parameters I'd set for myself! Even so, I haggled a little, as one always does when buying a new car.

"Well . . . okay," I eventually said to the salesman. "Write it up. I'll take it."

Of course it took some time, but a lot less than it might have, since I'd gone online in anticipation and fed in my financial situation. My credit, such as it was, was preapproved.

And when I was done, I was the proud owner of a new Escape! Me and the credit company.

I called my insurance carrier and got a commitment for a binder starting this very second—although the premium they quoted me made me shudder.

I needed some assistance after that—not to keep me from assuming I'd gone nuts for doing this, but because I had to dispose of my rental car. I considered who to call . . .

and decided on Dante. It would give me a neutral excuse to
see him—one unlikely to provoke any argument.

Unfortunately, he was unavailable. "I'm really sorry,
Kendra," he said. "I'm in the middle of a meeting that I
can't get out of for an hour or so. Can you wait till then?"

Possibly, but I wouldn't. Rachel was in class that day. I
considered calling Darryl. I felt certain my dearest friend
would drop everything to get one of his employees to drop
him at the car dealership.

Instead, I did something a lot more practical. I called
the company from which I'd rented the little sedan. Turned
out they were quite accommodating, and sent someone over
with appropriate credentials and paperwork to permit me
to hand their car back to them right there.

I was in business—ready to Escape!

I picked up Lexie at Darryl's. I called Wanda to ensure
she was on schedule to take Princess home and sit for her
there. All was well on that front. Then Lexie and I headed
off for our pet-sitting. She spent time exploring the backseat of our nice new vehicle. I could put it down to create
an entire platform for her, but thought she'd feel more secure with seats of her own. Plus, this way, when I braked,
she hadn't the entire area behind me to slide through.

Why wasn't I surprised later, when we reached home, to
see that Dante had beaten me there? I used the control I'd
remembered to retrieve from the rental to open the wrought
iron gate. I drove through and shut it behind us. Dante's car
was already inside, and he stood in the yard with Rachel,
both of them observing Beggar and Wagner at play.

They came up to me as I parked at my usual spot near
the steps to my apartment. "Nice wheels," Dante observed,

doing the guy thing of striding the length of my new car to study it. A Santa Ana wind had whipped up that day, and his dark hair wafted in the breeze.

"It's really cool, Kendra," said Rachel, staring inside. "What are all the gadgets?" Her snug T-shirt of the day was an orange one with piggy noses on the back. She was really into *Animal Auditions* in a big way.

"Heck if I know . . . yet. But I'll learn. And I'll give a demonstration when I figure them out."

"I heard about Detective Noralles and his sister," Rachel said in a low voice, apparently so Dante couldn't hear. But he did anyway.

"Not a good situation," he said. "I gather that the detectives on this case think they have it solved, so they've probably given up looking for the real killer."

"Then you still think it's someone besides one of the Noralles siblings, too?" I asked, watching his expression closely to see if he gave himself away.

If he was the killer, he was certainly cool about it. "I'm on your side," he replied with an absolutely innocent smile.

Rachel had other plans, and Dante and I went out for dinner that night, in my new car. I even let him drive part of the way. He appeared to enjoy the gadgetry, and none of it intimidated him. He even showed me a trick or two.

Jeff called just after Dante and I returned to my place. "Damn detectives," he fumed. "I always thought Wherlon was a fool, but I didn't think Vickie Schwinglan was so bad."

I could tell by Dante's ironic expression that he guessed who was on my cell, so I sidled into the kitchen to continue the conversation. Lexie followed, as did Wagner.

"I can't believe they really think that Nita could have

killed that guy," I told Jeff, which, as I pondered it, was in fact the truth.

"Whoever killed him hit him over the head before choking him with that leash. I don't think Nita's buff enough to do that, but apparently they do. Ned's barely restraining himself from a false confession. I'm still on it, and so are Althea and the rest of my crew. Keep me informed about what you're up to. With all of us working on it, we're bound to save Ned's butt—and his sister's, too."

"I hope so," I said fervently, then hung up, fed the pups treats for the heck of it, and rejoined Dante in the living room. He'd turned on the TV and was watching CNBC market news—which made my eyes glaze over, but someone with as much money as he had probably had to keep up with where to put it to make more.

He stayed till morning once again. We talked a lot about all sorts of stuff, including his business and mine, locales where he'd traveled, and places I wanted to see someday. I really enjoyed his company . . . not to mention our steamy sex.

I was glad, when we parted ways first thing the next day, that I'd see him again that afternoon at the next _Animal Auditions_ taping—a doggy scenario.

And I tried hard not to admit to myself just how much I was coming to care for Dante DeFrancisco.

NITA NORALLES CALLED me midmorning while I was busily drafting answers to a legal complaint at my law office. "It's so horrible, Kendra," she wailed into my ear.

"Where are you calling from?" I asked. Last I'd heard, she was incarcerated in North Hollywood.

"I'm home, out of jail—not really under arrest but not

truly free, either. That nice attorney Martin Skull represents me now, and Esther Ickes is Ned's lawyer. I hate that either of us needs legal representation, especially on something like this. And for both of us to be suspects . . ." I heard her soft sob.

"Where's Ned?" I inquired with trepidation.

"He's under further interrogation this morning. Honestly, Kendra, neither one of us knows where that potbellied pig harness came from, the one that's supposedly an exact replica of the one used to strangle Sebastian. It's unusual enough that there aren't many around. In other circumstances, I might actually have wanted one just like it for Sty Guy. But certainly not now."

"Where did the cops find the one they say is yours?"

"At my house, hidden under a stack of plastic bags in my garage. I didn't put it there, and neither did Ned. And even if it was mine—which it's not—that wouldn't be enough proof that I owned another one and killed someone with it. That's what Ned says, and I agree."

So did I, but I was a civil litigator, and my knowledge of what constituted sufficient circumstantial evidence was scant.

"Of course I despised the guy," Nita said. "And I was angry with him. But kill him? No way." Okay, that was what I wanted to believe, so I'd keep on trying to find the actual culprit. Nita promised that Ned and she would stay in touch. "And you'll let us know, won't you, when you figure out who really killed that awful judge and why?"

"It's a big assumption to think I'll solve the case," I warned her.

"Oh, Ned has talked about you before—not always in the nicest terms, I admit, Kendra. But one thing he says is that when you're interested in a murder case, you seem to

solve it right more often than anyone else he knows. Even
him, although he didn't exactly admit that." And he surely
wouldn't have requested my help if he genuinely believed
his sister could have done it.

But as I hung up and stared, unseeing, at the documents
on my desk, I could only shake my head and hope this situation wouldn't become the first I couldn't unravel.

Those damned harnesses! How could I get more info
about them? I'd already asked Dante, who was in the business, but if he'd learned anything so far, he hadn't shared.
So, I called Althea. She said Jeff already had her working
on it, but she'd found nothing useful yet. She'd found nothing out of the ordinary on Nita Noralles, either, and was
still working on Rick Longley.

Frustrated, I called Dante with the intent of being
pushy. Instead, he responded right away. "Sure, my purchasing manager tracked it down." he said. "Brody's called
and gotten the information you're after."

I phoned Brody, who gave me the contact data for the
owner of the small eastern manufacturing company, Rosalian Products, that had unleashed those scary pig harnesses on the world. "But the lady didn't want to talk much
when I called," he warned. "The LAPD's already been in
touch, and her local authorities, and the media, too. She's
upset, and all she'd tell me—so far—was that the type of
harness in question is their most popular, that they sell by
mail order and not retail in stores, and that there've been
probably a few dozen sent to various locations in California in the last few months, all of the same design."

"Thanks, Brody," I said.

And then I made my own call to that harness seller.
"I'm sorry." Cora Rosalian sounded more exasperated than
apologetic. "I can't talk about this."

"I understand." I turned to stare out my window into the parking lot behind my law office. My Escape hadn't yet escaped. It sat there, shimmering in the sunlight. "I'm an attorney who sometimes represents clients who are unjustly accused of wrongdoing, and I know this whole situation must seem really awful to you. You were just making the nicest and prettiest harnesses you could. It isn't your fault that someone used one for a murder weapon."

"Are you calling because you want to become my lawyer?" she asked suspiciously.

"Not at all," I assured her. "It's just that some friends of mine who might"—or might not—"have bought one of your harnesses—or so the cops allege, but not the one that was used to commit the crime—are under suspicion. I'm trying to help them out, so I need information."

"I see," she said. "I actually have talked to a lawyer here. He says I shouldn't give out information without a search warrant."

"I won't ask for specifics," I said—though I wished I could. "But have you sold your harnesses in bulk to any retailer either in this area or one large enough to distribute here?" Like HotPets, but I wouldn't put words in her mouth.

"No, I sell only by mail order. And I checked my records. I sometimes send out more than one harness in an order, but I haven't ever shipped more than one at a time to any address in Southern California."

A dead end, then. Maybe.

"I know you're not supposed to give out information, but if I were to e-mail you a list of names, could you tell me if you ever sent one of your products to any of them, and, if so, how recently?"

She hesitated. "I suppose . . . Who did you say you were?"

"My name is Kendra Ballantyne," I said. "And I was once unjustly accused of murder myself, so I make it a point to help others I think are innocent."

"I see. Well, send your list and I'll look it over." She gave me her e-mail address and we hung up.

I put together a list of my possible suspects, then forwarded it to her—along with a bunch of names I made up at random. If she said she'd sold to one of them, I'd figure she was just acting agreeable and not planning to assist me at all.

And I also didn't necessarily want to libel all my other suspects by labeling them as such in writing.

But I hoped that Ms. Cora Rosalian would give me the lead I'd need to finger whoever had strangled Sebastian.

Chapter Twenty-four

No RETURN E-MAIL from Cora by the time I finished drafting the court documents I'd been working on. I grabbed my lunch from a nearby fast-food place and brought it back to the office.

Still nothing.

I had to leave, since a new canine episode of *Animal Auditions* was on track for that afternoon. It was Friday, so I wished all the attorneys and support staff a great weekend. At least some might have an opportunity to relax.

Not I. But, then, a pet-sitter's job is never done.

Neither, it seems, is a murder magnet's.

I drove my fun new Escape to the SFV Studios, keeping half an eye on the computer on my console to see when I was in hybrid mode and when I was gobbling up gas. When I arrived, I felt as if I'd been good at keeping the environment somewhat green.

The gang was all there, surrounded by doggies instead of potbellies. The scenario we'd set up to test for a new judge had gone so well that we'd decided to start shooting a new set of shows in tandem, starring dogs. Each week, a couple of canines would be eliminated, just like on the piggy shows, so that we'd wind up with one dog champion a few weeks later than our swine champion was crowned. Fortunately, the Nature Network folks had leaped at the opportunity to air the new shows, too.

Charlotte, Rachel, Charley Sherman, and Shareen and Corbin Hayhurst all hustled around the set. So did host Rick Longley, schmoozing with the canine contestants and their owners. Cute terri-poo Mooch was present, as were Corina Carey with her Puli, ZsaZsa, and others I'd seen onstage the last time we did a pup performance, when our scenario was doggy baseball. Some sat, others leaped at one another, and a couple barked eagerly.

Dante wasn't there, though, so neither was Wagner. I approached the judges' table. I wasn't sure how much Brody was willing to share, and I couldn't outright ask him where things stood in his investigation on Dante's behalf. Nor did I wish, without an information exchange, to spew out the results of my conversation with Cora Rosalian about piggy harnesses, and my frustration that she hadn't yet responded to my e-mail. Of course everyone here except the dogs was on the list I'd sent to Ms. Rosalian as possible suspects— including Brody.

In the interest of discretion, I just said hi to the three judges. Brody's grin was inevitably perfect. Eliza seemed somewhat distracted as she shuffled through papers on the table before her, but she gave a friendly wave. I wasn't certain what to expect from Matilda, but she rose and motioned me to the side. I bent my head to hear what she had to say.

"Kendra, I want to apologize for the way I've been acting." Her voice was soft and sounded emotional, yet not way out there. "I know I seem flaky sometimes. I mean, that burglar alarm at my house . . . I might have set it off myself. Who knows? But the thing is, I know now how much Sebastian's death has gotten to me, especially since it was intentional." She shook her head, not budging even a single hair of her short blonde cap.

I noticed out of the corner of my eye that Corina Carey had edged up behind us, eavesdropping. I really didn't want the results of this conversation to wind up on *National NewsShakers*, so any questions I had for Matilda would have to wait.

"I understand," I whispered. "We're all on edge. But as you know, I'm trying to help some friends whom the cops consider suspects—two owners of potbellied pig contestants."

"That detective and his sister," Matilda all but spat. "They were really upset about how Sebastian criticized them oncamera. You may be wasting your time, Kendra, if you really think you can clear them."

"But—" I caught myself quickly. I'd really be wasting something—my breath—if I argued with her. But why was she so convinced that the Noralles siblings could be guilty?

Did *she* have a guilty conscience?

No opportunity to ponder then. Show time! Hosts Rick and Rachel, both dressed delightfully for the camera, announced that *Animal Auditions* was about to begin. They introduced each other, the doggy contestants, and the judges. Matilda had returned to the table, and smiled and waved along with the rest.

Tonight's scenario would be a sequel of sorts to the last—a slightly more advanced canine baseball game. I watched each contestant carefully, along with their owners. And our production staff. And especially our judges. Not to mention those in the audience I recognized—including, surprisingly, detectives Howard Wherlon and Vickie Schwinglan. I thought they'd already made up their small minds and weren't seeking other suspects. Or did they simply enjoy the show?

I got a kick out of this day's contest. The dogs were adorable, and even when they didn't obey their owners, they appeared to have a good time.

The judges were critical, but none was as nasty as Sebastian. Brody cracked jokes, earning occasional glares from his companions, but even Matilda sometimes smiled. And Eliza laughed a lot.

When it was over, I felt as exhausted as if I'd run with the dogs. And as frustrated as I'd ever felt. I had a feeling I was missing something in my investigation of Sebastian's death—but at that point I had no idea what it was.

A LITTLE LATER, his judging duties dispensed with for the day, Brody accompanied me to my new car. "Hey, I like it," he said, eying my Escape. "Anything new to report in your investigation?"

"Not much."

"But there might be something?"

I pushed the button to open the door. "Not necessarily, but I'd be glad to keep you filled in if you promise you'll keep me in the loop with whatever Dante has you doing."

"As much as I can," Brody said with a shrug that might have seemed apologetic from another man. But considering his unrevealed relationship with Dante, I suspected it simply meant "Deal with it."

I called Dante as I headed toward Darryl's to pick up Lexie, but only got voice mail. Where was he? Why hadn't he come to this taping?

As I slipped inside Doggy Indulgence, Lexie spotted me from across the room and lunged in my direction. I noticed that Princess, the crying Brittany spaniel, was still here, and wondered when Wanda would pick her up to hang out at home with her. I'd call her shortly to make sure all was in order.

Then I noticed that Lexie wasn't the only Cavalier present. Was that Wanda's Basil playing with a rag toy in one of the doggy play areas? I looked around but didn't see my pet-sitting friend. Maybe she'd left Basil here in anticipation of picking up both Princess and him later.

"Is Darryl here?" I inquired of the ungracious Kiki, who shoved the papers at me to log Lexie out. Holding my pup's leash, I signed where I should as Kiki nodded slightly toward Darryl's office.

I knocked but didn't wait for his response before pushing the door open. He sat facing his desk instead of behind it, and Wanda was there beside him.

"Oh, you're here," I said unnecessarily. "Is everything on for tonight? Will you be with Princess till Annie gets back to the Jeongs'?"

"Sure." She stood up. Wanda wore one of her usual gauzy tops over jeans. I looked down to meet her gaze. There was something uncomfortably bright about her demeanor. I was about to ask if she was okay when she said, "Darryl and I have been discussing a possible solution for Princess and her family. I need to make some calls. If it seems feasible, I'll tell you about it and you can suggest it to your clients."

"That's a bit obscure, don't you think?" I folded my arms.

"I don't think Wanda wants to disappoint you if it doesn't work out," Darryl said. My lanky friend also seemed discomfited. At that moment, I wished I could read minds. How offbeat was their possible suggestion for Princess? And if they were that embarrassed to present it, how could it ever work?

"Well, let me know as soon as you can, okay? I hope it works. I could use something definitive to resolve a problem right now." I took Lexie's leash and walked out.

I let Lexie into the backseat of the Escape and got behind the wheel. "Let's go pet-sitting," I said, and was rewarded by some hefty tail-wagging that I watched in the rearview mirror.

I was disappointed when we returned home. Dante's Mercedes wasn't parked in our driveway.

After Lexie and I grabbed a quick dinner, hers from a can of specially prepared doggy food and mine a nuked frozen dinner, I booted up my computer.

I still hadn't received the information I'd hoped for from Cora Rosalian on locally shipped piggy harnesses. Was she intending to respond, or had she simply humored me to get me off the phone?

I watched TV, first an improbable crime-solving drama that gave me no ideas at all about how to help Ned and Nita, and then local news.

Ned and Nita . . . I couldn't help worrying about them, so, despite the late hour, I called Ned. He answered, and it was especially good to hear his voice, since that meant he wasn't incarcerated for the murder . . . yet, at least.

But he still sounded despondent. "I didn't confess to anything yet, Kendra," he said. "But my so-called friends are still trying damned hard to get enough to hold Nita. You know, I get so angry with her at times for losing her temper. I even thought for a while that she could have done it—but that was so stupid! At least that lawyer Skull's a good guy and isn't letting them get away with holding her . . . yet. I don't suppose you've figured out who really throttled that jerk Sebastian."

"I'd tell you if I did. How about Jeff?"

"Nothing there, either. But I appreciate you both for trying."

No word from Jeff that night, which was okay with me. Nor from Dante . . . which wasn't.

Where was he? And why did I care so damned much?

Chapter Twenty-five

THE NEXT DAY was Saturday. Though Darryl kept Doggy Indulgence open on weekends to accommodate customers in the entertainment industry, I decided Lexie could stay home alone for a few hours. I engaged first in some pet-sitting, and then began the research into Sebastian's background that I'd been looking forward to for a while.

I aimed my Escape toward Anaheim and that day's agility trials there. Although Dante had expressed an interest in coming with me, it turned out he was too busy that day. Probably a good thing. I didn't need his distraction or designation of what I should do.

The event was in a large, open field with parking in a paved area at one side. I knew I was in the right place when I saw several people whose frisky leashed pups cavorted beside them.

Unlike regular dog shows, where conformation counts, agility trials don't require that entrants be purebred pups any more than we did at *Animal Auditions*. As a result, when I reached the dual dirt rings inside the earthy-smelling arena, I saw doggies of all sizes and shapes. The people with them—also of all shapes, sizes, and ages—had slapped entry numbers on their shirts or hats, sometimes multiple ones, indicating they might have more than one dog to run through literal hoops.

Things were already under way when I arrived, so I watched for a while, enjoying the excitement as dogs started off after a mechanical voice saying "Go." Their handlers urging them on, they leaped over hurdles and raced through tunnels, then stopped on the five-second pause table while those same humans encouraged them to stay still. Then they were off again, basking in applause as they finished.

I'd watched some agility shows on TV, but never before in person. I knew enough, though, to understand that the people in the rings in addition to the encouraging trainers were judges. When judges raised their hands, it sometimes spelled doom. They were in control. As I'd already been told, agility dogs started with 100 points, and each lift of a judge's hand signaled the scorer sitting at a table with a timekeeper to take off some of those precious points. The dog with the highest remaining number was the winner. Plus, the canine entrants strived to meet standards that would give them titles starting with Novice and going all the way up to MACH: Master Agility Champion.

But I wasn't here solely to enjoy the show. No, what I needed was to understand how Sebastian Czykovski had started his canine-oriented career as an agility trainer and had become an agility judge, which somehow had led to his last role on *Animal Auditions.*

He had been a member of this very club, Agility of Anaheim. I had stood around gawking long enough. I admit, though, that I got a kick out of the doggies who pranced around on leashes outside the rings, awaiting their turns to show off inside.

I sidled over to where someone who appeared involved with the show stood making notes on a pad. "This is really something," I said. "It's the first time I've ever come to an agility match."

The lady with glasses perched at the end of her nose looked over them at me with what appeared to be incredulity. "Really?"

I nodded. "I have a dog at home I'm considering training for agility, so I'd like to learn as much as I can."

"How old is he, and how well trained?"

I made it up as I went along. In actuality, Lexie—a *she*—was four years old and was her own dog, training me as much as I trained her. I doubted she'd do well on an arduous agility course. But the dog I described was younger and absolutely trainable.

"Maybe," the woman drew out the word dubiously, still not sure about committing any confidence to me.

"But what I want to understand is the judging. How does that work?"

"Judges do a lot," she said. "They arrange the courses before each match. They decide where to put the numbered pylons that tell the order in which the dogs are to approach each obstacle and which way they're supposed to go."

"And they also decide who gets points taken off for taking too much time or refusals to jump or missed contacts with parts of the obstacles, right?"

She nodded, smiling for the first time. "Sounds as if you've at least done some research. I'm Janice Adams, president of the Anaheim Agility Club. And you're . . . ?"

"Kendra Ballantyne. Actually, I'm here under false pretenses. I'm one of the producers of the reality show *Animal Auditions* on the Nature Network, and I'm considering whether to use any agility scenarios on the show."

Janice frowned. "That's the show where Sebastian Czykovski was a judge, isn't it?"

I nodded. "That's what gave me the idea to consider an agility scenario. Did you know him?"

"Yes." Her response was curt.

"I gather he was as hard to get along with as an agility judge as he was on our show."

By then, all contestants had done their rounds through the closest course, and several people with dogs on leashes approached us, happily discussing who had won and why.

"You could say that," Janice agreed. She waved over one of the people. "Kathy, this lady is with *Animal Auditions*. She wants to know about Sebastian."

Kathy immediately froze. She had bright auburn hair and a soft, wrinkly face. "He was a real S.O.B.," she said. "He just loved to lord it over everyone when he judged, just like on TV. Impartial judging? No way, when Sebastian was in the ring."

Who here hated him enough to want to kill him? I wanted to ask. Instead, I inquired, "When was the last time he did any judging for you?"

"A couple of months ago," Kathy said. "The thing was, he really did know his stuff. And . . . well, as a trainer, he had a large following. He had his own school and lots of people from there joined our club. He kind of controlled our purse strings, so we couldn't just dump him."

"So why did he stop judging?" I asked.

"His school started to get some really bad publicity,

thanks to some of the stuff he pulled." That came from a guy who had a miniature dachshund at his side. "Hi, I'm Marc."

"My husband," Janice explained territorially, not that I had any interest in the man twice my age and girth.

"What kind of stuff?" I inquired of Marc, as I bent to show his little dog the back of my hand for an interested sniff.

"Judges are supposed to have the sport at heart," Janice answered. "Not Sebastian. He had his own ego and pocketbook at the forefront of his mind, whatever he did."

"I'll say," Kathy added. "First he'd give people a really hard time in the ring, taking points off for refusals and other faults he caused himself. Then he'd hand them his card, suggest they'd do better if they entered their dogs in his school."

I'd watched from the corner of my eye as people went in and picked up hurdles, placing them elsewhere and sometimes adding or removing height. An apparent judge stood near them, directing what went where.

Soon, they finished, two people resumed their places at a table, and a mechanical voice said "Go." A mixed-breed resembling an adorable mop on legs started the closest course, and Marc said, "Sorry. Hans and I need to get ready." Hans, I assumed, was his dachshund, who followed him toward the opening in the fence surrounding the agility field. That pup with the little legs could leap hurdles? Amazing!

But I was here with an ulterior motive, not just admiring agility trials. I turned back to Janice, who was also watching the course. "Did anyone ever criticize Sebastian for his actions as a less than competent judge?"

"Sure," Janice said. "We all did."

"I could take what he said, since I considered the source," Kathy added. "But some of our newer members really had their feelings hurt."

Now we were getting somewhere . . . maybe. "Did anyone get mad?"

"You mean, did one of us wait a couple of months, then kill the guy?" Janice looked at me over her glasses with a sardonic smile. "No one I know."

"Well, remember, Janice," interjected Kathy, "there was that time last year that one of the guys punched Sebastian out after he got held up on the course because the so-called impartial judge stood right in his dog's way."

"Who was that?" I asked without trying to sound too eager. I'd heard the story before without any hint of an identity.

The women looked at one another. "I don't remember his name," Kathy said. "He wasn't from this area, and I don't think he really knew how to train dogs well anyway. His spaniel was extremely agile and bright, though, so I don't blame him for getting upset at Sebastian's nastiness."

"I remember seeing him around occasionally at other agility trials after that," Janice said. "He didn't compete, though, and stayed in the background—avoiding Sebastian. He seemed to make it a point to try to cheer up other participants Sebastian criticized."

"Mostly, though," Kathy said, "Sebastian hurt feelings with impunity. Hardly anyone complained. He even criticized those he judged in the TV and magazine interviews he did—although there he at least didn't name names. But I have to say I was really upset when one of our best members, Beth Black, apparently attempted suicide after her American Eskimo dog had a huge number of points taken off by Sebastian at an important match."

"She loved that dog," Janice said, nodding. "And he was so far along—his title was Excellent B, almost up to MACH—but he was getting old and had just been diagnosed with arthritis. She couldn't keep him competing, and was so frustrated that his career would end so cavalierly."

Aha! I'd heard rumors before that Sebastian's nastiness had been alleged to spur someone to attempt suicide. Now, I'd get the particulars. I'd gathered the woman survived. Had she decided to slay Sebastian instead of herself?

"Go" shouted the mechanical voice, and we all looked over as large Marc put his little dachshund through his paces. The pup was amazingly good, leaping over hurdles as if his legs were twice as long, and disappearing into canvas tunnels, then reappearing at the other end.

"He's doing great!" Janice exclaimed. "Now if he can just get to the time sensor fast at the end."

"What's that?" I asked.

"Things are mostly done electronically now," Kathy explained. "The dogs go between one set of sensors at the beginning of the course and another at the end, to ensure that they don't take more than sixty seconds total. Their time is automatically recorded, and the scorers at the table just note if there are any points taken off for faults."

"That's cool," I said with absolute interest. I cheered right along with them as Marc and dog finished the course to cheers and excited accolades.

Only after he'd returned to us and received even further congratulations did I resume the previous discussion with

Kathy. "So that poor dog with arthritis didn't get his MACH title?"

"No. Fortunately, Beth didn't die during her suicide attempt. She claimed she hadn't meant it anyway—didn't want to leave her poor dog alone. But she was still upset enough to want nothing to do with any of us, or agility, anymore. She moved away and we've all lost touch with her."

"That's awful," I said.

"Sure is," Marc interjected. "We all liked Beth. She was really active with the club. She had a boyfriend who always hung out at our matches, but since he didn't have a dog, no one got to know him very well. He seemed a quiet and nerdy type till something went wrong in the match for Beth, and then he'd sometimes start to try to take charge, fix things—till she shut him up. Anyway, I heard he was really broken up when she left."

I knelt to pet the agile dachshund. "You did great, Hans."

"Arf," he responded, wagging his tail. We all laughed, and for a moment I felt part of this agility-aspiring group.

Enough to ask Janice, "Would it be possible to take a look at any of the records, to see if I could figure out who punched Sebastian?" There was only a flimsy possibility of that, although I wasn't sure what else I might find. Some familiar names, like people who'd shown up at *Animal Auditions*?

"'Fraid not," she said. "Privacy laws and all that. And you wouldn't find that answer there, anyway. But I thought you were here for ideas for your TV show."

"I am, but it might help our ratings if we solved who killed Sebastian." Not to mention Ned's and Nita's well-being. I handed out my cards—pet-sitter sort, not lawyer.

"If you happen to think of anyone else who was particularly peeved with Sebastian, I'd appreciate it if you'd let me know." But I didn't hold out a whole lot of hope I'd hear from any of them—unless they aspired to a role on *Animal Auditions*.

I wandered around a while longer, watching and asking more questions—including quizzing one of the judges between rounds.

"This is all so fun," I said. "I admire you for being a judge. Does anyone ever get mad at you, though, for your calls?"

"Sure. Lots of people do." Her name tag said she was Gladys, but her expression did not suggest she was glad about my interruption.

"Enough to . . . well, do something about it afterward?"

"Like yell at me? Sure, but then I simply disqualify them."

I supposed that people here could be serious enough about their dogs' performances to do something nasty if disqualified.

Like that one woman who'd been mentioned—Beth Black? She'd attempted suicide, or so they said. What had actually happened to her? But Judge Gladys didn't know, either.

"Did you know Sebastian Czykovski?" I inquired next.

Gladys glared as if I'd sworn a blue streak at her. "Unfortunately. You know he's dead?"

"Yes." I explained who I was and my affiliation with *Animal Auditions*.

"We're all interested in a show like that," Gladys said, "and I'll probably watch it now that Sebastian isn't on it. But I wouldn't before."

"I don't suppose you could give me a lead on who might have hated him enough to kill him?"

"We all hated him. And even if I had a clue who offed him, I'd applaud, not tattle on him. Or her."

I didn't hang around a whole lot longer after that now familiar refrain. As fun as this was, I'd likely learned all I was going to. And I still didn't have a genuine clue about who might have killed Sebastian.

He sure didn't have any friends here. Did he make enemies who remained angry enough to do something months later? Or had this trip simply been a waste of time?

Chapter Twenty-six

As MUCH AS I prided myself on my prowess in unraveling my multiple murder magnet situations, I also knew when to call in assistance—a sounding board, if nothing else.

So, on that drive home, I used my hands-free phone to call one of the most savvy folks I knew. Who?

Dante.

Used to be I'd rely on my own private P.I., Jeff. But I preferred not using that particular resource often, if at all, now—except when I needed Althea's input.

Fortunately, Dante responded right away. "Kendra? Where are you—still at the agility match?"

"No, I'm on my way home, but I had a really delightful time there. Maybe you could sell these people some of the equipment they use, like hurdles and flexible tubes and that electronic timer they install at the beginning and end of each course."

A teensy pause before he said, his tone tinged with a smile I could almost see, "I do."

"Oh. Of course." And he probably made a fortune from that stuff, too, as he did with all his pet paraphernalia at HotPets. Well, why not? Someone had to profit. And he did it with such flair. "Anyway," I continued, "I got some additional insight into Sebastian, pre–*Animal Auditions*. Even before he started showing up as a pet pundit on national TV. He wasn't exactly a beloved judge."

"That's news to you?"

"No way. But I learned specific circumstances where agility people really loathed him. Only problem is that even though I've nailed down some situations, I don't have the names of who was involved in them."

"We can probably find that out."

I hesitated while I changed lanes, not wanting to be sucked off onto the freeway to downtown. "I'm not so sure. At least not in all cases, although I did get one name. I asked the president of their organization for a membership list when she couldn't recall some of the specifics. She didn't cooperate."

"Tell you what. When you're done with your pet-sitting rounds tonight, bring Lexie and come to my place. I'll get Brody to join us, and we'll brainstorm."

DANTE DEFRANCISCO WAS as private about where he lived as he was about giving live interviews.

I'd already looked. Googled him and checked all the print and online directories I could find. All I knew was that he lived in Malibu, one of the primo areas around L.A.—and also one that went up in smoke a whole lot during our annual fire season.

It was as if he didn't live anywhere. Or at least nowhere

the public could find out about from any possible source.

But tonight, he told me exactly where to find him. And I delightedly drove Lexie and me in our nice, new blue Escape over the Santa Monica Mountains by way of Malibu Canyon Road. Didn't need to get as far as Pepperdine University—with a law school in one lovely location. The turn off for Dante's was before that.

Some narrow, twisting roads with frequent glimpses of the Pacific—and then we were there. Or at least we got to the gate at the end of a driveway from which, even peering upward, I still couldn't see the house.

I pushed the intercom button. "Dante? It's me."

"Is this Ms. Ballantyne?" inquired a man's voice with a vaguely Hispanic accent, not my host's. Well, duh. I already knew he had a personal assistant. Maybe he had a whole house staff.

"Yes, it is," I confirmed, and the gate swung open. My gate at home also swung open when I pushed a button, so why did this one appear so much more imposing?

Maybe because much of my property could be seen through my fence, including my rented-out house with its garden and the garage where I lived. Here, there were massive hedges, possibly ficus, flanking the sides of the climbing driveway and obscuring whatever lay beyond them. They seemed perfectly well groomed, as if a landscaping staff ensured they were watered and pruned as often as needed.

At the top lay a circular driveway paved with really pretty stones. Beyond was an even more beautiful stone mansion at least two stories tall, its entry flanked by two long wings.

The front door was wide open, and Dante stood there, smiling. Wagner sat at his feet, utterly obedient as always.

I parked the Escape, and Lexie and I got out. "Nice place," I commented as Dante approached. I felt pretty pleased to see the guy. Not that I'd admit it to him. But his welcoming kiss suggested he felt similarly.

"Come in and I'll show you around," he finally said.

Unsurprisingly, it was equally stunning inside, with a huge entry foyer from which a curved stairway rose to the second floor. I loved the look—but wondered what one man did with a place this large.

Then again, Dante sometimes seemed larger than life, at least in his public persona, so why not this?

Once we'd completed the tour through perfectly decorated rooms and a kitchen many top chefs would undoubtedly die to use, he led me back to the living room. On the beige-on-beige patterned sofa sat Brody Avilla.

"Where'd you come from?" I blurted.

"Just got here. You got the grand tour?"

"Sure did." But before I could express how impressed I was, a guy who looked more like a personal assistant than a butler entered the room with a bottle of wine and some glasses on a tray. He seemed deferential in his actions but was clad in a plaid shirt and light slacks.

"This is Alfonse," Dante said. Alfonse was apparently a real gem, since he darted in and out for the next hour or so but I hardly knew he was there. Even so, my wineglass on a stone-topped table beside me never got empty, and delicious, beefy sandwiches were soon served.

Meantime, Dante, Brody, and I talked. I told them what I'd learned at the agility trials about Sebastian.

"The woman who was so devastated that she apparently considered suicide was named Beth Black, but I couldn't find the name of the guy who punched Sebastian out. Even so . . . well, I have an intuition that some of it's related to what happened to Sebastian, but I can't quite put my finger on it."

"Give me till tomorrow to see what else I can find," Brody said. And in a while, after we'd talked some more, he left.

Lexie was on the Oriental rug at my feet, nestled against Wagner. They'd become a pack of sorts, which I thought was cute.

Dante came close on the divan where I sat. "I know you'd need to leave early to do your Sunday morning pet-sitting, but will you stay the night with me, Kendra?" His kiss was soft and inquisitive at first, but soon grew so heated that I had to decide whether to sizzle or scamper away.

I chose the former.

I AWOKE THE next morning in Dante's stately bedroom, on his firm and comfortable bed with the regal red plush headboard, snuggled up to his incredible body. He awoke at the same time.

"I need to get going," I said sadly, already a little out of breath from recalling our exquisite acts of the night before.

"One for the road?" he asked softly before kissing me again.

It was therefore some time before Lexie and I piled back into my Escape and . . . escaped.

We enjoyed our pet-sitting rounds as always—especially a new client, a Greater Swiss Mountain Dog to whom Darryl had referred me. I'd visited his home a few weeks ago and gotten keys and instructions, but the owner had left just that day. The sweet Swissy's name was Mountie, and he was a big, beautiful short-haired pup with flopped-over ears and coloration similar to my tricolor Cavalier Lexie's.

But even as I concentrated on my canine and cat visits, in the back of my mind I kept thinking. About Dante? Absolutely. But also about Sebastian and agility and . . .

Well, hell! Did I honestly have an answer? It seemed fairly far-fetched, and I absolutely needed additional info, but just maybe . . .

I called Dante. What good was it to have a filthy rich lover without taking advantage? "I have an idea," I told him. "Some of how it comes off may depend on what Brody finds in his search today, but I want to do something tomorrow to see if we can unearth our killer. It'll work only if it's one of our *Animal Auditions* regulars, of course. And as odd as it sounds, I remembered something as I was pet-sitting that I think tells me who it is. It'll be interesting if Brody's inquiry supports it."

"Are you going to tell me what you're thinking?"

"Maybe later, if you humor me and have a little errand run for me . . ."

After I explained it, he laughed and asked, "Is it really necessary to go through all that?"

A bit affronted, I said, "Maybe not, but similar stuff has worked for me before when I've needed to ferret out a killer."

"Both literally and figuratively," he said, and he was right. He knew that ferrets had actually helped me in an investigation. "Well, okay. I want to see how this all comes together . . . or not."

I wished I could make some guarantees—but I'm a lawyer. I know better than to make representations and warranties with no basis behind them besides a really intelligent hunch.

But I really hoped things would unfold tomorrow exactly as I wanted. And maybe even with the killer I anticipated.

Chapter Twenty-seven

DANTE CALLED ME back in the early afternoon while, although it was Sunday, I was at my law office.

"I miss you," he said almost gruffly, as if that wasn't exactly how he'd anticipated spending this day. Maybe he resented missing me. I didn't exactly fit into his wealthy, ordered world, after all.

Any more than he fit into my scrimping, saving, pet-sitting, and lawyering life.

"Ditto," I responded, probably as irritably as he'd been.

"Then how about coming back tonight?"

"We'll see," I said. No sense in inflating his ego any more than it already was.

A short silence, and then he said, "I actually called for a reason. Brody's got some more information about the Sebastian stuff that he followed up on, thanks to your agility trial research yesterday."

"Really?" That perked me up.

"Yes. I have a conference call this afternoon, or I'd join

you, but I've set things up for the two of you to meet to discuss what he found, if you have time."

"I'll make time," I said. *Unlike you.* But I only thought that. I was just as glad he wouldn't be there, attempting to control what I did with whatever useful info Brody imparted to me. If any.

Even so, I felt a pang of regret, as I hung up my office phone, that I probably wouldn't see Dante again today. But I would tomorrow, on the set of *Animal Auditions*. By then, he should have accomplished the act I'd requested of him. And I'd have a better idea of how to use the fruit of his work to figure out Sebastian's killer.

OKAY, IT WAS neither the most private nor the most elegant location, but I had Brody meet me at an unofficial dog park near Universal City. I never liked letting Lexie run free, but she had a good time sniff-festing with the other hounds who were off their leashes and came over to meet her.

Brody came striding up to us at midafternoon. Maybe this wasn't such a great choice. I wasn't at all amazed, but most eyes—female human, at least—were on the nice-looking film star dressed down in jeans and snug T-shirt. He seemed not to let it swell his head any more than it was already.

As he reached me, he held out a file folder that appeared to be filled with papers. "Here are some copies for you of what I found. Interesting stuff regarding Sebastian and those agility folks—one thing in particular."

When he told me what it was, I stared. "You're kidding."

But of course he wasn't. And I realized, the more we

discussed the who, what, where, when, and why of his findings—especially the who—that my speculations might be actual fact. But until I had done more checking—and played out the scenario I had in mind—I hesitated to make any assertions that might defame my new suspect.

All I said to Brody was, "This works right into the kind of game I've played before. And what I've asked Dante to do will only reinforce it." I did, however, explain my scheme, and he laughed out loud.

"Excellent! Dante will love it, too. He's in the middle of something this afternoon, though, so we can't let him in on it immediately. But he'll be there tomorrow, I'm sure."

"Hope so." We hung out together for a while longer while he played with Lexie and the other dogs who came over to romp—not to mention his offhand flirtation with some of the female owners.

When we left the dog park a little later, Brody walked Lexie and me to my new car.

"I don't have time today, but one of these days I want a demonstration drive," he said. "Dante told me all about your new wheels and the deal you struck to buy it."

"I'd be glad to take you for a ride soon," I said. "But let's get tomorrow behind us first."

As we left, my mind swirled even more around the stuff Brody had said about Sebastian Czykovski and its many implications. Surely, the person I suspected couldn't be the killer.

But in a really offbeat way, I supposed it made sense.

I called my fellow production people later that afternoon, not to tell them my specific suspicions but to elicit their support the next day for the different piggy scenario I had in mind.

For this one week, we'd take time out from our usual pig contest. No one would be eliminated. Afterward, the game would go on.

But this special scenario, if it worked, would clear Ned and Nita Noralles—and net us Sebastian's actual killer.

OKAY, I COULDN'T not call Dante. I tried him a while after Rachel left but before Lexie and I took off for our evening's pet-sitting. All I got was his voice mail, so I left a general sort of message.

And got a return call a couple of hours later when I was again in my car. "Kendra? I haven't talked to Brody yet, but was he of any help?"

"I'll say," I said. "And that little favor I asked you—will you be able to have it all together for tomorrow?"

"Of course." He sounded slightly miffed that I even asked. "I've asked Brody to meet me this evening for a drink. Can you join us? We can make it somewhere near you."

"Sure," I said, trying to sound casual. "Why not?" Such a meeting would allow us to make more plans for tomorrow's possible showdown with the killer.

And if it led to yet another hot night with Dante . . . ? Worse things could happen.

WORSE THINGS *DID* happen. Oh, not in terms of sending us in a different direction for solving Sebastian's murder.

But by the time I met Dante and Brody for drinks at a nice British-style pub near where I lived, my mind had gone even further in rehashing my earlier discussion with Brody.

One thing hadn't made sense: How could Dante have discussed with him the deal I'd cut to acquire my Escape? I hadn't talked it over with Dante. It wasn't his business, only my own.

The pub was noisy, partly because it had a huge-screen TV at one side where a British football—soccer—game was being rebroadcast, and rooters for both sides were far from subdued.

We sat in a corner enjoying Guinness stout, fish and chips, and our discussion of what could occur tomorrow. Though I hadn't fully described to the two of them how I'd solved other killings with the help of animals, including those ferrets who'd helped ferret out the truth, they knew enough about it, often thanks to the stories my buddy of sorts, tabloid journalist Corina Carey, broadcast about the results.

Even so . . . "This scenario you have in mind for tomorrow?" Dante said. "It has some flaws." He wasn't at all shy pointing them out, but I nevertheless stuck to my idea.

"Let's see how it goes," I said. "If it doesn't work, we can go to Plan B."

"Which is?" he yelled over some raucous shouting behind us.

"I'll figure it out." I hoped. I stared into his handsome face, waiting for this sexy but controlling guy to attempt to thwart my theory.

"How about—" he began.

"How about you tell me exactly how you knew the details of my deal to buy my Escape," I inserted instead of letting him finish.

He shot a baleful glance toward Brody, who shrugged and rolled his eyes toward the ceiling.

When Dante looked back at me, I simply stared, waiting

for his response while taking a healthy swig of stout. As good as it was, it didn't obliterate the sudden bad taste in my mouth.

"I knew what kind of car you were after, Kendra," Dante finally said. "I also knew it would be difficult for you to afford at normal financing rates. It wasn't any problem for me to let drop to the Ford financing arm that I'd appreciate their fixing the loan to something a little easier for you."

"That was all?" I was utterly skeptical, feeling certain that in some manner he had backstopped the loan.

"Pretty much." Which clinched my suspicion as being true.

"I should thank you," I said coldly. "I like the car a lot, and I can certainly live with the terms. But why didn't you simply ask if I wanted a little help?"

"What would you have said?" he asked shrewdly.

I hesitated. "Point taken. Even so—"

"Even so, you're right. I won't do it again."

I tried to conjure up some warm and fuzzy feelings that this wealthy man I cared about had fixed a situation to make it work better for me.

Instead, I felt resentment still swirl inside.

He was again attempting to control, if not me, then at least stuff going on around me. For my own good? Perhaps.

But I wouldn't put up with it.

That night, Lexie and I retired early in our home-sweet-garage. Alone.

While I stewed sleeplessly about all that would occur tomorrow.

Chapter Twenty-eight

FIRST THINGS FIRST, and that meant, the next morning, that I took my dear Lexie to Darryl's so she'd have a delightful day, notwithstanding whatever happened to mine.

I didn't see my best bud Darryl when I arrived, and his staff seemed preoccupied with a couple of oversize pups who'd apparently decided to mix it up in a doggy play area. After I ensured Lexie was properly ensconced in her favorite place filled with people furniture, I decided to seek out Darryl in the most likely locale, since he wasn't refereeing canines.

As I'd been permitted to do in the past, I opened his office door without knocking—and found the answer to one mystery that had bothered me for the last few weeks. One that, had I truly thought it through, I might have solved for myself. Or maybe could have seen without bursting in, had I peeked discreetly through Darryl's office window.

"Wow!" I spontaneously exclaimed as I discovered

Darryl and Wanda Villareal engaged in one heck of a sexy kiss. "Excuse me."

The two pulled apart, red-faced and clearly sheepish. "Good morning, Kendra," Wanda said with a too-bright smile.

"Hi," Darryl blurted simultaneously.

I ceased my polite and embarrassed retreat to stare at them suddenly. "So why didn't either of you tell me what was going on?" I glared pointedly at Darryl. I always confided the worst of my love-life stories to him—almost, although never with graphic detail. So why hadn't he confided the best to me?

"We're really sorry, Kendra." Wanda approached first and sort of engulfed me in a big hug for such a petite person. "But . . . well, this is kinda new for both of us, and we were afraid that if we mentioned it to anyone, especially someone whose opinion we both care a whole lot about, like you—"

"It would go away before we could give it a chance," Darryl finished. My lanky buddy looked defiant now, as if wanting to suggest I get lost.

"This is really cool," I said, hoping I'd feel that way when I'd had a chance to think it over. At the moment, most of what I felt was hurt. Surely they could have told me. "Congratulations. You deserve each other." Maybe.

"Thanks!" Wanda's exclamation sounded genuinely grateful. "And we have something for you, too. About poor Princess's separation anxiety. You know we thought we had a solution?" I nodded, full of sudden optimism that something good might actually occur—for me, not just for them.

And wondering whether, on some level, this particular problem had helped to draw them closer as they pondered the possibilities. "We checked with other Brittany spaniel owners, who said that the best thing would be for Princess to have company. So, we've visited a breeder with Brittany puppies nearly ready to go to a new home." She squatted on the floor, lifted her purse, and pulled out some papers. "Here! You can have your law clients go check out the pups when they get home later this week. Okay?"

How simple a solution—maybe. It absolutely had ADR possibilities: a feasible solution short of going to court.

One that I could suggest to the attorney representing the Jeongs' neighbors if we ever ceased putting off our often rescheduled meeting.

Yeah!

I thanked them both and, swallowing my hurt at their prior failure to disclose, gave them hugs and kisses. "Thanks so much," I said. "And I'll stay out of your love life. But—"

"Yes?" Darryl said somewhat hesitantly.

"I'd be happy if you'd keep me informed." I headed out the door . . . pleased that, at least to some extent, this day that could be full of misadventures had at least started in a manner with plenty of possibilities—if I stopped worrying about my hurt feelings and focused on my happiness for my friends.

I RECEIVED A call from Althea on my way from Darryl's. "I wanted to give you the last tidbit of information you requested," she said. Turned out that Rick Longley had had a teensy glitch in his path to weatherman stardom, which was why he wound up back in L.A. "Some station muckety-muck in New York threatened to fire him," Althea said, "and Longley punched him out."

"So the guy's got a temper," I mused.

"Maybe it grew enough to cause him to kill Sebastian," Althea said. "Better find out if the judge ever threatened to can your host."

Could what I had planned for today be a mistake? Maybe. But it certainly wouldn't hurt.

I called Rachel on my hands-free. The approach I decided on wasn't exactly fair, but it would provide the info I needed. "Why didn't you tell me that Sebastian threatened to fire Rick?" I asked—not knowing, of course, if it could be true.

"Because I knew you'd start suspecting poor Rick of murder, Kendra," my assistant retorted. "But he didn't do it. I'm sure of it."

Okay, I'd pretty much concluded that Dante was no longer on my serious suspect list. Maybe because I didn't want him there. Even so, I hadn't fully eliminated a lot of others as potential perpetrators—and now that I'd zeroed in on the person I felt fairly sure did it, I didn't exactly like the fact that my list of possibles kept expanding.

Well, if all went as anticipated, it would shrink down to one . . . today.

FOR MY NEXT act, I had to accomplish the possibly impossible. I needed privacy, and a whole lot of luck.

Inside my Escape, I made a critical phone call, on which the entire day's pending circumstances hinged. To my surprise and delight, I reached the object of my call immediately. More important, I ascertained that the person was alone.

Our conversation at first was full of my fielding incredulity, which I had anticipated. I tried to keep it light, as if what I intended was actually a practical joke. And after a few minutes of frantic attempts at convincing . . . lo and behold—it worked!

Now, we were all set for this afternoon's activities. I only hoped they resulted in the consequences I intended—as long as my initial assumptions were, in fact, true.

Which, hopefully, we would find out within hours.

I ARRIVED EARLY at SFV Studios. Taking a deep breath, I exited my Escape and headed inside the three-story front structure, passing the offices and heading for the sound stage we used for *Animal Auditions*.

I gave a deep sigh of relief when I saw that at least some of my setup was already in effect. Charlotte was there, running around with her clipboard and frazzled expression. Rachel stood at the side of the stage area with Avvie Milton, whose adorable potbelly, Pansy, was at her side. A few of our remaining piggy contestants were there, too, with their owners, mostly staring out of the dressing rooms, awaiting our signal to come out for the start of the show.

That included Ned and Nita Noralles.

I approached Avvie first. I'd especially requested her appearance without going into any of the gory details. "What's going on, Kendra?" she asked softly.

"You'll see as things go on," I told her. "Right now, I particularly want Pansy to demonstrate some of her most perfect piggy sniffing prowess." I explained in vaguest generalities what would occur. "I'll use this scenario with some of the other piggies, of course, but if none delivers the exact result I need, I'll count on Pansy."

"And me, I suppose," Avvie said. I nodded, and we went over some of the signals that might be given to the pigs.

Pretty pig Pansy seemed to nod her large head as she lifted her big, expressive snout in agreement. I laughed. "I knew I could count on you," I said.

Next it was time to visit the dressing room containing Ned and Nita. I'd have to be especially careful with them. One word from Ned, in particular, and today's whole event would be toast.

Ned was dressed in a nice casual outfit for filming: light blue button-down shirt and dark slacks. "I'm counting on you, Kendra," he said, stooping to pat Sty Guy distractedly. "Jeff promised to come today, too, but I'm afraid this is the last *Animal Auditions* either Nita or I will be able to participate in, the way things are going."

Nita knelt on the floor, decorating Porker's standard black nylon harness with artificial pink flowers. She didn't even look up at me as she spoke with extraordinary emotion. "I hate this. I never thought my swan song would be a piggy performance, but those damned colleagues of Ned's . . . they won't leave us alone, Kendra." She looked up, and tears swam in her dark eyes. "They'll really arrest me next time, not just ask questions. And I'm afraid it'll even be today." She stood, looking highly photogenic in her long, dark skirt and frilly white blouse.

I wanted to reassure her that today's activities would end with her total exoneration—but I couldn't. Who knew if my piggy plot would succeed? And even if it did—well, my assumptions on whodunit could be entirely incorrect. I didn't think so, but . . . gee, even I'm not perfect. Sometimes.

One critical component of my plot arrived a minute after I excused myself from Ned and Nita: Dante. He had Wagner at his side . . . and a nice, large HotPets totebag over his shoulder.

I hurried over to him. I still wanted to sock him in that

almost-perfect nose after what he pulled regarding my Escape. I didn't dare address that particular gripe again now, when I needed something so important from him.

"Hi," I said in an anticipatory tone. "Did you get it?" I glanced tellingly at his tote.

His smile was almost chilly, which made my heart sink to way beneath the low but classy heels I'd put on this morning to set off my slim and stylish red dress. I really wanted to look good in case I got oncamera with my crime-solving scenario. I'd also donned a lawyerly jacket over it, in case that was the image I decided I needed at the time.

"Do you have any doubt?" he asked sardonically.

"Nope." I smiled almost apologetically. "Is Brody on board? He needs to get the other judges in sync." I glanced toward their table. Eliza was there, and Brody, too.

Not Matilda. Uh-oh.

I was just about to call her on my cell when I saw her come through the increasingly crowded soundstage's door.

Good. I could talk to her first. "Excuse me," I said to Dante and headed in her direction—only to find him still at my side, with Wagner keeping pace. "She might not talk to me if you're along," I hissed.

"Good point." He peeled off toward the judges' table.

He actually paid attention to something I said? That could be a first.

I reached Matilda, who looked especially frazzled. Her short blonde hair stuck up on one side, and the lapel of her brown suit jacket was twisted and tucked inside. I almost reached over to remedy that, but our production people would handle it. I didn't want to do anything at that instant to annoy her.

"Hi, Matilda," I said cheerily. "Ready for a fun day judging our potbellied contestants?"

She stopped and stared as if she'd never seen me before. Her complexion was pale, and I was afraid that even standard onscreen makeup wouldn't make her appear as upbeat and charming as she'd been on our first shows.

Surely she didn't know what to expect here today. But if not, something else was clearly upsetting her.

"Is everything okay?" I inquired. Maybe my suspicions were completely wrong, and her conscience was bothering her enough to change her personality. After all, I'd made assumptions about why she'd behaved as she did because of interference by my now primary suspect, but perhaps I'd gotten it backwards.

"I . . . I don't know," she said. "I just learned on my way here— Never mind." She suddenly put on a burst of speed that carried her toward the judges' table . . . and Dante, who greeted her effusively. She regarded him with discomfort, I thought, but took her place at the end.

I hurried toward Charlotte, who stood at the sidelines, surveying the crowd of pigs, owners, and production people. I made my own mental survey. The usual suspects were all there: Charlotte, co-hosts Rachel and Rick, trainers Corbin and Charley, all three current judges, Dante, and the primary pig folks—Ned, Nita, and other contestants who'd railed against Sebastian before his demise.

Then there were the members of the audience filing in whom I especially needed to see. One in particular. Was she there?

Yes! I saw her—Detective Vickie Schwinglan—at the edge of the bleachers, looking around as if seeking someone . . . me. Her usual companion, Detective Howard Wherlon, already sat at the edge of the front row. I gave a hopefully subtle nod that Vickie instantly got, and sidled off to an edge of the huge room.

"Glad you could make it, Detective," I said in a low voice. "Everything okay on your end?"

"Yes, but I think this is stupid." Detective Vickie Schwinglan glared down at me. "I bet it won't even increase your dumb show's viewership, the way you want. It's just one of your tricks, Ballantyne, the kind you use when you try to show up the police department. I'm only playing along because this time I'm going to demonstrate how wrong you are."

Whatever. But I didn't say anything that might antagonize the tall, arrogant, irritable cop. On my further inquiry, she confirmed that she had even gotten someone from SID—the Scientific Investigation Division—to come that day to assist with my showmanship.

She might think my suggestions foolish, but, despite her sniping at me, she must think the plan had at least a little merit—even just for police department public relations—or she wouldn't have played along this far.

"Hello, Vickie, Kendra," said a familiar voice from behind me. I shouldn't have been surprised at Jeff's presence, but I also wasn't excited about it. He could act as a distraction—and I wasn't about to include him in my list of those in the know about what I really was up to.

"Hi, Jeff," I said without much enthusiasm. The former cop glared and started asking Vickie questions about her murder investigation, which gave me an opportunity to sidle away.

I went into the audience area to greet guests—including Detective Wherlon. I pulled my hand out of my jacket pocket to shake his hand. "Glad you could make it, Howard."

The detective was, as always, dressed in a drab suit and surly expression. "Sure you are. What's going on, Kendra?

Detective Schwinglan was eager for us to come here today but wouldn't give much information. What did you tell her—that you're solving Sebastian Czykovski's murder here, today, oncamera?" His tone clearly scoffed, and I wasn't about to enlighten him.

"We just have a particularly interesting show planned today."

"Yeah?" he said. "Well, I'll be the one in the audience snoring."

We'd see about that. "Excuse me." I'd just noticed someone else I needed to say hi to.

Also in the audience, two rows up, was Flossie Murray, Sebastian's ex-wife. I was delighted Dante had gotten her here. Of course, as manager of the Long Beach HotPets, she probably wasn't about to say no to the company's big boss.

She didn't seem thrilled to be there. "Hello, Kendra," she said as I excused my way through seated audience members to get to her. "Do you know why Dante wanted me here? I've made it a practice to stay far from things where my ex was involved."

"I just think it'll be an interesting show," I said. Gee, hadn't I said that before? Well, not to her. "Stay tuned."

One audience member not far away resembled the photo I'd just seen of the agility guy who'd slugged Sebastian. Brody had shown it to me, and I figured he was responsible for this particular person's attendance.

I hurried toward the judges' table, where Dante still hung out. I first caught Brody's eye, and he winked. The guy who'd helped me get this far was obviously ready for what was to come.

I only hoped I was.

"Everything set?" Dante asked.

"I think so." I tellingly eyed his tote once more, and he nodded and grinned.

Together we went over to explain all to Charlotte. Then we would get started.

Chapter Twenty-nine

ALL THE INFORMATION had been passed down the line—to a point. Usually, it was up to primary host Rick Longley to explain the scenario to our piggy contestants' owners and our audience, but because of these special circumstances, I'd enlisted a thrilled Rachel to do it.

Why her? Well, unlike most of the others affiliated with the show, I didn't think she was ever considered seriously as a murder suspect. And I wasn't so sure anymore about Rick.

We were down to six pigs this week—Porker and Sty Guy among them. Avvie Milton had just joined us with Pansy as our unofficial seventh. As our guest, she'd be first to participate, though Pansy couldn't win our contest.

I only hoped someone did.

Dante, Avvie, and I stood on the side, Pansy and Wagner with us. I was just as glad that Lexie was at Darryl's. She was too small to compete with potbellies, and although

I felt sure things wouldn't get too ugly here oncamera, my little Cavalier was better off not in the way.

"We have a very special show for you tonight." Rachel's smile was radiant. Her hands-free microphone doodad, wrapped around her head, worked fine. "We've had our potbellied pig players act like detectives before, using their extraordinary sense of smell to find contraband we planted around our set. Our remaining contestants have shown they can really sniff things out."

She gestured toward the edge of the stage where the six contestant pigs and their owners stood in a row—fortunately, all quiet and getting along well.

Rachel's tone grew more somber. "And I'm sure everyone watching this show knows we suffered a tragedy a couple of weeks ago. One of our original judges, Sebastian Czykovski, was brutally murdered, and although the police have some suspects, they haven't arrested anyone yet."

I glanced toward the audience, where the detectives in charge were seated, glowering. I hadn't mentioned their presence to our camera crew, but I still checked the monitors to make sure they weren't being singled out and embarrassed. At least not yet.

It was time for Rachel to explain the scenario I'd set up. "We're going to try something different," she said. She motioned toward someone almost hidden in a corner behind one of the cameras. A short, balding man in a suit shuffled over, looking nervous. He held a paper bag in his latex-glove-clad hands. "This is Jarrod Krone, with the Los Angeles Police Department's Scientific Investigation Division. We've been given special permission for our scent competition this evening. Mr. Krone has with him the actual pig harness used to strangle poor Sebastian. Isn't that right, Mr. Krone?"

I heard murmurs everywhere in our audience, and saw Howard Wherlon standing and scolding Detective Vickie Schwinglan, whom he correctly assumed had prior knowledge of what would occur here. She stood with arms folded and face firmly focused on the stage, not her companion cop.

"That's right," Jarrod Krone said. He explained all that had been done via official investigative practices to determine the source of the fatal harness. They had discovered where it had been purchased, but not by whom. They had run fingerprint and other tests, but nothing had conclusively pointed out the perpetrator. "So when we were approached by *Animal Auditions*, we figured the special test that was suggested was probably a bunch of malarkey, but if it happened to work, that would be wonderful."

"And what special test is that?" Rachel asked on cue.

"Well, this harness is specially woven, mostly nylon or other artificial materials, like the majority of such straps, but this particular kind also has some decorative leather in it. Nylon won't always hold smells very well, but leather might. The idea is that the killer might have left a scent in the leather that the pigs could smell, and use to point out a suspect."

"And would this be usable to try the suspect for murder?"

"Not likely, but at this point we're willing to accept assistance in focusing in on a suspect or two. We'll collect additional evidence once we zero in on someone."

Talk about malarkey—the whole idea was probably as absurd as many of the things that went on in the supposedly scientific TV shows about crime scene investigation. But the idea here wasn't to be scientific—or even logical.

We'd asked Jarrod to play along to see if a suspect who happened to be here would buy into the idea of the possibility of being fingered by a piggy nose and grow defensive. And give him- or herself away.

Our first pig contestant was Randall, who'd gone first in our initial episode. He sniffed the bag containing the harness—which, unsurprisingly, wasn't the actual murder weapon.

It was the thing I'd been hounding Dante about. He'd used his clout and financial status to have a couple of new ones flown in over the weekend from the Ohio manufacturer, expressly for today's show.

Randall smelled it, and was then encouraged by his owner to sniff the other piggy owners, who were somewhat suspects in Sebastian's murder. Maybe their motivation was sparse, but Sebastian's nastiness had been the supposed reason the cops had zeroed in on Nita and Ned Noralles as prime suspects.

Randall seemed utterly friendly to his competitors' people, and not inclined to associate any of them with the scent of the harness. Good.

Next was Nita with Sty Guy. Her job was to get her potbelly to sniff the harness and compare the scent with those of the judges. Of course Brody hadn't been around back then, but it didn't hurt to keep him in this scenario.

Sty Guy seemed more of a ham than Randall. He butted his adorable big nose at Brody, who only laughed. Eliza, too, seemed to enjoy this potbelly's attention, although he quickly moved on.

To Matilda. Who looked utterly upset. She didn't move

at all as black-and-white Sty Guy nosed at her and made some excited piggy noises.

Was this it? Had Sty Guy zeroed in on Sebastian's killer?

I had to remind myself that this scenario was an utter farce. But Matilda didn't know that.

"I didn't—" she stuttered. "It isn't me. I couldn't. I . . ." She quickly shut up as Sty Guy moved on.

But this was the kind of reaction I'd counted on from the actual killer. Matilda was once again near the head of my suspect list.

Still, we weren't through with *Animal Auditions*. We needed to complete the entire process before I'd feel satisfied that all piggy assistance had been utilized.

Next was one of the other potbellies, whose goal after sniffing was to check out our whole production staff. That included Rick Longley, Rachel, Charlotte, our camera folk, me, . . . and Dante.

The big, lumbering white boar seemed to spend an inordinate time checking out Rick—but the guy had apparently decided to play games of his own, and pulled a small packet of popcorn from his pocket.

Was this a ploy to keep suspicion off himself as the real killer? Rick laughed a lot, and I sensed no unease at all. So what if Sebastian had threatened him with firing? The fact that Rick had punched someone else out in a similar situation didn't mean he'd commit murder. And even though the guy was oncamera a lot and probably was a fair actor, wouldn't he seem somewhat uncomfortable if he was, in fact, guilty? I wouldn't delete him from my suspect list, but he didn't stay especially high on it, despite my earlier surmises.

Dante, though . . . this large piggy seemed quite taken

with our show's biggest benefactor. Of course I'd wondered about Dante, and whether he could have killed Sebastian strictly for fun—or for the promotional value of having a murder on the show he was funding. But he, too, made a huge joke of the pig's unyielding attention.

I reminded myself why the piggy would zero in on Dante, if any of this silly scenario could be true. Dante had undoubtedly touched the harness, since he'd had it flown in for us. He'd probably even packaged it up as supposed evidence for this show.

Gee, could there actually be some reality to this idea of potbellies smelling out someone who'd touched a harness—like the real killer, if the cops would make the actual strap used for strangulation available?

Interesting. Once we zeroed in on a real, live suspect, maybe we could give it a genuine try.

Next was Ned Noralles's Porker. He was allowed to sniff the harness, then ambled over to our studio audience. As planned.

Right then, I had Avvie get Pansy to smell the evidence, too. Wouldn't hurt to have two porcine opinions—with Porker's first and Pansy to back him up.

Our ushers this day were film school interns who sometimes hung out at SFV Studios. They urged everyone down onto the floor to be sniffed out in turn.

Flossie Murray was first. Sebastian's ex-wife seemed excited about getting to meet Porker the piggy up close and personal. Porker seemed friendly with her, too. But the potbelly didn't give any indication he'd ever come across her scent before—and more important, she didn't act at all guilty.

Then there was the dog agility guy who'd punched out Sebastian. I'd learned his name: Chip Fong. I'd never had a chance to chat with him, but Brody had checked him out. Now, he seemed somewhat defensive, yet he, too, acted as if he got a kick out of this meeting more than he felt singled out by it.

To save time, I asked Avvie to have Pansy check out other audience members. They all reacted in different ways. Most were there because of their affinity for potbellies and appeared to enjoy being part of the show. Dante joined the ushers and me in helping to get the audience folks scented, then reseated.

One, of course, was my former flame. Jeff played along fine, even when his former nemesis Ned Noralles seemed inclined to get Porker to pick on him.

"Hey, piggy," he said. "And you, too, Porker."

Ned just glared.

Then Porker approached the detectives. Vickie Schwinglan was clearly uncomfortable, but she smiled and played along.

Detective Howard Wherlon glared at potbelly person Ned Noralles, his fellow cop. But he must have known the cameras were on him, so he simply stood still and took it.

Until Porker started butting him like a bully with his big nose.

"What the hell?" Howard hollered.

Porker didn't let up. And shortly thereafter, he was joined by Pansy, who started a loud piggy campaign—and when piggies are loud, they're earsplitting!

"What's the story, Detective?" inquired Vickie, shouting over the melee. "I went over it all with Mr. Krone—the entire chain of custody of that harness. You aren't on it."

Avvie gave a command, and smart Pansy quieted down. But she still stood steadfastly with her piggy. Likewise Ned and Porker. Dante and I remained beside them.

"But you apparently touched it enough for the pigs to smell your scent on it," Ned said to Howard with a huge but snide smile. "Gee, Detective, are you the murderer you've been supposedly looking for?"

"This is all bullshit," Wherlon said, his face red as he glared furiously from Ned to Porker and back again.

"If anything," I said, coming closer, "it's pig poop. But actually, I suspect it's the truth—right, Detective?"

"I was here before only to watch the show—and see Detective Noralles, here, embarrass himself in front of the whole world." As Wherlon was now embarrassing *himself* . . . "What motive would I have for killing that damned Sebastian?"

I knew the cameras were now on me. Corina Carey had been invited to other shows, and I knew the *National News-Shakers* reporter would be utterly irked that I hadn't invited her here this afternoon. But I'd call her once we had what we needed on film. Then she could get her scoop.

By then, Brody Avilla had also joined us at this side of the stage. His movie-star face was on high alert. He looked like one of those guys in a high-adventure film, ready to pounce on the bad guys. But he waited along with the rest of us.

Unsurprisingly, Jeff Hubbard stood by his side. Jeff had a quasi-official reason, as a P.I., to play this game. Brody had some sort of supersecret claim to it, too, but even if I'd known what it was, I wouldn't reveal it.

"How about this, Detective?" I slipped around Dante, who attempted to get in front of me. Protecting me? Or wanting to confront the possible killer himself? "Does the name Beth Black mean anything to you?"

Howard's ruddiness suddenly faded to ash. "No," he lied hoarsely. "Should it?"

Chip Fong stalked over. "She was one of our best agility contestants, and you know it. I recognize you now—you used to come to our meets. You were with her and her really great dog—I don't remember his name, but he was a real winner, at least until Sebastian Czykovski started getting on Beth's case. He kept harassing them both, subtracting points for faults the dog never made. Kept the poor, aging dog from making MACH—which caused Beth to try to kill herself, then leave the Anaheim area. You yelled at Sebastian, threatened him, but then I didn't see you again after Beth left."

"Yeah, like he said," I told Howard.

"And let me guess why you chose me to take the fall, Wherlon," Ned said, getting in his face. "I'm a whole lot better homicide detective than you'll ever be, and I've told anyone who asked. I stopped you from getting a nice, healthy promotion, didn't I? That was around the time your girlfriend left you. Of course I didn't know the circumstances then, but I did know you weren't working worth shit. You didn't see that I was right, or I'd have stood up for you later, once you were doing the job okay again. So you took advantage here, two birds with one stone—right? You offed Sebastian for chasing off your girlfriend, then tried to frame me and my sister for it."

"You're all nuts," Wherlon said. He shoved past Ned and started to leave.

Dante began to react, but Detective Vickie Schwinglan took charge. "Hold it, Detective Wherlon," she said.

"Why? You gonna arrest me for the murder of that bastard Sebastian Czykovski? With no evidence?"

"There's enough for me to ask you a few questions," Vickie replied. "Let's just go to the station and talk about it."

"Forget that," Wherlon said. He suddenly reached inside his jacket and extracted a nasty-looking police-issue weapon. "I'm outta here. And I'll be happy to shoot anyone who tries to stop me—people, not pigs."

With that, he started backing from the soundstage, waving the gun from side to side.

I felt, rather than saw, Dante react beside me.

Damn! He was going to get himself killed. I couldn't let that happen. Like it or not, I cared about the tycoon with his delusions of control over me.

But before I could shove him aside, I heard an enraged bark, followed by a growl, and Wagner leaped out of nowhere, chomping his muzzle hard on Detective Howard Wherlon's wrist.

I heard a huge report as the gun fired. I felt Dante fall to the floor.

"No!" I screamed.

Chapter Thirty

I THREW MYSELF over Dante, crying, oblivious to whatever Wherlon was doing. Let him run! I didn't care—as long as Dante was all right.

"I'm okay, Kendra," said his deep voice in my ear. Was it my pleading imagination pretending everything was fine?

No. Dante seemed unharmed. But he was hugging Wagner. His dog had been shot.

Thank heavens the wound appeared superficial, perhaps because of the gun's odd angle. Dear Wagner hadn't released Wherlon's wrist, and the cop hadn't been able to aim.

Now, Wherlon was being cuffed by Vickie Schwinglan.

"Where's the nearest good vet?" Dante demanded.

There were a lot of veterinary hospitals around. I chose one nearby that I'd used for Lexie lately—now that I wasn't especially friendly with a vet I'd nearly dated before, Dr. Tom Venson. He was farther out in the Valley, anyway.

"He'll be fine," the nice lady vet told Dante a while later, over the examination table where Wagner lay. The bullet had barely grazed him before slapping into the soundstage floor, fortunately not ricocheting to hit a person or pig. "Just keep him on these antibiotics till they're gone, and wash the area with antiseptic a few times a day. If he starts chewing on it, bring him back and we'll fit him with a collar to stop him."

Wagner was able to walk out on his own four feet, tail wagging.

Only then did I remember to call Corina Carey. "Sorry you won't get a scoop on the story," I told her, "but I'll be glad to get you personal interviews with me and others who were there and experienced the whole thing." When I hung up, I told Dante, "I figure you won't participate in further interviews with her, but that's your call. Me? Well, you never know when you'll need a press person as a friend. She's scratched my back now and then, so I also scratch hers."

"And her Puli's?" he asked with a smile.

"And ZsaZsa's," I agreed.

I'd driven to the vet's, which I was sure drove Dante crazy, since as fast as I'd gone, I was sure he'd have gone faster. But he'd been holding Wagner. Besides, it was my car, even if he was the moneybags behind it. I suspected the way he'd arranged my reasonable rate was to guarantee I'd pay it . . . or he would. I couldn't really stay angry with him about that. I'd gotten my car, and I wouldn't miss any payments. End of story. Sort of.

I asked if he wanted to drive my Escape back to SFV Studios.

"You bet."

When we arrived, things were still busy but seemed to be winding down. The place was a crime scene, after all. Again. Detective Howard Wherlon, while stopping short of admitting to murdering Sebastian, had shot poor Wagner and might have hurt others, if he hadn't been quickly subdued.

Brody came over as we stood outside the yellow crime scene tape. "You're really something, Kendra," he said admiringly. "That whole setup with the pigs was almost out of some farcical film comedy, but amazingly it worked."

"Guess so," I said modestly, even as three pigs and their people joined us—Avvie, Ned, and Nita. "But I give all the credit to our potbellied friends." They all looked so pretty in their nonlethal harnesses and almost appeared to smile at my compliment. "Thank you all for what will be an amazing show. I assume it'll still air on the Nature Network tonight?"

I looked inquiringly at Charlotte, who had joined the crowd, along with Rachel and Rick. "Yes," she said. "I got the authorities' okay, although it'll need to be edited to take out the stuff Wherlon said and did, so we don't taint the case against him. All our participants will have their faces blurred and their speech rendered unidentifiable."

"It's news!" said Corina Carey as she slipped in among us.

"If you don't show it, or even if you do, *National News-Shakers* will take its chances and throw it out there. First Amendment, and all that. Now, who wants to be interviewed first?"

THE SHOW DID go on TV that night with IDs obscured by design. It was, of course, a whole new pig scenario, and no one was eliminated this week. We'd go back to our original idea next week, including inviting the losing piggy to go home.

Long after our pet-setting duties were enjoyed and completed, Lexie and I watched it in high def, curled up on the beautiful beige-on-beige sofa in Dante's living room. Dante, to his absolute, pet-loving credit, had Wagner up on the furniture beside us, too, despite the ointment on his wound. There was a gorgeous doggy blanket—a HotPets special— tucked up beside him, but for comfort, not to protect the couch.

Dante's personal assistant, Alfonse, had gone home, but Brody stayed with us. Not on the sofa, though, but on a nearby chair.

"You're an amazing judge of character," Dante said when the show was over, holding me tight in the middle of the dog sandwich. He kissed me, and I smiled.

"So I know the information I found out for you before helped you figure out it was Howard," Brody said, "but I had the impression you'd already guessed—true?"

I nodded. "Not that I was sure, of course. But one day while I was pet-sitting, some really disparate stuff I'd heard started to congeal in my mind. Ned had mentioned that Howard once had a girlfriend who'd had something awful happen—she'd died, or had nearly died then dumped him. And a guy I met at an agility match said that Beth Black had a quiet boyfriend who tried to turn all officious when something went wrong for her, till she turned him off. Howard himself seemed inordinately interested in showing up at the *Animal Auditions* shows even before Sebastian was killed, although I don't think the two of them ever talked. Even so . . . my mind blended it all and came up with the possibility that Howard Wherlon had been Beth Black's boyfriend . . . and had finally wreaked his revenge on Sebastian, the man who'd chased her out of Howard's life."

"Great job!" Brody said. "And here I thought I knew a lot about investigating—what I learned from playing cops in films." And whatever else he'd done in the past to pick up covert investigation techniques. But neither Brody nor Dante talked about that. "And your idea to get the pigs to point Howard out—extraordinary!"

"I'm a murder magnet," I reminded them. "Using animals to figure out the killers is what I do. Now, if you have a cure for that particular disease hidden somewhere in your HotPet storage warehouse, Dante, I'll take a million of them."

He laughed—as my cell phone rang.

It was Ned. "I'll never be able to thank you enough, Kendra," he said. "Nita, too. And Porker and Sty Guy."

"You can pay me back by telling me everything you know about the case against Wherlon. Oh, and I've got all sorts of speculations about Matilda Hollins, too. Got anything on her?"

"Sure, both of them."

So Dante and Brody could hear—no attorney–client privilege involved—I turned on the speaker phone feature.

"Matilda knew about Howard's affair with Beth Black. She'd have kept track of such things, especially since she'd had her own fling with Sebastian and therefore knew the agility crowd. I gathered that, even though she's a pet shrink, she'd also been aware of human agility trainer Beth's emotional issues. And Matilda also knew how angry Howard was at Sebastian for causing Beth's breakdown and flight from the area. Apparently, when Howard came to *Animal Auditions* to harass me, he got angry all over again when he saw Sebastian and how he treated the contestants. He confronted Sebastian after the second show and killed him—probably a premeditated act, since he'd brought a unique pig harness with him. Beth had bought it for him at a flea market a while back so he could give it to me as a present when I supported his promotion—only I didn't, so he'd kept it . . . then used it to kill Sebastian."

"So he figured he'd frame you?" Dante asked.

"Apparently, although I'm not positive whether he had me in mind specifically at first, just a pig owner. But the harness still had its sales tag on it, and he'd bought another one under an assumed name and had it delivered to one of those sham post office boxes, so I figure he was probably already planning what he ultimately did. After the murder, Matilda confronted him, intending to blackmail him with what she knew. Instead, he turned the tables and threatened her—both physically and professionally—if she didn't help him. Even though she'd been exonerated when her professionalism was called into question once before, he said he'd make sure former patients he happened to know went to the veterinary board with all sorts of allegations. By then, he'd definitely gotten the idea of making sure I went down for the murder—both to get me out of the way of his promotions within the department, and to pay me back for not supporting him before. He'd pin it either on me or on Nita, since if she was charged, I'd go ballistic."

"Who, you?" I asked innocently.

"Yeah," Ned's voice shot back. "Anyway, he made Matilda plant the second harness at Nita's."

"Any idea when she got possession of it?" I asked. I had a feeling it had been in her house on the day I'd visited but she didn't let me inside.

"Not yet, but that'll come out as she talks. In any event, once she planted it, she was into the conspiracy up to her veterinary shrink eyeballs. And she was scared, figured he'd dispose of her whenever his plan was done, if not before. He purposely ran into her car and broke into her house, but she was afraid to let anyone know. Now that he's been arrested, she's singing like a cheerful pig."

"Great!" I exclaimed.

"So, you did it again, Ballantyne. I used to get damned mad at you for showing me up in murder cases. Now I want to kiss those pretty feet of yours."

"Hey!" Dante interrupted.

"But I'll gladly turn that pleasure over to you, Mr. De-Francisco. Bye . . . and have fun!" I heard the click, and Ned was gone.

"Looks like you've increased your fan club," Brody said. "A cop in your pocket? Good position to be in."

"Better than the antagonism that used to be between us," I agreed.

"Well, one of these days I'll want to hear more of your story. Maybe I can make a movie about it."

"No thanks," I said. "The publicity tonight for *Animal Auditions* is about as much as I can stand."

"I still may take some lessons from you someday," said Brody. "Murder Magnet 101."

"So are you ever going to tell me how you learned to conduct investigations the way you do it now?" I asked.

A loud silence. And then a grin with a hearty, "Nope!"

"Then . . . Dante, you made an odd comment once about fixing things so you wouldn't be arrested. Will you elaborate now?"

I was expecting a "no," so I was pleased when he shrugged and said, "Since you wouldn't be my alibi, I made sure the one I actually gave would work. Thing was, it was real. I'd been on a video conference that night with one of my overseas suppliers, so I had to get my high-tech guys to get their act together and provide evidence of timing, plus proof it wasn't prerecorded."

"And you didn't tell me that. Why?"

"Just wanted you to worry a little."

About whether he could be a killer? On the other hand, it would give me good reason not to get too involved with him. And I'd gathered, from stuff he said, that he genuinely wanted to keep his distance. Or at least he genuinely *wanted* to want to . . .

A little like I genuinely feared letting my heart get wrapped around any man, especially one as controlling and unpredictable—and utterly irresistible—as Dante DeFrancisco.

Brody left a short while later. "It's been a big day, and I have some scripts to read tomorrow."

Maybe. Or perhaps he was conducting some other undercover investigation for Dante that neither disclosed to me.

When Brody was gone, I had something else important to ask Dante. "Ready to kiss my feet?" I inquired huskily.

"Anytime," he said, and turned off the TV.

I ALL BUT danced back to the Valley to do pet-sitting rounds the next morning. Afterward, I headed my Escape toward Darryl's to drop off Lexie. I wanted her to have a fun day, and it wouldn't be if she stayed with me.

It was Tuesday. I had a big day planned at the law office to help make up for my lack of attention over the last few weeks.

Now that Sebastian's killer was caught, my time spent on *Animal Auditions* was bound to go down. But I'd gathered from calls and a quick check of the Internet this morning that the show had gotten fabulous reviews—not to mention the huge audience, all of whom would undoubtedly frequent the show's excellent main sponsor, HotPets.

Dante would do well from this, too.

Dante. We'd had such a glorious night, celebrating my success in finding Sebastian's killer, his success in all the additional promotion for HotPets, our success in finding each other . . .

Well, yes, I guess I'd admitted to myself that I'd really fallen fast for this guy. Maybe I was foolish, after all the bad relationships I'd gone into in the past, including recently. But sometimes, even when a fellow won't answer all your questions, you just have to make a romantic decision and run with it.

Then there was Darryl. When I got to Doggy Indulgence, Wanda was there again. We all went into Darryl's office, and I smiled as the two of them stayed close together. Hey, this was August. A prime time for love? Apparently, even though this month didn't usually have that reputation.

"Have you told the Jeongs about the possible separation anxiety solution for Princess?" Wanda asked.

I had to admit I hadn't. Darryl understood immediately. "I guess you were a little preoccupied yesterday, what with figuring out the solution to Sebastian's murder."

I nodded. "But I'm not going to wait a minute longer." I had the Jeongs programmed into my cell phone, and I called them where they were still conducting business, in New York, but due home in a couple of days.

Treena answered immediately. "Hi, Kendra. Is everything okay with Princess?"

"I haven't talked to Annie today," I told her as I attempted to get comfortable on one of Darryl's office chairs, "but I'm sure everything's fine. Not only that, I've had one of the best pet-sitters I know, besides me, helping out—Wanda Villareal. You've spoken with her, I'm sure."

Wanda nodded.

"I have, and she sounds wonderful. And I haven't heard threats from our neighbor for days. Is everything resolved?"

"Depends. Do you foresee much travel in the near future?"

"Probably, in spurts. On trips that we're not so far away, I'll bring Princess. At least we'll have a few months coming up really soon when we'll be in town, so we'll just have to worry about what to do with her when we're not at home."

"Great. Perfect. Wanda has come up with a solution that can't be beat. You need to get Princess a new best friend—a Brittany spaniel puppy that you can train while you're here, and who'll keep Princess company while you're gone."

A pause. "Maybe. I'd considered doggy day care, but she hated the few times we tried. But a puppy of her very own . . ."

"Not only that, but Wanda's done some homework. There's a breeder nearby who'll have puppies available in a couple of weeks."

"Oh, Kendra, thank you! That sounds like such a good solution. And . . ."

"Hey!" I interrupted. I turned to Wanda. "How many puppies do they have?"

"I'm not sure. Why—would the Jeongs want more than one?"

"Treena, didn't you say your neighbors lost a dog recently? What if you offer them a new pet? Imagine how the wife would stop complaining about a noisy puppy if she happened to have its brother or sister." It was a solution I'd used at least once before, and it had worked then.

"Hey, I like that!" Treena exclaimed. "Let's try it."

"Right away," I suggested. Within the next half hour, after a bunch of cell phone calls between Treena and her neighbors, and between the neighbors' attorney—who, amazingly, was accessible—and me, we'd reached a tentative solution. I told Darryl and Wanda about it. "The other lawyer got us on a conference call, and his client all but cried into the phone about the prospect of getting her own crying puppy. It's amazing!"

"It's wonderful," Wanda said, grinning.

"Super!" Darryl agreed.

"Thank you both so much." I gave them a joint hug.

"Glad we could help," Darryl said. "In any case, you know you can always run things by us."

As Wanda nodded, I felt happy that my dear friend Darryl had graduated from "me" to "us." Which, if I wasn't in a kinda relationship, might otherwise have made me feel left out.

But tonight, Dante and Wagner were joining Lexie and me for dinner at my place. And—would you believe it?—I was cooking! Something simple, a really excellent pasta dish I'd learned some time ago. One with aphrodisiac implications.

I headed for my law office, where I was greeted by Mignon's chirp and Borden's high-toned congratulations. They, and it seemed everyone else in the office, had watched *Animal Auditions* last night. Everyone was impressed.

That evening, I let Lexie accompany me on pet-sitting rounds, including to our old standbys Abra, Cadabra, Stromboli, and Piglet, not to mention Beauty, the golden retriever, and Mountie, the Greater Swiss Mountain Dog, the latest additions to our client list. Then we headed home.

Rachel saw us as we entered the gate. She'd already let Dante and Wagner in, and along with Beggar they were sitting in the front yard of my big, rented-out house.

"Hi," she said, running over to greet me. And then, worriedly, she whispered, "I know you and Dante are an item now. Are you going to let him pay your mortgage so you can move back into the house we rent? It's your right, of course, but Dad and I would really miss living here."

"Is that what Dante told you?" I gritted my teeth in exasperation.

"Oh, no," she hastened to say as he started sauntering toward us, stopping to pick up a rubber ball to throw for all three dogs to chase. "I just assumed . . ."

"Things are staying status quo," I assured her.

Later, I couldn't help mentioning it to Dante. Over coffee, after dinner, when we'd already imbibed a bunch of delicious Chianti; my pasta dish, which had turned out well, was arguably Italian.

"I need to set some ground rules," I told him.

"Uh-oh. This sounds serious." But his dark eyes twinkled seductively, and it was all I could do not to grab his hand and tow him into my bedroom.

I took a deep breath. "I care a lot about you, Dante. And I want to keep seeing you, see where things go with us."

"But I hear a *but*." Even so, instead of fleeing, he scooted his chair even closer beside me in my tiny kitchen.

"But I need some space. To take care of myself, I mean—not to stop seeing you. I appreciate your helping me get the Escape. I love it. But as we discussed before, you need to talk to me before doing me financial favors." I told him what Rachel had said. "People may make assumptions about us, and that I can't help. But. . . . Well, maybe I'm being too presumptuous. Do you even want to continue to see me that way?"

"Absolutely, Kendra," he responded, then shared a humongously hot kiss with me. "Honestly, I had no intention of falling for any woman the way I care for you. Brody knows that—he keeps razzing me about it."

Which explained a comment I kept recalling, in which Brody had said something to Dante about never thinking he'd see the day . . . Interesting!

"It even scares me a little, damn it," he continued. "Hell, it scares me a lot. The only other woman I really cared about died on me—a car accident. I'll tell you more about it eventually, if you want to hear." Hell, yes! "But I really want you, Kendra. And I'm willing to take it as slow as you want . . . at least for now. But someday—"

"Let's worry about that someday as it comes," I said. One that would include more insight into him. And learning more about his lost woman.

"Fine. Meantime . . . well, I want you with me a lot. I've been putting together some plans for HotPets products and services that I'd like your opinion on. Like . . . how would Lexie and you like to join Wagner and me on the first cruise ship that specializes in people bringing their pets?"

"Really? That sounds fantastic! When? Where will it go?"

"Details are still being worked out, but I'll ask your input as things progress."

"Excellent!"

"And I really want you to visit HotWildlife with me soon. There are some legal issues I'd like your advice on."

"Anytime."

We soon went out to walk the dogs for the last time that night. Dante and Wagner were going to stay over.

I was feeling all warm and fuzzy. Could it be that, for once in my life, I'd picked out the perfect man to care for?

Maybe so, if perfection came with flaws like holes in one's Googled—and hacked—past.

But as we returned inside and rushed right into each other's arms—Lexie and Wagner happily wagging their tails beside us—I figured I just might have the most enjoyable time ever while unraveling all the knotty questions I had about Dante DeFrancisco.